About the Author

Susan Tennyson is a Bristol wife and a Mum to two daughters. She spends her days home schooling her eldest daughter. When she is not teaching, she enjoys spending time with her family on day trips and holidays in the UK. She loves entertaining friends at home and enjoys music and television series. She has dreamt of writing a book for long time but only recently found the courage to do it.

The Habit I Cannot Break

Susan Tennyson

The Habit I Cannot Break

Olympia Publishers
London

www.olympiapublishers.com
OLYMPIA PAPERBACK EDITION

Copyright © Susan Tennyson 2024

The right of Susan Tennyson to be identified as author of this work has been asserted in accordance with sections 77 and 78 of the Copyright, Designs and Patents Act 1988.

All Rights Reserved

No reproduction, copy or transmission of this publication may be made without written permission.
No paragraph of this publication may be reproduced, copied or transmitted save with the written permission of the publisher, or in accordance with the provisions of the Copyright Act 1956 (as amended).

Any person who commits any unauthorised act in relation to this publication may be liable to criminal prosecution and civil claims for damage.

A CIP catalogue record for this title is available from the British Library.

ISBN: 978-1-80439-882-1

This is a work of fiction.
Names, characters, places and incidents originate from the writer's imagination. Any resemblance to actual persons, living or dead, is purely coincidental.

First Published in 2024

Olympia Publishers
Tallis House
2 Tallis Street
London
EC4Y 0AB

Printed in Great Britain

Dedication

This book is dedicated to my habit I cannot break, Ian.
My strength, my support, my soul.
My life, my love, my everything.

Part One

Chapter One

The stage is set. The lighting is dark except for four spot lights shining down on four glittering microphone stands marking the places where we will stand for the final time. Emotions are flowing through me and I am unsure of how I am feeling. Do I want this to end? I cannot wait for my freedom to be able to do what I want when I want, but I do not want to leave the three best people in the world. My heart is breaking. The four of us stand on the edge of the stage, ready to face our final concert. I can see sadness in all their eyes. We hug each other tightly, not wanting to let go. I take one final glance at a certain person and my heart skips a beat; I wish we could have had our time again in a different world, how amazing it would have been. The music starts up and we step on to the stage to a huge roar and I am taken back five years, to the day that we all first met. We did not know where our lives would take us and how the journey to get here would go…

It is a Wednesday morning in the middle of March, the sun is shining, and I am full of nervous energy. I put on my dark blue jeans, a white t-shirt and a black jacket. I ruffle my hair in the mirror.

"Do I look like a pop star?" I ask my reflection.

I am about to go to an audition for a new pop group. I have been to a few auditions before, but for some reason this time feels different.

I grab my phone and keys and leave my parents' house to get a taxi to the hotel in the centre of town where the auditions are being held. As we drive through the busy streets, I go over the song that I am going to sing, making sure I know all the words so that I don't come across too nervous. The taxi pulls up near the hotel and there is a large crowd heading towards the entrance. Looking around at all these amazing people, I wonder if I have any chance at all. I get out of the taxi and make my way across the road, there is an electric atmosphere coursing through everyone around me.

I walk through the open doors and make my way to the conference room where we all have to wait for our turn to sing. I check in at the desk before finding myself a chair near the window. I sit and watch everyone around me; some are talking excitedly to others, some practicing their songs out loud and others like me just sitting quietly, watching what is going on.

One by one, a girl with red curly hair and a clipboard calls out a name and they are ushered into another room. They are not seen again so they must be being sent somewhere else after performing. I have been waiting for just over an hour when my name is called. My heart is beating as if it is trying to escape my chest; I stand up and make my way over to where she is stood.

"Hi, are you Jacob?"

"Yes, that's me," I say, my voice slightly shaking with nervousness.

She replies, "Hi, I'm Shelly. Don't be nervous, I'm sure you will be great. Follow me."

I follow Shelly through the door into a room which is predominantly empty apart from a table at one end with three people sat behind it. The lady in the middle speaks first.

"Come in, I'm Harriet, this is Jasmin" – pointing to the lady on her left – "and this is George" – pointing to the man on her right. Trying to convey confidence, I stop in front of them and wait.

"Okay, great, tell us a little about yourself," says Harriet.

Clearing my throat, I reply, "Hi, I'm Jacob Adams, I come from just up the road, Rusholme. I am eighteen years old."

"It's lovely to meet you, Jacob. What song are you going to sing for us today?"

"George Michael, 'Faith'."

"Excellent, off you go when you're ready."

After taking a deep breath, I start singing. All my nerves suddenly disappear and I am feeling confident, my voice sounds great and I'm really hoping that it is coming across well to everyone else. Glancing at them, I can see that they are writing things down and showing each other what they have written. I come to the end of my song and I look over at the table and I can see that they are all smiling. They discuss me amongst themselves, very quietly.

Eventually, George speaks. "That was fantastic, Jacob. We would like you to hang around for a bit longer and we will talk to you again later. Shelly will show you where you should wait."

I look at the others, Harriet and Jasmin are smiling and nodding at me.

"We'll see you soon," Harriet confirms.

Shelly walks over to me and starts to guide me to a door on the other side of the room. She opens it and leads me out into a corridor.

"Well done. Now all the other shortlist group members are in a room just down here. You will be waiting in there for a while as we have lots of others still to see." Shelly continues as we walk towards another door, "We have about twenty others waiting to be seen again. When everyone has sung for the first time, we will bring you all back up here to sing in groups, then they will hopefully make their final decision."

We stop outside another door and Shelly opens it. As we walk in, the other hopefuls are sat around a large table in the centre of the room. They are all looking slightly apprehensive and staring at me. I smile nervously at them and find a chair at the table.

Shelly then announces, "Someone will be along soon with some refreshments for you all, see you in a bit." Shelly leaves, closing the door behind her.

I sit quietly for a short time, taking in the atmosphere of the room, watching everyone else. Sat next to me is a girl with long blonde hair. She turns and smiles.

"Hi, I'm Jacob."

"Hey, I'm Alice."

She has a warm smile which puts me at ease straight away.

"This is crazy. I didn't think I would get through. I'm so happy I'm in the final group of people. How are you feeling?" Alice asks me.

How am I feeling?

"I'm not sure really," I reply, "it's a bit surreal at the moment. I wonder how long we are going to have to wait."

As we are talking, the door reopens and in walks the most stunning-looking boy I have ever seen. He is tall, unlike me, slight build, with light brown hair and the most amazing brown eyes I have ever seen. My stomach gives a little leap as I watch him walk into the room. He looks around and walks over to the table, pulls out the chair next to me and slouches into it.

"Hi, I'm Leo."

"Jacob," I reply, looking into those sparkling eyes, shocked by the way that he looks back at me with a cheeky smile. Before I can say anything else, a trolley comes through the door, stacked with drinks and food which two members of hotel staff start placing on the table. Leo stands to reach over and grabs a drink.

"Do you want one?" he asks, turning to look back at me.

"Thanks, I will have a water."

He takes another bottle of water and as he hands it to me, our hands brush each other's and I feel electricity run through me. He looks and smiles at me again and then the moment is over.

Leo starts talking to Alice and as I sit listening to their conversation, a few more people are brought into the room. I join in with Leo and Alice talking about where we are from, our families and what we like doing. We talk for hours and time goes by so quickly, I really like these two. We are in the middle of talking about our families when suddenly, Shelly enters the room.

"All the auditions have been completed and you are the finalists. They would like you all to come back into the other room and they will explain what will happen next."

Shelly turns and walks out and we all start to follow her back down the corridor and into the other room.

There are about thirty of us left and as we all enter the room, Harriet, Jasmin and George are standing, waiting.

"Well done, everyone. Come in and we will let you know what's going on," George says and waits for everyone to file into the room. Then, he continues, "We are now going to split you into groups. We have had someone watching the holding room to see how you have been interacting with one another and with your solo performances, we have decided who we think we would like to see you sing with."

I am secretly hoping that they put me with Leo. He has made

such an impression on me. Jasmin then goes around the room and starts putting people into groups of four or five, when she walks towards me, she moves me to one side to stand on my own. She reaches Alice and asks her to stand with me. As Alice walks over, she has a big grin, she seems happy to be with me. Jasmin then puts another boy into our group and, finally, there are two boys left; Leo and another. Jasmin discusses something with George and Harriet then asks Leo to join our group. *Yes!* He is with us, I am so happy; it's such a strange feeling flowing through me. *I have only known him for a few hours, how can I feel like this?* I try and calm myself down and listen to what we are being told.

"We would like you all to go and find a quiet place in the hotel and for an hour, pick a song and practice singing it in your group, then we will call you back one group at a time to hear what you have done and we will then make our final decision," Jasmin announces.

We move towards the door and we are first out, so we head towards the room we were in previously.

"Oh my god, can you believe this?" Alice says in a very excited voice.

I turn to the boy who we have not yet spoken to. "Hi, I'm Jacob, this is Alice and Leo."

"Hi, I'm Xander. Do you know each other then?"

"No, we've only just met," Leo replies. "So, what are we going to sing?"

"How about keeping it classic with an old Beatles song?" suggests Xander.

We all agree on this and we try a few different songs. We finally decide on 'Love Me Do' as this is the one we sound the best singing. We all chose an individual bit to sing, then join for the chorus. We go through it a few times and it is sounding great.

The hour goes by so quickly and all of a sudden, we are being called back to sing again. I am so nervous as this will be our final chance to impress them.

We stand in front of Harriet, Jasmin and George.

"How have you got on?" asks Harriet.

Xander replies confidently, "I think we've got on well and the song we have chosen sounds really good."

"Excellent. When you are ready, let's hear what you have been doing."

We all take a deep breath and Xander counts us in and we start to sing.

Everything is going well and we sound good. I really hope they can see how much we all want this. I will be so disappointed for us if we don't get it. We finish the song and wait for their reaction.

"That was great, guys. We have a few more groups to hear and then we have a lot to discuss afterwards, but we will try and not let you wait too much longer. Thank you." Harriet points to the door.

We look at each other and make our way back out of the room.

"What was that about? Did they like us? They didn't give much away," Alice comments.

"I think we did really well," I reply.

"We will just have to wait, let's go back into the other room and wait in there." We all follow Leo back into the room to wait again.

This time, the wait is torture; no one is speaking, and we just sit there with our own thoughts. Time just seems to have stopped. Eventually, after what seems like an eternity, Shelly comes to tell us that they are ready to see us.

As we stand up to leave, we all hug and wish each other good luck. When I hug Leo, I hope that this will not be the last time I will be with him. I pull away from him and look into his eyes and wonder if he feels the same way. I'm sure he doesn't, he's probably not even gay and he is just too beautiful to want to be with me. He must have so many girls after him. I shake these thoughts from my head as this is not the time to deal with them.

We make our way back down the corridor; all the other groups are making their way back to the room too. We enter for the final time and the atmosphere is totally different than before; it's not excitement any more, it is a nervous energy. This moment is going to change people's lives forever.

Harriet stands and looks around the room at everyone, then starts to talk. "Thank you to all of you for coming today. You have worked so hard, and I can see promising futures for a lot of you. We have made our decision on which group we are going to sign and they are…"

I am so nervous. I'm going to be sick. I look over at Leo and he spots me and gives me a wink, this does not help. I turn to look back at Harriet. *Please let it be us, please let it be us,* I chant in my head.

"… Xander, Alice, Leo and Jacob."

What did she just say, did she say it was us? I am in total shock. I don't believe it until the others jump on me. We've done it, it's us!

Everyone else in the room is clapping and after a minute or so of celebrating, we face back to Harriet.

"Well done, you guys. Sorry to the rest of you. You are free to go."

As the rest of the groups leave, we keep looking at each other in disbelief. Shelly is moving four chairs around the front of the table and gestures to us to sit down.

"Well done to you all. Now, we have a lot of work to do," Harriet says. "The first thing we have done is booked you a room each in the hotel for tonight and you also have a table reservation at seven this evening in the restaurant. This is so you can have some time together and get to know each other a little better."

George hands us all a folder. "Here are your contracts that you will need to read and sign, but we won't be doing that today. I want you all to go and contact your families and tell them the good news. If you go to the reception, they will tell you where your rooms are and then spend the evening relaxing and taking everything in."

Finally, Jasmin speaks, "We want to see you all in here again tomorrow at one. We would like you to come with some family members, if that's possible, and we will answer any questions you have and we will sign your contracts then. Now off you go, share your news and have some fun."

As soon as we are outside and the door closes, we scream and jump around, hugging each other in sheer delight.

Chapter Two

"I can't wait to tell my mum and dad. Let's go and find out about our rooms," suggests Xander.

We all make our way to the reception; Xander goes to the desk and explains who we are and that there are some rooms for us. The man hands over four keys and tells Xander the numbers of the room. Xander thanks him.

"Come on, we are in rooms 376 to 379. Let's take the stairs."

We follow Xander. As we arrive at the stairs, we all start running, racing up them, laughing, so full of excitement we can't contain it. We reach the third floor, and we are all out of breath but still laughing. We push open the door and fall into a corridor full of doors. We look for a sign to tell us which way to go. We take a left turn and look for our rooms. When we reach the first one, Xander hands the key to Alice.

"Thanks, see you all in an hour."

Xander takes the next room and hands the other keys to myself and Leo. We then find ourselves alone, and my heart starts thumping again. I look at Leo and smile. He reaches out and touches my arm; I am breathless from his touch and I wonder if he can tell what he is doing to me. He looks at me with his amazing eyes. I could stare into them forever; they are so hypnotising.

"See you soon." He opens his door and goes inside.

I'm left standing in the corridor by myself, I can still feel his touch on my arm. I enter my room, close the door and lean against it, images of Leo going around in my head. What is he doing to me? I have never felt like this about anyone before. Yes, I have liked some boys before, but they didn't do this to me.

I stay there for a while just trying to take everything in, but I need to phone Mum and Dad to let them know how I've done and that I won't be home today. I get my phone out of my pocket and sit on the bed. I find Mum's number and it starts to ring. She answers straight away.

"Hi, love, how did you get on? You've been gone a long time." She sounds excited.

"I got it, Mum, I'm in the group."

All I can then hear is Mum screaming and shouting at Dad that I am in the group. Mum and Dad are then both on the phone shouting congratulations and well done.

"Mum, Dad, just listen a minute. I have to stay at the hotel tonight; they have given us all a room and we have to go to dinner at seven, so I can't speak long."

"Okay, love, what are the others like, I hope they are nice?"

"There are four of us including me. There's Alice, Xander and Leo. They all seem really nice."

"That's great, I hope you all get on well, have a great time tonight."

"Mum, they need you and Dad to come to the hotel tomorrow at one as they want us to have someone there when we sign the contracts."

"Of course, we will be there. We will get to you about twelve so we can have a chat about it all first."

"Thanks, Mum, I've got to go now as I want to take a shower before dinner."

"We will see you tomorrow, we love you."

"Love you too, see you tomorrow."

I hang up the phone and lay on the bed. I close my eyes and start to envision all that might happen in the future. Eventually, I open them to check the time; it's 6.45 p.m. I can't lay here forever, so I get up, get undressed and jump into the shower. I have a quick wash, dry and put my clothes back on, just as there is a knock on the door.

I answer it and it's Alice. "Come on, let's go, the others are waiting."

I grab my key and close the door behind me. Xander and Leo are waiting by the stairs. Leo has wet hair from being in the shower and it is dripping on to his shirt, he looks so good.

"Come on, let's find the restaurant, I'm starving," Leo says as he pushes the door open to the stairs.

Alice puts her arm through mine and smiles. "Come on, Jacob."

And we follow Leo and Xander down the stairs.

When we get to the restaurant, they have a table ready for us with champagne on it. We all sit down, Alice sits one side of me and, to my delight, Leo sits the other. I glance at him and I want to keep looking, but he catches me, making me blush. I quickly advert my eyes back to the menu we have been given. We all order our food when the waitress comes over and Leo opens the champagne.

"Who wants a glass?"

We all nod. I have never had champagne before but have wanted to try it. Leo fills all the glasses and hands them around.

He then raises his glass. "To us, the best group there will ever be."

"To us." We all cheer and clink our glasses together.

I take a sip of the champagne and it tastes lovely, so I have some more.

Our food arrives and we sit quietly as we eat and drink. After we have finished, another bottle of champagne is brought over to our table. Leo opens the second bottle and starts to refill everyone's glass.

"I better not have any more, I don't drink very much," says Alice.

The conversation then turns to what we should call ourselves.

"Should we keep it simple?" asks Xander.

"I think so, short and snappy," replies Leo.

A few names are mentioned but none seem right.

"How about UsFour?" suggests Leo.

"I like it," Alice says.

"So, what do we all think of UsFour for our name? Jacob, Xander?"

"Yes," replies Xander and raises his glass.

We all raise our glasses.

"UsFour," we all cheer again.

The evening goes by so fast, the champagne keeps flowing and I'm starting to feel a little tipsy. It's just before midnight; Alice and Xander decide to go up to bed, but I decide to stay for one more drink with Leo.

"Do you have a girlfriend?" Leo asks.

"No, I don't, do you?" I'm not brave enough to tell him I'm gay. I haven't told anyone, not even my parents.

"I've liked a couple of girls, but no one at the moment," Leo answers.

My heart drops; he likes girls, I definitely have no chance. I need to forget about anything happening between us and this makes me feel really sad, and it must show on my face as Leo looks at me with concern.

"Are you okay? What happened?"

I can't tell him so I just say, "Nothing, I think I've had too much to drink. I'm going to bed."

I stand up to go, but my foot gets caught in the chair and I start to fall. Leo moves so fast; he stands up and catches me before I do. We lock eyes and he smiles at me.

"Come on, I will take you up to bed."

I grab on to Leo's arm and he walks me back to our rooms. When we get to my door, Leo reaches into my pocket of my jeans to retrieve my key. My heart beats faster and I catch my breath; this time, I don't have the feeling in my stomach, it's somewhere else. I look at him. Can he sense how I am feeling? He looks back at me and reaches out and brushes my hair out of my eyes. Then he moves closer. *Is he going to kiss me?* But he reaches past me and opens my door. I'm so disappointed but not surprised.

"Good night, Jacob, see you tomorrow."

He smiles again and turns to head for his room. What just happened, that was bordering on flirtatious. Could Leo also like boys?

I fall into bed and I'm sleeping within seconds, my head full of dreams of me and Leo.

I wake up the next morning and my head is pounding, but I feel so happy. I get up and have a drink of water, it feels so refreshing. I splash water on my face and decide to go down to the restaurant for some breakfast. I text Mum on the way down to ask her to bring some clean clothes with her for me to change into.

Walking into the restaurant, Leo, Alice and Xander are sat at a table.

"Morning, sleeping beauty" – laughs Leo – "how are you feeling?"

"Bit of a thumping head, but I slept well." *Because I was dreaming of you,* I add in my head.

"Have some breakfast, it will make you feel better," says Alice.

Breakfast is a quiet affair; I think the excitement and the champagne from last night has affected us all. As I am eating my breakfast, I feel something touch my foot. I look down and I see Leo's foot touching mine. I look up at him, he is not looking at me but he has a slight smile on his face as he eats his breakfast. So, I move my foot against his to see what his reaction will be. He continues to smile and starts to move his foot against mine too. Then our legs touch and he glances at me and smiles. At that moment, we hear someone call our names across the restaurant. It's George making his way over to our table. This breaks the spell, and Leo moves his leg quickly away from mine.

"Morning, all, I hear you had a good night last night. I also heard you have come up with a name for your group?"

Xander replies to George, "Yes, we've decided on UsFour. What do you think?"

"It's not up to me, I'm afraid, you will have to run it past Harriet. Well, I will see you later." And George makes his way back out of the restaurant.

"I hope Harriet will let us keep the name, I really like it," Alice says as she stands up to leave the table. "My parents will be here soon, so I'm going to wait for them in the lobby. See you later."

"I'm going back to my room too," announces Leo. "My brother is coming and he's bringing me a change of clothes, my mum couldn't get the time off work. See you later."

As I watch Leo and Alice walk away, I think about what just happened and last night. These moments between the two of us.

Does he like me the way I like him? I sit and finish my food with these thoughts running through my mind.

I make my way back to the room. Mum texts to say she will bring some things with her, so I text her again to see if they could come earlier, I really need to see them. She replies that they will leave straight away and will be there as soon as they can.

Back in the room, I sit and wait until my parents arrive. Half an hour passes when my phone goes, they are here. I text back to tell them the room number and to come straight up. They arrive within a few minutes. I open the door to let them in and give them both the biggest hug. So much has happened since I last saw them.

Mum hands me a bag and I go into the bathroom, take a shower and put on the fresh clothes which make me feel so much better. Mum and Dad want to hear about everything that has happened. I go through everything with them, but whenever I mention Leo's name Mum gives me a knowing look. *Does she know that I like him? But she doesn't know I'm gay so I'm probably just imagining it.*

We then take a look through the contract together, discussing all the points that are in there, and after an hour we are happy with it.

"Shall we go down and get a drink at the bar before we have to see Harriet?" I suggest.

Mum and Dad agree. Dad goes to order some drinks at the bar, and we make our way over to a table. Leo is sitting in the corner with who I assume is his brother. I catch his eye and wave. He waves back and gestures for us to come and join them.

"Mum, Dad, this is Leo," I say with a big smile on my face. Mum gives me that look again.

"Hi, Mr and Mrs Adams, this is my brother Mark."

Everyone shakes hands and I'm just disappointed that I couldn't shake Leo's hand just to feel his touch again.

We all sit down and talk about yesterday's events and speculate about what might happen later today. I try and catch a look at Leo every now and then and I catch him looking at me too, but they are only brief glances.

One o'clock comes around too fast. I have really enjoyed our families being together as it all seems so natural, but it's time to make our way to the conference room.

In the first two hours of the meeting, we go over the contracts and answer everyone's questions and change slight details. Eventually, they are all sorted and signed. It is now official; we are a group and Harriet even agrees with our name choice.

"I'm sure you are all wondering what will happen next. I would like you all to move to London in apartments we have set up for you. This will happen about the end of April, when we have some songs finalised. You will then go into the recording studio and start working on your first album. How does that sound?"

Move away from home, that sounds a bit daunting, but I'm sure it will be so much fun I can't wait. Everyone seems happy with this. Mum has tears in her eyes, but she is still smiling.

"Once we have a date we will be in contact again and then we will be in touch with you all, but until then that's everything for today." Harriet finishes speaking, stands up and starts shaking everyone's hand. Jasmin and George then follow her as she leaves the room.

"That's that, then. Let's get each other's numbers so we can keep in touch," suggests Xander.

We all put each other's numbers into our phones and one by one we hug each other. Leo hugs me last and says, "See you in

London, I can't wait."

"Me too," I reply. I can feel Mum watching us both.

We then all say our goodbyes and make our way out of the hotel.

Chapter Three

The day has finally arrived; I'm moving to London. I can't wait to see everyone; we have talked and texted over the last few weeks, but it will be great to see them again. I've packed all my things in my room and it is strangely empty in here. Mum has been a bit teary the last few days, but Dad has been keeping her spirits up. A car will be arriving shortly to drive me to London. I take a final look around my room, I don't know when I will be back again.

The car is here. The driver introduces himself to me, "Hi, I'm Jim. I will be yours and Leo's driver from now on." I can't believe we have our own driver.

It's time to say goodbye. Mum and Dad are both crying, but they assure me that everything will be fine.

I jump into the car, as Jim puts all my things into the boot. The car moves away and I wave out of the window at Mum and Dad. This is the most exciting thing I have ever done, although, I am a little worried about leaving home. I have a long journey ahead so I make myself comfortable and listen to some music on my phone, whilst looking out of the window watching the world go by.

Four hours later, we pull up outside a modern apartment block, it looks really nice. I have been given Shelly's number to ring as soon as I arrive so she can show me where to go. I phone the number and she answers after a few rings.

"Hi, Jacob, I'm on my way."

Two minutes later, she appears at the door.

"Hey, how are you? You are the first to arrive. Let me show you your new home."

"Hi, Shelly. I'm good, thanks, I can't wait to see it."

Shelly heads into the building and towards the lift, we get in and Shelly presses level four and we move off.

"Here's your key, you are number forty-one. The others are also on the same floor as you."

The lift door opens and Shelly leads the way to my new apartment. We arrive at a door. "This is you, I will leave you to have an explore. You have my number if you need anything."

I open the door and walk into a hallway, there's another door at the end. This opens into the living space. It is all open plan, there is a living room and kitchen diner and it is all dark blue and white. There is one more door at the side of the living room and this leads into the bedroom which has an on-suite next to it, these rooms are gold and cream. It's all amazing. As I'm trying to take it all in there is a knock on the door, it is Jim with all my things. He leaves it in the hallway and I thank him as he closes the door.

I take my stuff and start putting things where I want them. I unpack my clothes and toiletries first. Then I start adding my few special things from home around the living room. As I am finishing unpacking my phone goes, it's Leo. He has texted me saying that he has arrived and he wants to know if I'm okay and if I would like to come to his for a drink. I reply that would be great and that I will be there in ten minutes and ask him what number he is in. He replies that he is in number forty-two, he's next door to me.

I look at myself in the mirror and realise I cannot go looking like this, so I quickly change, try and do something with my hair and give myself a spray of my favourite aftershave.

"That's better."

I'm feeling a little nervous, even though we have spoken, it has only been as friends, we haven't mentioned anything that happened at the hotel, perhaps I did imagine something happened there.

I reach Leo's door and knock, my heart is pounding in my chest again. Leo opens the door and he is just as stunning as I remember.

"Hi, Jacob, it's great to see you. I've missed you." He gives me a hug, I can smell his aftershave and he smells amazing.

"Hi, I've missed you too." I can't believe he's missed me.

"Come in, let's have a drink."

I go into Leo's apartment it is set up just like mine but his is in a light blue. I sit down as Leo grabs two bottles of lager from the fridge. He hands one to me and sits on the sofa next to me.

We tell each other what we have been doing since we last spoke and we are so comfortable in each other company.

"I've texted the others to come in when they are all settled but I haven't heard from them yet," Leo says as he gets up to get us another drink.

"Have you heard from anyone about when we will be going into the studio?" I ask.

"No not yet, but I can't wait."

Leo sits back down, but this time he sits much closer to me than before. He is so close I can smell his aftershave and feel his leg against mine, excitement runs through me again.

We continue to talk, I am feeling so happy, after another drink Leo's phone goes.

"It's Alice, she's here and will be over in about half an hour, shall we order some food? I found some take away menus in a drawer."

"Yes, that will be great. I will text Xander to see how long he will be. You text Alice back to see if she wants some food."

I text Xander and he is in his apartment too and will also be over in half an hour. So, we decide to order some pizza for when they arrive.

The evening has gone by so fast, we have been eating, drinking and laughing so much. I notice throughout the night Leo has been very touchy with me. He has been placing his arm on the sofa behind my head and he brushes my hair every time he does it, there has also been little touches as we pass each other. I need to talk to him about it as I don't want to get my hopes up thinking things could happen between us if he doesn't realise he is doing it. Hopefully, I will get a chance this evening.

It's late and we have had a lot to drink, we all have one more, then Xander and Alice decide, it is time for them to go back to their apartments. I stay behind to talk to Leo.

"I will help you tidy up."

"Oh, great, thanks."

We are tidying the kitchen and as Leo moves past me his hand brushes my back once again. This is my opportunity.

"Leo," I begin nervously, "do you like me?"

"What do you mean, of course I do."

"No, I mean more than friends?"

Leo looks at me and goes to sit on the sofa, he puts his head into his hands. I go and join him and wait.

Finally, Leo starts to talk. "I don't know. When we first met, I thought you were amazing and we had some moments that made me think that you liked me. Then, we went back home and I thought of you so much."

Oh my god, he does like me.

Leo continues, "But then, I was out with some friends and I

liked some of the girls, I was with as well."

No, please like me, I'm shouting in my head.

"Now, we are here, all the feelings I have for you have come back again. I'm so confused. I have never had feelings for boys before it has always been girls. I thought I had enjoyed being with them, so I don't understand what is going on."

He stops talking and looks into my eyes, his amazing brown eyes looking deep into me trying to read me.

"Do you like me?" he finally asks.

"Yes, I think you are amazing. I have liked you from the first time I saw you. I thought you were stunning. I am gay. I have always liked boys but I haven't had a boyfriend before." I stop, full of relief to finally get it out in the open, to let someone know. "I've never told anyone that before, even my parents don't know."

I look at Leo wondering what he is thinking, is it too much for him.

"We don't have to do anything if you don't want to, not until you know how you feel. Let's just enjoy our time together, get to know each other better."

Leo looks at me smiling and nodding.

"That would be nice."

"Come on, let's get this place tidy for you."

I jump up and continue tidying the kitchen.

The next morning, a text message on my phone wakes me. It takes me a moment to realise where I am. I reach for my phone and it's from Shelly, our cars will be picking us up at midday today to take us to the studio. I check the time and it is only ten so I lay back down and think about what happened last night with Leo. I can't believe he has feelings for me but will anything actually come of them, I really don't know. I'm just going to have fun with him and the others and wait to see what will happen.

I decide to get up, have a quick breakfast before getting ready for the day.

Two hours later, we are all ready and waiting by the main doors for the cars to arrive. Five minutes later, they pull up.

"Jacob, you are in the car with me, aren't you?" asks Leo.

I walk over to the car Leo is in and join him in the back. The car sets off and as I'm looking out of the window to see where we are going, I feel Leo place his hand on my leg. I look over at him.

"Is that okay?" he asks, looking a little embarrassed as there is a pink flush on his cheeks.

I nod and place my hand on top of his, he gives me one of his cheeky smiles and turns to look out of the window. His hand stays on my leg until we arrive at the studio but as the car starts slowing down, he moves it away quickly. Is he afraid someone will see?

We get out of the car and join Alice and Xander and make our way into the studio. Shelly is waiting for us just inside.

"Hi, follow me and I will introduce you to some people who you are going to be working with, George is here too."

We follow Shelly into a room, George is stood talking to two men we haven't met before and five other people are sat around the tables. George turns around and welcomes us in,

"Hello, how are you all? Looks like you've all been having a bit too much of a good time. Enjoying the free drinks at your apartment?" Laughing at us all, we all must look a little hungover.

Shelly then introduces us to the two men talking to George.

"This is Luke and Dan. They are your song writers. Luke

writes your lyrics and Dan sorts the music side. They have been working hard, coming up with songs for your album. I will let you all get acquainted and I will see you all later." Shelly leaves the room.

We all say our hello's and George gestures for us to take a seat.

George then introduces us to the others. "These five wonderfully talented people are your band. This is Megan, Fred, Harry, Tori and Jack. Now we have a few songs ready for you to try today. The first one we are going to start working on hopefully will be your first single. We are hoping to release that in about six weeks if we can get it together in time."

"What is the song called?" asks Alice.

"I want to go dancing with you," George replies. "It's an upbeat song that should be good for a first single. I'm going to leave you with Luke, Dan and the band. They will talk you through that song and the others that we hope will go on your album. See you later."

Luke then speaks up, "Right, guys, we have a lot of work to do to nail this song as soon as we can so we can make you into a famous pop group."

We all look at each other, we are ready.

The next four weeks go by in a blur, during the day we are in the studio working on the songs. The evenings are not fun filled like the first night, we are just so exhausted when we get back from the studio. On occasions, we have gone into each other's apartments to have a meal but mainly we go straight to bed, not at all how I thought it would be. A few of the evenings me and Leo have been able to spend some time together just the two of us, talking and watching television. These nights have been lovely, we are really getting to know more and more about each other. Some of these evenings when we have been snuggling together, I have really wanted to kiss him, but he always moves away when I have lent in to try and he has still not said that he wants to start a relationship with me, but I realise that I still need to give him more time.

It's Friday morning and we are making our way to the studio. I can't wait for this day to be finished as Leo again rejected me last night and I just need some time to myself and we have got the whole weekend free. Mum and Dad are coming to visit Saturday afternoon and they are staying the night. I can't wait to see them.

We get to the studio and waiting for us there is Harriet. We haven't seen her since we have arrived, it has been either George or Jasmin that have been meeting with us.

"Hello, how are you all? I have been hearing good things about you. We have got something different for you today. You are not going to be recording today, we are going over to a photography studio and doing a promotional photo shoot for your single."

"That sounds amazing." Alice is excited, I am too.

We get back into the cars and go to the photography studio. When we arrive, Harriet ushers us into a room. On one side are four areas set up for our hair and make-up. On the other side are four rails of clothes. This is going to be so much fun.

"Take a seat, everyone, and we will get started."

We all sit in our seats and we are introduced to our personal team. I have Steve for my hair, Jackie for my make-up and Taylor who is in charge of my outfits.

"We will be working with you for any photo shoots, television appearances and on tour," Taylor tells me.

Steve starts on my hair first; he cuts a bit of my hair but we agree that it should stay a little longer on the top and left a little messy. When he finishes, Jackie does my make-up; she only puts a little bit on just to stop any shine on the photographs. Next, the bit I have been looking forward to, the clothes.

Taylor starts looking through the clothing rail and as she is deciding what I'm going to wear, I look over at Leo and he seems to be having a good time too. He has also had his hair done and he looks so good.

Taylor picks out a pair of dark blue jeans, a white long sleeve shirt and a navy jacket. I love this outfit, it reminds me of the outfit, I wore at the audition.

"Put these on and let's see how it looks."

She points to a door where I can get changed. I put the clothes on and look at myself in the mirror, I look good. I really like this outfit and my hair has never looked like this before. I step out of the changing room, and I catch Leo looking at me. He checks no one is looking at us and he walks over and whispers in my ear, "You look absolutely amazing," then walks away, slightly blushing.

I catch Alice looking at us and she gives me a smile. *Does she know?*

"You look great," Taylor says as she starts adjusting things to the outfit. She pulls up the jacket sleeves a little bit to show more of the shirt sleeves. She then unbuttons two buttons on the shirt to show more of my chest. Leo is watching me the whole time, he can't seem to take his eyes off me. I can't help smiling to myself.

When Taylor is happy with the outfit, she sends me to another room, where I get some photographs taken on my own. When the others are ready, they come into the room too. Xander comes in first, he is wearing light blue jeans and a black t-shirt. Then Leo enters, and that exciting feeling returns. He is dressed in tight beige trousers and a dark red shirt, he is looking incredible. Finally, Alice arrives and she looks so different with her straightened hair, make-up and grey suit and sheer blouse on. When everyone has had their individual photographs taken, they start the group ones. We soon come to a decision that Alice is not allowed to stand next to me if she is wearing high heal shoes as she towers over me, everyone finds this extremely funny, but I don't.

Leo must have noticed it, he whispers to me, "Never mind about them, I think you're perfect." This gives me a funny feeling in my tummy. What is he doing to me, I want him so much.

We spend the rest of the afternoon changing outfits and doing different photo poses. We have so much fun. When the photographers decide that they have got what they need, we go back to the first room.

Harriet is waiting for us there. "That was a great photo shoot, we got some great pictures. These are going to be sent off to a few different magazines with information about you and your single. They should be out next week."

I can't wait to see us all in a magazine, that will be so strange. Harriet continues, "We have got another treat for you before you have a lovely weekend with your families. We have organised a night out for you, dinner and then a club. We are going to let you choose one of the outfits from today to wear if you would like to?"

We are so excited about this. We all choose our favourite items and get changed. I choose the first one as I think this was Leo's favourite.

When we are ready, the cars are waiting for us and they drive us to a restaurant where we have a lovely meal and champagne, I'm really starting to like champagne. After the meal, we are taken to a club, Jim lets us know that he will be waiting outside for us when we are ready to go back.

Me and Leo get out of the car. Leo gives me his cheeky smile and runs his hand down my back, sending shivers through my spine.

"I can't wait to dance with you, you look so good in that."

He's flirting with me again and it feels really good.

We go into the club and it is really busy, but they have a table set aside for us. We sit down and order some drinks. We are having a great night dancing, drinking, laughing. Xander, Leo and myself are getting a lot of attention from the girls when we are the dance floor. I don't really like it, so I go and join Alice at the table. I order another drink and as I am sipping it, I watch Leo. He has forgotten all about me and is loving all the attention from the girls.

Alice is looking at me. "Are you okay?" she asks.

"No, not really." How has the evening gone from him wanting to be with me to him wanting to be with every girl in the place?

"You really like him, don't you?"

"How do you know?"

"I have noticed little things between the two of you and you are not very careful at hiding your feelings for each other when it's just the four of us together and earlier I heard what Leo said to you."

"He doesn't know how he feels about me. He likes me but as you can see, he likes girls too. He's never had feelings for a boy before. I can't watch this any more. I'm going." I stand up to leave.

Alice stands up too. "Wait, I will come with you. I will let them know we are going."

I nod and wait for her to make her way through the dance floor to Xander and Leo. She tells them we are leaving. Leo looks over at me with a guilty look on his face, but before he can see my reaction I turn and walk towards the entrance.

Alice catches up with me. "They are staying. Leo asked me if you were okay, I told him you weren't."

"What did he say when you said that."

"Nothing, he just looked a bit worried. Come on, let's get out of here."

The cars are waiting outside just as they said they would be. As we get in, Jim asks, "Did you have a good night?"

"No, not really," I reply.

As we drive home, Alice holds my hand, she knows that I'm upset. Why does he make me feel like this? It's not fair.

We arrive back and I reach my apartment.

"Good night, Alice, and thanks for tonight."

"Are you going to be okay?" she asks.

"I will be, I think I need to see Leo just as a friend like you and Xander and not someone I want to be with. It hurts me too much that he doesn't want to be with me."

Alice gives me a hug and kisses my cheek and makes sure I get into my apartment.

Once in, I put the kettle on, I need a cup of tea before bed to calm me down. I can't believe it. Why did I ever think he would want to be with me? As I'm sitting drinking my tea, there is a loud knock at my door. I get up to go and see who it is. I open the door and there's Leo. He's not looking very happy, he walks straight into the living room.

"Why did you leave?" he asks in an angry voice.

"You looked like you were having a great time and I didn't

think you would miss me."

"I thought you were having a good time too?"

"I was, but then all those girls started hanging around and I don't want any of that kind of attention. But you seemed to love it, so I left you to it." I am beginning to get frustrated with him.

"It was just a bit of fun. If the girls like us, then they will, hopefully, buy our records. I didn't want any of them."

"It didn't look like that and I think if Alice hadn't told you I was leaving, you would still be there." The fury is building inside me and I don't like it.

"Jacob, what's wrong? It was just a bit of fun." Leo calms down and starts to look worried.

"I feel like you are using me for company when you are alone, then when something more appealing comes along, you go for that."

"No, it's not like that." Leo is looking at me with pleading eyes.

"Well, what is it like, Leo, do you want to be with me or not? You are giving me such mixed messages. I don't know what to think."

"I don't know."

"I think you should leave."

"I don't want to go."

"I want you to go. I've had enough of you messing with my feelings."

Leo stands there looking at me not moving, I need him to leave. I'm close to tears and I don't want him to see me cry.

"Leave," I shout.

He looks at me one more time and leaves. I watch as he closes the door. I then throw myself onto my bed and I can't help it but the tears come. I finally fall to sleep, but I have a very restless night.

Chapter Four

The next morning, I wake up and for a brief moment I have forgotten about last night, then it hits me hard. Why can't he just be with me? I'm so glad Mum and Dad are coming today.

I'm sat eating breakfast when there is a quiet knock on my door. If its Leo, I don't want to see him. Opening the door, I'm relieved to see it's Alice.

"Are you okay? I heard you both shouting last night."

"No, we had a fight. He wasn't happy that I left the club and I'm not happy that he's messing me around."

"Jacob, I'm so sorry it hasn't worked out. I thought you two would have been really great together."

"I'm not going to talk about Leo today. My mum and dad are coming later and I just want to spend time with them."

"Maybe, you should talk to them about Leo, it might help."

"But they don't know I'm gay."

"Perhaps, it's time they do. What time do they leave tomorrow? I will come over to see how you are."

"I don't know. I will text you when they are gone. Who is coming to see you today?"

"My sister is coming later. I can't wait to see her. Please tell your parents, Jacob, they should know. It will make you feel better. Have a great day and I will see you tomorrow."

Alice is right, I do need to tell my mum and dad, it's time.

Mum and Dad are arriving at midday. Throughout the morning, all I do is check the time and my phone, not only to see if they have arrived but also to see if Leo has messaged me. He hasn't.

Mum and Dad finally arrive and I show them around the apartment and they are overwhelmed by it all, especially the fact that I have made them lunch. Mum keeps looking at me as if she is trying to read my mind; does she sense something is wrong?

We sit down to eat and I don't talk or eat very much, I am so nervous.

"Are you okay, love?" Mum eventually asks.

"I've got something to tell you both."

They look at me with very concerned faces.

"I have wanted to tell you this for a long time, but I have been too scared." I stop for a moment and take a deep breath. "I'm gay."

Mum and Dad look at me and they are both smiling.

"We know, Jacob. We have known for a long time. We were just waiting for you to tell us or just bring a boy home for us to meet."

All the pressure of carrying this secret for so long has suddenly lifted. Mum comes over to me and gives me a hug, then Dad does too.

"Something is still wrong though, what is it?" Mum asks.

How do mums know everything? I then tell them all about Leo and what has been happening.

"We thought you liked Leo when you were together at the bar. Have you talked to him this morning about what happened last night, now that you have both had time to calm down?" Mum asks.

"No, I can't at the moment. I'm so confused and feel messed around by him. I just need a couple of days."

Mum rubs the top of my hand and looks at me to say

everything will be fine. Then dad suggests we go for a walk and explore the area.

As we are on our way out, Leo is just going into his apartment with who I am guessing is his mum. He spots me and gives a small smile, I smile back. He goes inside and I wonder if he is going to tell his mum about us.

I spend a wonderful day with Mum and Dad; we walk, we talk and we eat too much food, I didn't realise how much I miss them.

Sunday afternoon comes around to quickly and it is time for them to go back home. I want to go back with them but I can't let so many people down, so we say our goodbyes and go back to my apartment. I text Alice to let her know that Mum and Dad are gone and she can come over whenever she is free. Alice replies to let me know her sister is still here and she will be over later.

Two hours later, there's a knock on my door. I assume it is Alice so I hurry to let her in but as I open the door, it's not Alice. Leo is standing in front of me.

"Can I come in?"

I nod and we head into the living room and he stands in the middle of the room not looking at me.

"What do you want, Leo?"

"I'm sorry." He looks up at me and he seems genuinely sorry.

"I have been thinking about you all weekend and I spoke to my mum about everything. I think I just needed to say how I was feeling out loud to someone that wasn't you."

"Why couldn't you talk to me?"

"Because you know how you feel about all this and I don't."

"What did your mum say?"

"She said, I should do whatever makes me happy."

"Your mum's right, but what does make you happy?"

"You do," Leo replies and I am shocked by his answer.

"Me?" He's choosing me.

Leo walks over to me and puts his hands on my arms and I think he is going to kiss me, when we are interrupted by a knock at the door.

"It's Alice, she is coming over to see how I am." I go to open the door for her.

"Hi." Alice looks in and spots Leo. "Are you okay? Do you want me to come in?"

"No, we are just talking."

She lowers her voice so Leo can't hear, "Are you sure?"

I answer in a quiet voice to match hers, "He has apologised and he has told his mum about us. I think he wants to be with me."

"That's great, but make sure it is what he really wants."

I smile at her and thank her for coming over, then I walk back to Leo.

The moment has passed and it looks like he is going to leave.

"Where are you going, don't you want to stay for a bit?" I ask him.

"No, not tonight, we have a busy two weeks ahead, what with the single being released and I want to get an early night. I'm glad we've spoken. Good night, Jacob." He hugs me and leaves.

I'm disappointed but can't believe what has just happened he has chosen me. I wished I had kissed him.

The next two weeks are chaotic; we do radio and television appearances, magazine interviews, all to promote the single. We also sung our song live on television for the first time which was the most nervous I have ever been, but Leo was always by my side giving me encouraging words and small touches when no one is looking to calm me down.

We made it to Friday, the single has been played all over the radio and television for the past two weeks. Today is the day we find out what position it has entered in the charts. We would love to have number one, but if it's not and it is in the top ten, we will still be ecstatic.

We are all gathered at the studio. Everyone is here; Harriet, George and Jasmin, Luke, Dan, the band and Shelly. Shelly has not stopped talking to Xander the whole time we have been here. I think they like each other.

I'm stood next to Leo and he has his arm around my waist and he keeps running his fingers along the top of my jeans, I think he's nervous. I squeeze his hand to reassure him. We look at each other and smile then we catch Harriet looking at us, so we move apart. We are not sure how we feel about people knowing about us yet and we don't know how they will react to the news either. Harriet whispers something to George and he makes his way over to us. He purposely stands in between us both.

"How are you boys, nervous?"

We both nod our heads. Why did he have to come over? This is our time.

We wait a few more moments. Shelly keeps checking the emails on her tablet in between talking to Xander. She checks it again and this time she goes over to Harriet and shows her something. Harriet looks happy as she stands up.

"Jasmin, open the champagne. We are number one."

What! No! We got number one. I can't believe it. Alice and Xander run over to us, screaming, and we all hug each other.

Then as I go to hug Leo, I can't help myself, I kiss him. But as soon as I do, I pull away.

"Sorry."

"Don't be sorry," and he grabs me and kisses me back. It is deep, long and full of passion.

As we pull apart, the room is in silence. I look around. Alice, Xander and Shelly are all smiling at us but Harriet has a face like thunder.

Harriet walks over to us, "What do you think you are doing? I want to see you both in my office tomorrow for a meeting."

Harriet then turns to Alice and Xander, "You two now have the day off."

Then she storms out of the room.

George looks at us. "It will be all right. Don't worry, I will speak to her. Go and celebrate having a number one single, it's great news." George leaves with Jasmin to follow Harriet.

I look at Leo and the joy I have just felt has gone. He holds my hand and squeezes it.

"It's going to be all right," he says, trying to reassure me. "Shall we go out for a drink?"

"I don't really feel like going out now. I'm going home. You all go out."

"I'm not going anywhere without you," Leo tells me.

All the others decide to go to a local bar. Me and Leo make our way home.

"Do you want to come in?" I ask Leo as we reach my door.

"Yes, of course, I do."

We go in and I get us both a drink from the fridge and we sit down. For a while, we sit in silence, then Leo puts his drink down and takes mine from my hand.

"You look so good in this outfit. I loved it the first time you wore it at the photo shoot. I wish that night didn't end like it did. I wanted to take it off you."

He then kisses me. I put my hands in his hair and kiss him back. Feeling his tongue brush against my lips, wanting to get inside. I open my mouth slightly and he moves his tongue in my mouth searching for mine. It becomes more passionate the more we kiss and I start to undo his shirt buttons and for the first time I see his very toned chest. I move my mouth down his neck, making small light bites then running my tongue over his chest. I hear his heart beat faster and feel him take in deep breaths. He then takes my jacket and shirt off and as we kiss, I feel his bare skin against mine. This makes me moan out loud and I can no longer control myself and I reach down and touch him over the top of his trousers. I look at him and he seems a bit surprised.

"Is this okay?" I ask slightly breathless.

He nods, so I touch him again and I can feel his jeans becoming tighter, he is excited. I stand and pull him up and take him into the bedroom.

I wake up and I look over and there naked in my bed is Leo. The sheet only covers his bottom half. I stare at him for a while taking in his beautiful face and his toned arms and chest. I then lean over and kiss him which stirs him from his sleep. He opens his eyes and I wonder if I will ever get used to the amazing colour of them.

He smiles, "Good morning, how are you?"

"I'm really good, how are you?"

"Wow that was amazing last night, I have never felt like that before." He has a sparkle in his eye.

I kiss him again and with this he throws me over on to the bed and rolls on top of me kissing me back. We spend another wonderful hour in bed but then it is time to get up to face the meeting with Harriet.

Chapter Five

Two hours later, we are on our way to Harriet's office. Leo is holding my hand tight. We are both worried about what is going to be said.

We arrive and Shelly is waiting for us.

"I'm sure it's going to be fine," she says kindly as she takes us to Harriet's office.

We are asked to wait outside, and I feel like a naughty school boy waiting for the head teacher. After keeping us waiting for another ten minutes, she opens the door.

Looking very serious, she says, "Come in and take a seat."

We both sit down and wait to hear what she is going to say. Eventually she starts talking.

"Now, you know why you are here, I want to talk to you about what happened yesterday."

Neither of us say anything back to her.

"If you are thinking about starting a relationship, I advise you not to."

We both look at each other in shock.

"Why can't we?" Leo asks.

"This would not look good for the group. The female fan base is the largest group to spend money on you all. They want to think that it is a possibility that they could be with you. But if you two are together they will not think of you this way. One because you are taken and two because you are gay. They may not want to spend their money."

I can't believe what she is saying, surely people won't care we are together and I don't care what girls think, I just want to be happy. I wonder what Leo is thinking, I look over at him and I'm so surprised he looks furious.

"What will happen if we don't agree and we want to be together, it's taken me a long time to realise I want to be with Jacob and you're telling me I can't." He sounds so angry.

"Yes, that is what I'm telling you. You can't be together or say that you are gay. And what will happen if you continue, we may have to find someone else to be in the group. You are here to make money and the female fan base makes money."

Leo looks so angry. I want to comfort him but I can't. I also don't want him to do anything stupid but before I can say anything Leo stands up.

"I'm not having this. You can't make me do anything I don't want to. I like Jacob and want to be with him and that's final." He storms out of the room and slams the door behind him.

I go to get up to follow him but Harriet says, "Sit down, Jacob."

I look at Harriet then to the door, I want to run after Leo.

"Jacob, sit down!" she says more forcefully.

I sit back down but cannot look at her.

"Jacob, I know this is hard for the both of you. We didn't expect to have this issue or we would have mentioned something about not having relationships together. But can you understand why you can't be together."

No, I don't! I want to shout at her but I say nothing.

"If you continue this relationship, we will have to let you both go and we probably won't keep Alice and Xander either. You are all here to make money and if you can't then we will find others who can."

I'm shaking with anger and close to tears, but what can I say I look up at her.

She smiles but it doesn't reach her eyes.

"Jacob, do you really want to let down Leo, Alice and Xander? Do you really want to split the group up before it's really started to get good? It will get good, Jacob, you are all going to go so far, you will make so much money that the world will be your oyster."

What do I do? I don't want to ruin everything for the others but I think I'm falling in love with Leo. I feel Harriet watching me.

"Don't do anything silly, Jacob, you do not want to ruin everyone's lives," she says as if she has read my mind. "I want you to talk to Leo and tell him that you cannot be together, then we can all get back to work."

"Can I go?" I ask I just want to get out of here and find Leo.

"Yes, you can, but just remember what I said and, Jacob, I do mean it so think very carefully before you make any decision."

Looking at her, I'm suddenly full of hate.

I walk out of the room leaving the door open in defiance. I need Leo. I find him sat in Shelly's office it looks like he's been crying and Shelly is comforting him.

When they both see me, Shelly says, "I can't believe she is doing this. She can't, can she?"

"I think she can and will," I reply walking over to Leo.

"We need to talk but not here let's go home."

I hold out my hand for him to take so I can help him up. He looks at me, his eyes glistening with tears and I fall in love with him a little more at that moment. He takes my hand and stands up, as he does he reaches in and hugs me, I hug him back and hold him tight, I don't let go until he does.

"Come on, let's go home. See you later, Shelly."

We arrive home, Leo hasn't said anything in the car and I'm glad as I didn't want to talk in the car as we don't know Jim well enough yet and I'm not sure if he would say anything. I want the safe feeling of home before I speak to Leo. I have decided what we should do, I hope Leo agrees with me.

I take Leo to his, I think he will be more comfortable there. When we get in, I make us a cup of tea and sit next to him on the sofa.

"I can't believe what she said, I'm so angry. I just want to be with you Jacob and she's not stopping me." Leo's voice is shaking as he speaks. I need to calm him down.

"Leo, listen. She will break up the group if we stay together. I don't want to be the person who destroys four lives."

Leo looks at me he can't believe what I'm saying.

"What? Are you saying we can't be together after what we've been through? I don't care about the group."

"Yes, you do care, Leo, we all do, but I'm not saying we can't be together either. I want to be with you and I'm so happy that you feel the same way."

"But how can we be together?" Leo asks, finally calming down.

"We will stay together but we will have to keep it a secret from the outside world, this way no one gets hurt." Leo doesn't look convinced. "I wish I could shout about being with you to the whole world but I can't, we can't. When we are at home, we can be a couple, I think we can trust Alice and Xander to keep our secret. We can also let our close families know but no one else."

"I hate that, it's so unfair why we can't do what we want." Leo sounds so upset. I've never seen him like this before.

"I know it is very unfair but I would rather have it like this than not have you at all. And one day, hopefully we will be able to be a couple out in the open."

I lean over and kiss him, he kisses me back but this time it feels different than before. This kiss is full of feelings and emotions that is coursing through us both.

"So, do you think we can do it? We will have to be very careful but I don't want to ruin everything," I ask Leo.

"Yes," he replies as he kisses me again.

A few hours have passed and we have been snuggling up on Leo's sofa not wanting to move, to just be in each other's company. There's a knock on the door, Leo gets up to see who it is. It's Alice and Xander, Leo lets them in.

"How long have you been back, we have been waiting to see what is going on?" Alice looks worried.

"What did Harriet say?" Xander asks.

We tell them everything that has happened up to the point where we have decided to stay together.

"She can't do that, that's so unfair. So, if you had a girlfriend outside the group or you were not gay, that would be okay but because you are two boys and in the group they won't let you be together? It's disgraceful." I had never seen Xander so passionate about anything before.

"What are you going to do?" Alice asks quietly she is still looking worried.

"Look, we don't want to split the group up as that's not fair for any of us, so don't worry," I say looking at Alice. "But we do want to be together, we are going to keep it to ourselves. It's not what we both really want but we feel this is the only thing we can do at the moment."

Leo then says, "It took me some time to realise that this is what I want, who I want and I don't want to let it go. We will need your help. When we are home or with our families, we are a couple but when we are working or out in public, we can't be seen to be together. We don't want anything to happen that will jeopardise the group and our futures."

"Will you help us and be on our side?" I finally ask them.

Alice smiles, "Of course, we will, it's not fair but we will help you hide it."

"Thank you," we both reply.

"We will leave you to it. Do you know if we are back in the studio on Monday?" asks Xander.

"I don't know but I'm sure I will hear from Harriet to see what we have decided. I will let you know when I find out."

Alice hugs me and Leo and they both leave.

We are suddenly alone again and this is how I like it, just me and Leo. Leo moves towards me puts his hands on my hips, kisses me and says, "Do you want to stay the night?"

I nod my head and this time he pulls me into his bedroom.

We wake up Sunday morning in each other's arms. We have the whole day free to spend together.

Leo looks over at me with a big smile on his face, "I'm going to make you breakfast in bed." He jumps out of bed naked and I admire his perfect body.

"I would put something on first if I was you," laughing at him as he bounces out of the bedroom door, not taking any notice of what I said.

I can hear him clattering around in the kitchen and I am feeling very content but my thoughts are disrupted by my phone ringing. I pick it up and see that it is Harriet. I get out of bed and walk to the bedroom door and close it to hide the noise that Leo is making before I answer it.

"Hello."

"Hello, Jacob, how are you this morning? Did you talk to Leo? Have you decided ?"

I must remember not to sound happy, she can't know.

"I'm not good as you can imagine. I am very upset and Leo won't talk to me."

As I am saying this, Leo comes in with two cups of tea in his hands. I quickly put my finger to my mouth to tell him to be quiet.

"So, you have decided that its best for the group that you don't get together?"

As Harriet is speaking Leo crawls on to the bed and starts kissing my shoulder and neck I try and push him away as I'm going to laugh but he keeps coming back.

"Yes, that is what we have decided to do. It's the best for everyone," I say, trying to hold in my laughter.

"That's great to hear, I'm sure Leo will come around. We need to get back to work so I want you all in the studio early Monday morning. Can you tell the others?"

"Yes, okay I will."

"Great well goodbye, Jacob, you have made the right decision." And she hangs up.

Yes, I have made the right decision but it's not the one that you want.

I turn to Leo, "You are terrible. I couldn't think straight."

Leo laughs, kisses me and announces, "I will be back with breakfast, then we are having a lazy day in bed," he bounces off the bed again.

We spend all morning in bed, hugging and talking, it is total bliss. Finally, we decide we should get out of bed.

"Come and have a shower with me," Leo says as he walks

into the bathroom. I follow him in and I have never done anything so thrilling and romantic at the same time. I wish we could stay like this forever. When we get out, I put on a pair of Leo's tracksuit bottoms and a t-shirt, I didn't want to go next door to get any of my own clothes, I didn't want to burst the bubble.

"I like you in my clothes," Leo states as he pulls the waist band of the trousers pulling me closer and kisses me softly.

We spend the rest of the day not doing anything, just spending time together. Leo makes us a special dinner and I'm surprised how good he is at cooking. We've had the best day ever.

Later, I tell him that I think I better go home, to get ready for tomorrow and that I want to phone my parents as I haven't spoken to them all week. I am sad to leave but if I don't go now I may never.

Leo sticks his bottom lip out at me in a fake sad way and I can't resist, I lean in and lightly bite it.

"Hey! Please stay tonight, I don't want you to go," Leo pleads.

"I can't, I need to get ready for the week. I've not been home since you stayed and I have to get sorted."

I look around and start picking up all my things. "I will see you in the morning."

I kiss him and he holds me not letting me go. As he's laughing, I wriggle free and wave to him as I close the door.

As soon as I get in, I phone Mum.

"Hi, Mum."

"Hi, love. How are things?"

I tell her everything that has happened this week, well nearly everything!

"I can't believe that." She sounds shocked, angry and upset.

"Come home, Jacob, then you and Leo can be together properly."

"I can't, Mum, I can't let the others down."

"But it's not right what she is doing to you"

"I know, Mum, but me and Leo are still together so she hasn't won. We just have to be careful when we are out or at work."

"Are you sure you are happy about it, because I'm not?"

"Mum, we are good, we had a great day together today and I'm sure it will work, so you don't need to worry. I have to go now as I got stuff to do and I need an early night."

"Okay, but if it gets too much, just come home. I love you."

"Thanks, Mum, I love you too."

I put the phone down and I wish that this day would never end it has been extraordinary. Now comes the hard part, we have to make it convincing that me and Leo are not together.

Chapter Six

The last few months of this year have been crazy. We have released our album, and it has gone straight in at number one. We have been planning a tour for next year and now finally we have some time off.

We have been able to convince Harriet and everyone else outside our inner circle that we are not together whilst having a full-on relationship in private, it has been fantastic.

We have had a few moments where we have slipped up. One time was during a television interview, Leo put his arm around me whilst we were sat on the sofa and I put my hand on his knee, we were in our little world so much that we weren't listening to the presenter. Luckily, Alice and Xander are great at pulling us out of it, covering it up or saying the right thing to distract everyone. We are so thankful that they are on our side.

We are now leaving home to spend time with our families. I am going to Mum and Dad's, while Leo is going back to his mum's. Then he is coming up to me for New Year's Eve. I don't know what I will do without him for the next few weeks.

It's Monday morning and we are all packed and ready to go our separate ways, it is going to be really strange not seeing everyone for a month. We wish each other a good Christmas and say our goodbyes. Me and Leo have said goodbye inside just in case any fans or photographers catch us. We then all drive off in separate directions.

I can't wait to get to Mum and Dad's as I haven't been back since I left in May. I also can't wait for Leo to come and stay with us and spend some time with my family. We have planned a trip for just the two of us after New Year. On my way, my phone goes.

Hi Jacob, I'm back at mums and missing you already.

A big grin appears on my face and I type a message back.

Missing you too. Counting the days until I see you again.

Seconds later, I get a reply.

Me too xxxx

When I arrive, Mum and Dad have a party to celebrate my return. It's great to spend time with everyone I haven't seen for such a long time.

Christmas goes by and I have had so much fun. New Year's Eve has finally come around and Leo will be here in an hour. Mum is panicking, she hasn't stopped tidying the house and has made sure she has all of Leo's favourite things in. I have never seen her like this before.
"Mum, will calm down he is only here for today and then we are leaving tomorrow afternoon."
We have booked a remote cabin at The Lakes for just the two of us. We are so looking forward to it.
He's finally here, I see the taxi pull up outside.
"Mum, Dad, he's here," I shout out to them.

I go to open the door to let him in. As he gets out of the taxi, I notice that there is a photographer in a car across the road. What the hell is he doing? Leo spots him too, he quickly grabs his bags and rushes into the house.

"Mum, close all the curtains, there's a photographer outside trying to get pictures."

Mum and Dad rush around the house closing all the curtains as we wait in the hallway.

When it is safe, I hug Leo tight, he hugs me back then he pulls me away to look at me. He kisses me gently on the lips, "I've missed you so much."

"I've missed you too, come in and say hi to Mum and Dad."

We go into the living room where they are waiting.

"Hi, Mr and Mrs Adams. Did you have a good Christmas?" Leo sounds a little bit nervous.

"Yes, thank you, Leo, did you? And calls us Lisa and Ron," Mum says.

"Yes, I did, thanks, it was just, Mum, my brother, Mark, and his new girlfriend, Tessa."

"I bet it was good to catch up with them, we've loved having Jacob back," Dad says to Leo.

"It was. I haven't seen my brother since I left in May, so it was great to see him and meet Tessa."

"I'll put the kettle on. Do you want a cup of tea, Leo?" Mum asks.

"Yes, please."

As Mum is going into the kitchen, I say, "I'm just going to take Leo upstairs so he can unpack his stuff."

Leo follows me upstairs and into my room and as soon as we get in there, he throws me onto the bed and kisses me hard.

"I have really missed you," he says in between kisses.

I try and push him off. "We can't do this here, I don't feel comfortable doing anything with Mum and Dad downstairs," I say standing up off the bed.

"Spoil sport, so we can't do anything until we go away?" Leo asks looking a bit disappointed.

"No. You will just have to wait. Its only one more day."

"Am I at least sleeping with you in here?"

"Yes. You are sleeping with me in here."

"Good," and he seems happy with that.

We go back down stairs and Mum has the tea ready. We sit down and talk about what we've been doing over Christmas, we talk about Leo's family and wonder about how Alice and Xander Christmas was.

Leo then asks, "What are the plans for later?"

"Well, Mum has booked a table at a restaurant, if you fancy going out to eat? We can then go for a drink or we could stay in. It's up to you?"

"A meal sounds nice but could we come back here for a drink. I don't fancy being out to long on New Year's Eve. We won't be able to be ourselves as there will be to many people about."

"That sounds great, Mum's booked a quiet part of the restaurant so hopefully we won't be noticed."

"What time should we leave?" Leo asks.

"The table is booked for seven, so we should leave about half an hour before," Mum replies.

"Great. Is it okay if I take a shower and get changed before we go?"

"Of course, it is, Leo. Jacob will get you a towel."

It is time to leave and Leo looks and smells amazing I don't know how I'm going to keep my hands off him until we go away.

"I will go and check to see if it's okay for you both to come out, wait here," Dad says, as he opens the front door.

He goes to the car, opens all the doors so it's easier for us to get in. He then starts the engine.

"Come on," he shouts over the noise of the car.

We run out of the house and into the car. The photographer is still there but we have been to quick and he misses us as we pull out of the drive.

Me and Leo are laughing in the back of the car, happy to have not been caught. Leo holds my hand all the way to the restaurant.

At the restaurant, we are shown to our table in the corner. As we are walking through, we get a few glances and we hope people haven't recognised who we are.

We have a lovely meal and I enjoy being with my family and Leo together. I feel happy and free but as we are making our way out some people come up to us asking for autographs and selfies. We love our fans but we don't want any photographs taken of just us, when we are all together as the group, we are fine having pictures taken with them but not like this I don't feel comfortable about it. It starts to become too much as more people start coming over to us. Mum rushes out to get the car, while Dad tries to get us outside as quick as possible, by the time we have got to the car we have had so many photographs taken.

I sit in the car and I'm shaking, Leo doesn't dare comfort me in case we are seen. Mum drives away as quick as possible.

"Are you okay?" Dad asks as we get clear of the restaurant.

"I am but I don't think, Jacob, is," Leo replies.

"I'm okay, just a bit shaken up."

"I'm sorry, we shouldn't have gone out. Its ruined the evening for you both." Mum sounds upset.

"It's not your fault, Mum, so don't get upset. We both thought we could have a quiet meal. I thought people would not recognise us or if they did they would respect our privacy. Obviously not."

We arrive home and Mum pulls the car as close as she can to the house. Dad jumps out opens the house door and we make a run for it before anyone can see us.

Once inside and the door is closed, I relax. I hadn't realised how much I had been shaking. That really unsettled me.

"Are you sure you are okay?" Leo asks as he puts his arms around me.

"I am now." And I snuggle my head into his neck and take in his smell. It comforts me.

"Come on, you two, let's have a drink, put some music on and get celebrating New Year," Dad shouts from the living room.

From then on, we have a great night. We drink, dance and laugh so much. Mum has loved dancing with Leo, I'm glad they get on so well. Midnight approaches and we are all feeling a little tipsy, we count down the end of 2017, what a year we have had.

"Three, two, one. Happy New Year," we all call out. I hug Mum and Dad and so does Leo. Then I'm where I enjoy being the most, in Leo's arms. I look him deep in his eyes and we kiss.

"Happy New Year," I say to him. "Last year was the best year of my life, I hope this one can top it?"

After a few more drinks, we are making our way to bed and it's the first night we have gone to bed and just fallen to sleep in each other's arms. I like it but I wish we could have done more. Tomorrow and maybe we will go all the way whilst we are there. This thought fills my head as I snuggle into Leo even more than I was and drift off to sleep.

We wake up late, later than we should have. We want to get on the road, and I haven't even packed. We have a quick breakfast and I throw some stuff into a bag and say bye to mum and dad. I will be back here before going back to London. Leo will meet me there he is going back to his mums after our week away.

I am driving and it takes us nearly two hours to get to our cabin. When we arrive, the place is breath-taking, it is so secluded. Mum has ordered us a food delivery to arrive when we reach the cabin, so we don't have to go anywhere to public.

We go inside the cabin and it is stunning so comfy and warm.

"Alone at last," Leo states as he comes closer to me. He puts his arms around my waist and he has his cheeky smile on his face. I know that look. He kisses me and it's a long passionate kiss and I can feel that he is excited.

"We have to wait, the delivery will be here soon and I don't want to be caught in a compromising position or have to rush anything."

"Okay but after I am taking you upstairs and that's where we are staying." Leo lets me go and as I walk away he smacks my ass playfully.

An hour later, the food and drink has been put away, we are now able to be in our own bubble without any interruptions for a whole week.

Leo gets two glasses of champagne, gives me a glass, takes my other hand and walks me up the stairs. In the bedroom, we put our drinks down and he pulls me close. We kiss, our lips and tongues exploring each other's. He starts to undress me and once he has me naked, I sit on the bed and watch him get undress. There is no better sight in the world than watching Leo reveal his naked body. Once he's naked too, he climbs on to the bed and starts using his lips, tongue and teeth to explore my body. I let out a deep moan as it feels so good.

"Jacob?" he says as he breathes into my neck.

"Yeah!" I answer him, feeling breathless.

"I want to go all the way with you."

We both stop kissing and look into each other's eyes.

"You do, are you sure?"

"Yes. I've been sure for a while now. But you hadn't said anything, so I didn't. But if you are still not ready, then we can wait, it's not a problem."

I laugh and bury my head into his neck.

"What's the matter?" he asks, sounding worried.

I look back into his eyes and smile. "I've wanted to for a long time too, but I was waiting for you."

"So, you want to?"

"Yes, definitely."

"Okay, we will just take it nice and slow and easy for our first time."

He moves further down and I just melt under his desire.

We are both in bed and I have my head on Leo's bare chest, I can hear his heart beating. He is running his fingers through my hair. I turn and look up at him.

"I love you," I whisper.

He looks deep into my eyes and smiles.

"I love you too."

These words coming from Leo have melted my heart, I roll on top of him and kiss him deep and lovingly.

We spend a wonderfully free week together. We have done so much walking, it is so quiet here and we have hardly seen any people so we were able to walk holding hands, it's only a little thing but has meant the world to us to be able to do something so normal. We have been relaxing and we have even written some songs together, songs that we don't think we could ever record as they are all about our relationship, maybe one day.

But the time has come to go back to the real world, we really don't want to leave but we have to be back in London to start work in a week.

We pack up and I drive Leo to Manchester airport, he is taking a quick flight back to London to spend the last few days with his family at his mum's house and I'm going back to my mum and dad's.

We arrive at the airport. We have to be careful saying our goodbyes. We can't really kiss each other goodbye as there are too many people around, which breaks my heart and I am close to tears and Leo can see that I'm upset.

"It's okay," he reassures me. "I will see you in a few days at home."

"I just don't want to go back to living a lie again, I have loved being normal," I say feeling the tears rising.

He pulls me into a hug, not caring who can see us.

"I love you, when we get home would you like me to move in with you?" Leo asks.

"What? Yes, I would love that, are you sure?"

"I have loved every minute spent with you and I want it to be like that always," Leo says he now has tears in his eyes.

I look around outside to make sure no one is looking, when its clear I kiss him.

"I've got to go but I will see you in a couple of days, I love you." And he jumps out of the car.

"I love you too, have a safe flight."

Then he is gone.

Chapter Seven

I arrive back in London a day before Leo is due. I want to make the place nice before he moves in tomorrow, so I make sure everything is clean and tidy and that there is room for all his things.

Xander has arrived back and we have a quick catch up on how our break was. It sounds like him and Shelly are becoming close, he can't stop talking about her. Later that night Alice also arrives back and we catch up too. I tell her all about mine and Leo's trip away. She is so happy when I tell her that we are moving in together.

I didn't sleep much last night as I am so excited and I have woken up early. Leo said he would be here about ten, so I get myself ready and make sure I'm looking my best before he arrives.

He is finally here. Alice and Xander are going to help us move Leo's things into mine, I guess it's our home now.

It doesn't take long to move everything and find a new home for it. I can't believe he's here, we can go to bed together every night which I love doing.

Once we are all sorted, Xander asks, "Shall we go out for a drink and something to eat?"

I'm a little concerned about going out after what happened on New Year's Eve but we know where it's okay for us to go and we will be in a group. So I agree.

"Let's get changed and we can make our way out. I'm going

to see if Shelly is around and see if she wants to come out with us." Xander rushes out the door.

An hour later and we are in our favourite restaurant, drinking, eating and having a great time. Shelly did join us and we have all been catching up, when Shelly says, "I've got something to show you." Looking over at me and Leo.

We look at each other wondering what it is.

"You have been photographed together and they've put it online."

She gets out her phone and hands it to Leo. The headline reads, 'UsFour or is it UsTwo,' the article goes on about Leo meeting up with me over New Year and there is a photograph of Leo arriving at Mum and Dad's. It then goes on about how we looked very cosy together whilst we were out and there is a photograph of us sat next to each other in the restaurant and one when we are leaving.

"How did they get the photographs in the restaurant, that photographer must have bought them off someone who was there?" Leo sounds angry.

What do we say? I don't think Xander has told Shelly about us still being together. I look at Leo and I don't know what he is thinking. Should we tell Shelly about us but I can't do that without asking Leo first. Maybe if we do tell her, she might be able to do something about it and keep Harriet from finding out. Suddenly, Leo stands up and leaves the table. I watch him as he walks out of the restaurant. I get up and follow him and find him standing outside, he looks angry.

"Are you okay?" I ask him gently.

"No, I'm not, Jacob," he snaps.

Why is he angry at me?

"It makes me so angry that we can't just have a quiet dinner without any of this happening." Leo is getting so wound up, I need to calm him down.

"Leo, calm down, the photos just look like two friends meeting up, it should be fine."

"The article didn't sound like we are just friends," Leo shouts. People are starting to look over at us.

"No," I say back trying not to make him any angrier. "What are we going to do?"

"We can't do anything now, it's already out there for people to see."

"Should we talk to Shelly about us, she might be able to help?" I can see he is still fuming.

"It can't make it any worse, I suppose."

"Come back inside and let's see what she has to say." I touch his arm to comfort him but he moves it away abruptly.

I look at him shocked and he looks back at me. "Sorry," he says as he walks in.

As we are walking through the restaurant, people are looking around at us.

"Are you okay?" Alice asks.

I nod to Alice and then turn to Shelly.

"Shelly, we need to tell you something but not here I don't want us to be overheard."

"Well, let's go back to yours and we can talk there," Shelly advises.

We pay the bill and leave the restaurant. Twenty minutes later, we are home, I get everyone a drink and we are ready to talk.

"So, what's going on, I can guess but I need to hear it," Shelly asks.

"Well, me and Leo are still together and have been since we

had the meeting with Harriet. We have been keeping it a secret and only Alice, Xander and our close families know about us."

"I thought as much, I have been watching the two of you together when we have been doing any press events, I think you forget that it's meant to be a secret sometimes."

Me and Leo look at each other, we didn't realise we were being so obvious.

I then tell her about what happened over New Year and how they got the photographs of us.

"We know we shouldn't have gone out that night, but we thought we would be okay. We just wanted a normal night out."

Shelly looks at us both. "You can't have a normal night out. You are in one of the biggest groups of the moment and there are photographers everywhere who would love to get a story on you just so they can make a lot of money. You have also been told by the management team you are not allowed to be together. You know the consequence if you are caught."

Shelly looks over at Xander with a sad expression on her face. She continues, "Hopefully, this is a one off-article. So, we will just have to ignore it and if you are asked about it, you will have to say that you are just friends meeting up. Let this be a warning to the both of you that nowhere is safe for you, except in these four walls. You will have to be careful from now on. Harriett will not go back on what she said."

"We will be more careful," I respond to Shelly, "but what about you two?"

"What do you mean?"

"You and Xander obviously like one another. Will you be allowed to be together?"

Shelly glances over to Xander. "I haven't said anything to anyone," he replies to her look.

"Yes, we are close, but nothing has happened yet, we would like to be together but I don't know if we will be allowed either."

Xander then adds, "We have to talk to Harriet about it, but we hope that because Shelly isn't technically in the group, we will be allowed."

Leo is mad again. "I bet you will be. It's just because we are two boys that we are not allowed to be together. I hate our management team."

He gets up and storms into the bedroom and slams the door. We all stare at the close door.

"I'm sorry. Its great news. You two will make a great couple," I say to Xander and Shelly, "and I hope they let you be together. I wouldn't wish this on any one. I hate what me and Leo have to go through."

"Thanks," they both reply.

Xander then says, "I think it's time to go, say goodbye to Leo for us."

Alice, Xander and Shelly leave and I open the door quietly to the bedroom.

Leo is laying on the bed, not looking any calmer. I give him a small smile as I enter the room.

"Why is our life so unfair and complicated? I wish I had met you a different way."

I move over to the bed and sit by him, "We may not have met if we didn't meet this way, our lives may have never come together."

"I'm glad they did," he whispers.

"Me too, let's go to bed it's been a long day."

We both get undressed and climb into bed, Leo snuggles up to me and puts his head on my chest, I hold him until I feel him relax and is sleeping.

This is not how I imagined our first night living together would be but I wouldn't want to be anywhere else.

Our tour starts tomorrow. We have spent the last four months rehearsing and recording our next album. Xander and Shelly are officially together which made Leo so mad at the beginning that he stopped talking to everyone apart from me for a whole week, which made rehearsals a bit of a nightmare. He has now come around to the fact they are allowed to be together and is happy for them.

Me and Leo have been living together in total bliss, we love it. Luckily, no more stories have come out about us so thankful Harriet is still none the wiser about us. We have been so careful, sitting apart at interviews as much as we can and only going out when we are with others. We talk about what we would do if we could go out on a real date but it's just a fantasy, so we make it as special as we can at home.

Our first leg of the tour is throughout the UK, the first being in London. We have been to the venue to rehearse and it is huge. We can't believe that so many people want to come and watch us perform. Our families have been invited to come and watch our first performance. Mum and Dad are very excited to come and watch us.

This evening we have had a quiet meal together and then an early night before the madness begins.

Me and Leo are in bed, "I'm going to hate not sleeping with you every night while we are away," I say.

We have decided to stay in our own hotel rooms whilst on tour just in case any one notices we are sharing.

Leo looks at me with sadness in his eyes and replies, "Me too, it's going to be so hard being away from home not spending time with you alone."

"We must promise we will try to spend at least a little bit of alone time together whenever we can," I say back to him.

"I promise," he reaches over, kisses me and snuggles down to sleep.

I watch him for a while as I don't know when the next time we will be together like this. Eventually, I drift off to sleep and the morning comes too quickly.

Before we start getting ready, we make love and it feels so intense as if our bodies know that this may be the last time for a while. After, as we are lying in each other's arms, tears start flowing. Leo hugs me tighter and his tears come too. We know that the next six months are going to be torture for us both.

"I love you so much," I say to Leo through my tears.

"I love you too, we will be all right, won't we?" he asks.

"Yes," I reply, hoping that we will be but I know this is going to put a lot of pressure on our relationship.

It's time to leave and we take the cars to the studio where we are meeting up with everyone, the management team, Shelly, Dan, Luke, the band and the stylists. This is where we are all getting on the two tour buses which we will be using to travel around to the different venues.

Me and Leo are very quiet on the way there, we just don't know what to say to make each other feel.

When we arrive at the studio we put on a brave face and join in with the excitement everyone else is feeling. We all jump on the bus and travel to the venue, when we arrive our excitement becomes real as there are hundreds of fans outside waiting for us, this is unbelievable.

We do a final rehearsal on the stage and then we go back to the dressing rooms where our families are waiting for us. It is so good to see Mum and Dad. I say hello to Leo's mum, brother and girlfriend, but we must be careful that we don't come across to familiar as this might cause suspicion.

It's time to go on. We say goodbye to our families they are going to watch from the VIP area and we make our way to the stage.

We hug each other and then run on to the stage to a roar from the fans. We look out at all these people here for us, thousands and thousands, just cheering our names. I look over at Leo and he gives me a wink and we start to sing. What an experience.

We have gone through a few of our songs and now we are going to sing my favourite song 'Young love'. As we are singing it Leo keeps looking over at me as if he is serenading me. Also during some of our other songs he has ran past me and smacked my ass playfully this is becoming a bit of a thing and I like it. We come to the end of our final song and the crowd is screaming so loudly we wave at them all, thanking them and eventually leave the stage. That was amazing but there is no time to stop we have to get back on the tour bus to go to our next venue as we only have a few days for rehearsing. We say goodbye to our families hopefully we will see them again at some of the other gigs.

We are back on the tour bus and we are all buzzing from what we have just done and no one is able to sleep. We decide to have a little celebration as we are driven to the next city.

We eventually, arrive at the hotel, absolutely exhausted and we are shown to our rooms that we will be staying in until we move on to the next city. We all need to get some sleep, we say good night to each other and I want to kiss Leo so much but there are too many people around so we just say good night and go to our separate rooms alone. I find it hard to drift off to sleep. This is hell, I want Leo back in my bed, this is going to be a very long and lonely tour.

Chapter Eight

We have been touring for three months and what a three months they have been. It has been a roller coaster of emotions. There is immense happiness and joy on show night with so many fans turning out to see us. We have sold out every night.

But other times, I have felt so lonely. Me and Leo have hardly had any chance to be alone together and all our pent-up feelings and sexual frustration is coming out when we are in public. We have been flirting with each other at every opportunity. It doesn't matter if we are rehearsing or doing a press conference. We have said things we really shouldn't be saying out loud and we can't stop touching each other. We are at our worse on stage, we flirt with each other so much, we hug, slap each other's asses, touch hands and whisper things to each other about what we would like to do when we are alone. We must be so obvious but we can't help it.

We have finished our last UK gig and we have a few days off before we start the European leg. To celebrate we decide to go out for a drink, the four of us, Shelly, Luke, Dan and the band. Leo is sat drinking and talking to the band on the other side of the table. I sit and watch him for a while, he seems very animated around them nothing like the Leo I know. We have a lot to drink, it's getting late and I have had enough. I tell Alice, Xander and Shelly that I'm going up to my room. I look over at Leo to tell him but he is still too busy to notice that I'm going. What is with him today he has hardly spoken to me, he's been too busy hanging around with the band. Come to think of it he has been hanging around with the band a lot more lately.

I say night to the others and leave. I get to my room and sit on my bed. I feel so lonely at the moment. I hate feeling like this. I want to phone Mum and Dad to talk to them but it's too late so I just go to bed alone.

I have been sleeping a while when I'm suddenly woken by something. What's that noise? I can hear shouting. I look at the clock and it's just gone four in the morning. The shouting is getting clearer and it sounds like someone is shouting my name. It sounds like Leo, what is he doing. Then suddenly, there is a loud bang on my door.

I rush to open it. He is going to wake the whole hotel with the noise, he is making. Leo is standing there, I can see he has had loads to drink and is very drunk.

"Jacob, here you are," he says slurring his words. "Jacob, I miss you, I love you."

"Get in," I shout grabbing his arm and pulling him inside. "What do you think you are doing?"

He staggers into the bedroom, I follow him.

"I love you, Jacob, but I like girls too," he slurs as he lays on the bed.

"What are you talking about?"

Before I can question him, he has passed out on the bed. Great!

I go over to him, take off his shoes and cover him in the duvet and I climb into bed, next to him. There's nothing I can do about it now, that's where he's going to have to stay.

I wake up and Leo is still sleeping. He looks so good with his messy bed hair but then I remember what he said earlier I have to ask him about it.

I gently run my fingers through his hair, I miss him so much. He slowly wakes, looks around and he notices me.

"What happened? Why am I here?" he sounds groggy.

"You were very drunk. You came back shouting and banging on my door. Do you not remember?"

"I'm so sorry. Did anyone see or hear me?"

"I don't think anyone saw you but I'm sure they heard you."

I need to ask him about what he said but I don't know if he will remember.

I look at him and he knows something is wrong.

"What's the matter?" he asks.

"You said something and I'm worried about what it meant."

"What did I say?"

"You came in and said that you love me but you like girls too."

He looks away from me and puts his head down.

"I did something last night and I feel so bad about it. After you came up to bed, me and some of the band decided to go to a club. We had a lot to drink. Which I know is not an excuse but I ended up kissing this girl. She wanted to come back to the hotel with me and I nearly said yes but then I came to my senses and came back to find you."

I can't believe it. He was willing to sleep with a girl. What would have happened if he didn't come to his senses he would be in bed with her and not me.

Leo is looking at me, his deep brown eyes bearing into my soul. I can't look back at him, so I get out of bed.

"Jacob, I'm so sorry. Please look at me or say something."

I can feel the anger building inside me and I just explode.

"What if you had slept with her, what would that mean for us? You would throw our relationship away just for a one-night stand with some random girl."

I am absolutely fuming. Leo gets up and comes over to me and tries to comfort me but I don't want him near me.

"Jacob, I'm so sorry. I was stupid."

He reaches out to touch me.

"Don't you touch me," I yell at him and move back.

"Jacob."

"No, Leo, I don't want you here. You've cheated on me and right now I don't want to see you."

"Jacob, please."

"Get out. I can't look at you."

"No, Jacob, I'm not going, you need to know how sorry I am. I love you."

"Get out."

He just stands there.

"Leo, just fuck off."

I never swear but he's just not listening to me. I can't be in the same room as him and he's not leaving so I storm into the bathroom. I slam the door and lock it so he can't follow me. I hear him knock gently on the door and say my name but I ignore him.

I wait in the bathroom for what seems like an eternity. I listen at the door and I don't think I can hear him so I open the door, look around and realise he has gone.

I can't be here. I need to be away from all this. I want to go back to Mum and Dad's and be somewhere familiar and warming. I decide to phone George. I can't face speaking to Harriet.

"Hello," George answers the phone.

"Hi, George, it's Jacob."

"What can I do for you, Jacob?"

"I want to go and see my parents for a couple of days before we fly out to Paris. Is that okay?"

"Is everything okay?" George asks me but I can't tell him the real reason.

"Yes. I think I just need a few days to get some stuff sorted. Could you arrange for a car for me I can drive myself. I will be back here in a couple of days."

"I'm sure that will be fine. I will let Harriet know. I will arrange for a car to be dropped off at the hotel. What time do you want to leave?"

"Thanks, George. Could it be here in an hour? I just want to leave as soon as possible."

"Jacob, are you sure you are okay? Is it anything to do with Leo?"

What!

"No," I say quickly.

"I will get it sorted for you."

"Thanks, George. I will see you in a few days."

"Take care, Jacob," he says and puts the phone down.

Why did he ask about Leo, does he suspect something?

I have a shower, get dressed and throw a few things in a bag and I leave the room. I head towards the hotel lobby and ask at the reception if the car keys have been left for me yet. The lady at the desk hands the keys over and informs me where it is parked. Before I get into the car, I text Alice and Xander to let them know I'm going back to Mum and Dad's for a few days. But I can't text Leo to let him know I'm still so mad at him.

A few hours later, I pull up outside Mum and Dad's. They will be at work now, so the house is empty. I let myself in and once inside I feel better. They will be shocked when they get home. I haven't told them I'm coming.

I wait around for them to come home and Dad is first back. He is very shocked but happy to see me. He hugs me and knows something is wrong.

"What's the matter, Jacob, why are you here?"

"Me and Leo had a huge fight and I just had to get away from it all and come and see you and Mum."

"Are you okay?" Dad asks.

"Not really but I feel better being here."

Dad hugs me again.

"I'm sure everything will be all right. Does Leo know you are here?"

"I didn't tell him, I'm so angry with him. Alice and Xander know so I guess they've told him."

"Come on, let's have a cup of tea, Mum will be back soon."

We just sit down with our tea when Mum comes through the door.

"Hi, I'm back. Whose car is that outside?"

She walks into the living room, spots me and screams.

"Jacob, what are you doing here?"

Dad answers, "He's had an argument with Leo."

"Oh, love, are you okay?" she says as she hugs me.

"I'm okay, Mum. I'm glad I'm here though."

"Do you want to talk about it?"

"No, not really, I'm just to mad at him and I just needed a break from everything."

"They're working you all too hard. You need a break. How long are you here for?"

"Just a couple of days. I have to be back at the hotel to leave for Paris on Friday."

"Well, we are so happy you are here, we've missed you."

"I've missed you both too."

I have been at Mum and Dad's for two days now and I feel so much better than I did when I first arrived. Mum has been spoiling me and it's great to have a bit of normality in my life. I've been thinking about Leo constantly but I still can't bring myself to talk to him. He has texted and phoned me so many times but I have ignored them.

I have to leave tomorrow and I don't want to, being on tour is hard.

I'm sat having breakfast, Mum and Dad have just left for work, when there's a knock on the door. I hate answering the door as you never know who it will be. Mum and dad have had some random people coming to the house as they know where I live, so I ignore it. They continue to knock, so I go into the living room to see who it is. As I glance out of the window, I recognise that silhouette straight away, it's Leo. What is he doing here?

I go and answer the door but I don't say anything I just look at him.

"Can I come in?" he says with a small smile.

I stand aside and let him come in.

"What are you doing here, Leo, how did you get here?"

"Jim drove me. Why didn't you tell me you were coming here? I didn't find out you had left until yesterday when Alice came to find me as she hadn't seen me since Sunday evening and then no one was available to drive me here until today."

"I just needed to get away from you and everything else. I needed somewhere normal."

"Jacob, I haven't stopped thinking about you. I'm so sorry about what I did. I promise I will never do anything like that again. I miss us so much." He sounds like he is getting upset.

"I hate that you kissed that girl and I'm worried you don't want me and you really still like girls."

Leo moves towards me and I let him hold me and I melt into his arms. I've missed him so much.

"I'm so sorry, I do want you, I love you. Can you forgive me?"

I look into his deep brown eyes and I believe he is truly sorry. Do I believe that it won't happen again, I'm not sure but I need to trust him? So I nod in answer to his question. He smiles and kisses me.

"Are your mum and dad home?"

"No, they are both at work."

"Can we go upstairs then?

I smile at him, take his hand and lead him up to my room.

Once we are inside Leo kisses me. I have missed his lips on mine. He then starts kissing my neck and I can feel the excitement running through us both. It has been a long time since we have been intimate with each other. He pulls off my t-shirt and starts kissing my chest. He then pushes me on to the bed, pulls off his t-shirt, revealing his amazing body. He moves onto the bed beside me and reaches down and moves his hand over my trousers. I've forgotten how good his touch feels. He undoes my jeans and I'm suddenly lost in our passion.

We are laying in each other's arms, naked from making love and I feel so happy, we spend the rest of the day in bed.

"We have to get up, Mum and Dad will be back soon."

"Can we stay here a little longer, please? I miss just laying with you in bed," Leo pleads.

"Okay, another half an hour then we really do have to get up."

We finally make it out of bed and Mum and Dad are due home

any minute.

"Did you tell your mum and dad about our fight?" Leo asks, looking a little nervous.

"I told them we had an argument but not what it was about."

"I'm sorry, you felt you had to escape from everything. We made a promise to spend time together on tour but we've not managed it very well."

"I have felt so lonely since we've been away."

Leo hugs me. "Let's do better when we go back. I don't want you to feel so bad you need to leave ever again."

"Okay," I reply, hugging him back tightly.

Chapter Nine

Tour is finally over; we have travelled all over Europe and our final concert was in New York. Me and Leo are good, we have tried to see each other alone as much as we can. This has been made easier as we have had connecting rooms at some of the hotels. Leo hasn't gone out with the band on his own and has remained faithful. We have been a little bit more careful whilst in public because of spending time together behind closed doors but we still like flirting with each other on stage, it builds up so much sexual tension. I have been much happier this last part of our tour.

Now that the tour has finished, we will be able to spend some time with our families over Christmas. This year, I am spending it with Leo's family which will be fun. I'm seeing Mum and Dad before travelling back to London to be with Leo. We are staying at home and only spending Christmas day at Leo's mums, it's not too far away for us to travel and that means we can have our own space.

We fly back to the UK tomorrow but before that the management team have organised an end of tour party for everyone involved in organising it. The party is being held in a trendy loft downtown. We are all really looking forward to it. To be able to relax, let our hair down and to let off some steam.

I decide to wear my outfit that I wore the first night me and Leo slept together, the one from our first photo shoot, to see if he notices. I make sure I am looking and smelling amazing, I want to get him excited.

We are meeting each other in the hotel lobby, I make my way down in the lift. As I step out of it, I notice Leo talking to Xander and Leo is looking hot. Looks like he may have had the same idea as me and it's working. As I'm walking towards them Leo looks around, spots me and gives me one of his big cheeky smiles.

As I reach him, he whispers in my ear, "I prefer that outfit when it's on the floor."

I blush slightly at his comment.

We are just waiting for Alice and as we wait Leo cannot take his eyes off me. Eventually, Alice joins us and we make our way to our cars.

Once in the car, Leo puts his hand on my leg and is running it up and down my inner thigh. We need get to the party soon or I will be jumping on him in the car. Thankfully, it doesn't take too long to get there and we make our way into the building and up in the lift, when the doors open, the sight of the loft is stunning. There is a dance floor in the centre with hundreds of glittering lights hanging over it from the ceiling. At the end of the room is a bar and the room is shaped so that there's lots of dark corners.

Leo has not left my side on the way up here, he has been so close that I can smell his aftershave, it's intoxicating.

"Lots of dark corners in here," he says and winks at me. "Let's get you a drink."

We head towards the bar, Xander makes a bee line for Shelly, they look so happy together. Alice joins Megan who is our drummer in the band and they have become really close friends throughout the tour.

"Just me and you then." Leo puts his arm around my waist.

"Leo, we still have to be careful, what if someone sees us?"

"Jacob, tonight I don't care. You are looking amazing. I love this outfit you're wearing. I remember when you had that on, I hope this night ends like that one." He squeezes my waist.

"We can't do anything, Harriet is here."

"Well, I will have to get you into one of these dark corners later when she has gone. I'm sure she won't be here long."

I smile at him. I don't want to be caught but I would love him to take me into a corner.

We spot George coming over to us and Leo moves slightly away from me. See, he does care about being caught.

"Hi, you two. What do you think, it's all right here, isn't it?"

"Yes, it's great, lots of dark corners to do dirty deeds," Leo replies with his cheeky grin on his face. I can't believe he said that to George.

"Well, make sure you both have a good night. Harriet and Jasmin won't be here all night so you can let your hair down once they're gone."

He looks at us both and gives us a wink as he walks away.

Leo looks at me a bit shocked by what George has just said and done.

"What did he mean by that?"

I hadn't told Leo about what George said to me before.

"I think he knows about us. When I went back to Mum and Dad's at the end of the UK leg, I spoke to George to help me out and he asked if the reason I wanted to leave was because of you."

"What did you say?"

"I didn't say anything, I just ignored it I just said I needed time away."

"But it seems like he knows."

"I know, but Shelly guessed we were still together and

George is around us as much as she is. Perhaps he's just worked it out. We are not very discreet."

"No, we're not, and tonight will be one of those times." And he smacks my ass as he walks over to the bar to get another drink.

A few hours in and as George predicted Harriet and her shadow Jasmin leave. George is staying but he is good fun to have around so we don't mind him being here. This is when the party really starts, we play stupid drinking games, we do lots of dancing and we are all having a great time. As I go to get myself another drink Leo appears at my side. As soon as I'm handed my drink, he grabs my hand and pulls me towards one of the dark corners that he has been hinting about all night. He pins me against the wall, looks around to make sure we can't be seen and when he is sure it's safe he kisses me, his tongue is instantly running along my lips waiting for me to open my mouth to let him in. I moan as he kisses me harder this gives him his opportunity for his tongue to push in and explore my mouth. It feels so hot because it's so dangerous. He then puts his hand inside my trousers, I protest but he continues and his touch feels so good, I let him carry on. His movements become more rapid and intense, I have to stop him.

"Leo stop; I'm going to cum."

He moves his hand a few more times and takes it out of my trousers. He kisses me one more time.

"Come on, I want to dance with you."

"You are going to have to give me a minute and I think you need to as well before we go back out."

"I don't care," he says, as he puts his hand down his trousers and adjusts himself.

He kisses me and turns to leave our hiding place. I can't believe he just walked out of here with no cares of how he looked.

That was so exciting, we have never done anything like that outside our home because home is our only safe place, but that was amazing.

It takes me a minute or so to calm down and sort myself out. Eventually I am calm enough to leave as I do I spot Leo in the middle of the dance floor surrounded by all the team dancing up a storm with his unique moves. I walk around the edge of the room watching his every move and my heart soars, I love this man so much he makes me so happy.

Not paying any attention to where I am walking, I bump into George.

"Sorry, George. I wasn't looking at where I was going."

"That's okay. You were looking at a much better view."

I turn quickly and look at him shocked.

"It's okay, Jacob. I really don't mind. I won't say anything to anyone. It's just so nice to see you both so happy."

"What are you talking about, George?" It's best to act like I don't know what he's talking about.

"You and Leo, you're still together."

"How did you know?"

"I can see when two people are very much in love."

"We are. I'm sorry we didn't do as Harriet told us, but we were too far in by then. You definitely won't tell Harriet?"

"No, I won't. I'm really happy for you both. I thought Harriet was out of order not letting the two of you be together."

"Really, why didn't you say anything to her?"

"I did, I fought for the both of you, but you don't fight Harriet. She gets what she wants or you're out. I needed to stay to protect you both."

"George, why didn't you tell us?"

"I couldn't, I didn't want you to get too comfortable about

who knew you were still together. You're not the best at keeping it a secret as it is."

"I know, Shelly, Xander and Alice keep telling us that, but we honestly do try."

"Let's just say it's a good job, Harriet is not around much and she doesn't see everything that goes on." He laughs at me.

I look back at Leo on the dance floor, I catch his eye and he waves for me to join him, I look at George.

"Go and join him and have fun, just be careful. I think I'm going to leave you young ones to it. I will see you in the morning."

"Thanks, George, for everything," and I hug him.

He is taken by surprise but hugs me back.

"You're welcome. Now go to your lovely man, he's waiting for you."

He walks away and waves to everyone on the dance floor and shouts, "Have fun, everyone, don't stay out to late we've got a flight to catch home tomorrow."

Everyone waves back at him and as I watch him leave, I am filled with gratitude towards him.

I go and join Leo on the dance floor and we dance for hours. Midnight comes around and we decide it's best that we all make our way back to the hotel as our flight is in the morning and we don't want to miss it.

"Let's get you back to the hotel, I want you so much," Leo says a little too loud and a few people turn and looks at us.

He grabs my hand and leads me back out of the building into the car where he sits next to me instead of his normal seat. I feel his body against mine and I want him so badly. The night has just felt like one long foreplay session and we are both ready to explode.

We arrive back at the hotel. Alice, Xander and Shelly have arrived at the same time as us and as no one else is around, Leo holds my hand all the way up to our rooms.

"Night, you two, have fun," Xander shouts down the corridor, as he winks at us both before he goes into his room with Shelly.

Laughing, we go into Leo's room. Once inside, there is no stopping us. We kiss each other so passionately, as we undress each other.

"Shower first, I think." Leo drags me into the bathroom, we have uncontrollable sex in the shower it's what we both need after this evening and all the pent-up sexual energy inside us both.

After the shower, we lie in bed, wrapped in each other's arms.

"I can't wait to get home," I say to Leo.

"Me too. I miss being with you all the time."

"George does know about us. He has all along."

"How do you know?"

"He told me tonight. He tried to fight Harriet about us, he tried to convince her to let us be together. But she wasn't having any of it."

"Why didn't he tell us?"

"He didn't want us to be too comfortable about being together if we knew more people knew, but he is really happy for us."

"I'm really happy for us. I love you, Jacob."

Those eyes are on me again.

"I love you too." And I roll on top of him and kiss him and this time we make love and it is gentle and loving.

I have visited Mum and Dad for a few days and had an early Christmas celebration with them.

Me and Leo are now back home to celebrate our first Christmas together. We've bought a tiny tree to put in the living room and a few decorations to make it look more festive. We are so happy to be home again.

We spend Christmas day with Leo's family which was great fun, but the rest of the time it has just been the two of us.

New Year's Eve is a quiet affair, we have had a few drinks, a lovely meal that Leo cooked us, a relaxing bath together then to bed and this is where we stay until the next morning when there is a knock at the door.

"I'll get it," Leo says as he gets out of bed.

"You can't. We don't know who it is. Alice and Xander are not here, so it's not them and you shouldn't be with me. Stay in here." I get up and close the door behind me, hiding Leo in the bedroom.

I pull on some clothes quickly and open the door.

I'm shocked to see George standing there.

"George, what are you doing here?"

"I need to talk to you. Is Leo here?" He is looking very serious. I nod.

"Come in. I will get him."

I show George into the living room and tell him to take a seat and I head back into the bedroom.

"Who is it?" he looks at my face. "What's the matter?"

"It's George. He wants to talk to us, he looks really serious."

"Come on, let's go and talk to him, it can't be that bad." He puts on some clothes, grabs my hand and walks me into the living room.

George looks at us both. "I think you better sit down."

"What is it, George?" Leo asks as we both sit down. "Why are you here so early? Couldn't this have waited until we are back at work?"

"No, this can't wait. I need to show you something that has been put online." He gets his phone out just as Shelly did the last time a story had been written about us. Fear rises in me what is it about this time?

We take George's phone and there is an article and photographs taken of us on tour. One is of Leo kissing that girl, but worse there are photos of us at the party in New York. One is of Leo holding my hand leading me into a corner of the room, the other two are of us individually coming out of the corner looking happy and a bit bedraggled and you can clearly see Leo is excited.

"How the fuck did they get these?" Leo snaps.

"I don't know, maybe the staff at the place took them, hoping to make a bit of money," George answered.

"That's not all, there has been a social media group set up by some of your fans."

"What's wrong with that?" I ask him.

"The group is about a theory that the two of you are a couple. They have been posting videos and photos of the two of you on tour. It seems that they have been gathering lots of evidence of every time you've touched each other on stage or on a television interview and also any time you look at each other during songs."

I can't believe it. I look at Leo and he is fuming. He absolutely hates this kind of thing.

"What are we going to do?" I'm close to tears as I know how much this will be upsetting Leo.

He looks at me and sees I'm upset so he holds on to my hand.

"I don't think there's much we can do, but you can expect Harriet to have something to say about this. This can't be kept from her this time. The article has been reposted on lots of other sites and it won't be long before it makes it into a magazine. If by a miracle Harriet doesn't see it, I can bet you Jasmin will and she will let her know."

"George, we don't want anything to happen to the group. Can you please talk to Harriet again, try and make her see that it would be okay for us to be together?" I plead with him.

"You know that I would, but she won't have it. The best thing we can do is deny it all. You two will have to stay apart at all times when you are out of here so not to give journalists and fans any more ammunition. I'm so sorry, boys, but there is nothing else I can do."

The tears now start to fall. Leo pulls me into him and hugs me.

"I will leave you two alone and I will see you Monday. Just be prepared for the wrath of Harriet."

"Thanks, George." Leo gets up to see him out.

Leo sits back down next to me. "I'm so sorry, Jacob. It's all my fault. I shouldn't have made you do what we did that night."

"It's not your fault. I went willingly with you," I say through my tears. He hugs me again. "They would have got other photographs of us somehow if they hadn't got those ones. What do you think of this fan page?"

"I don't know. Should we have a look?"

"I don't know if I want to."

"We need to know what we are dealing with."

We search for the site and we can't believe what we are looking at. There are hundreds of posts of me and Leo together.

"Oh my god, I knew we weren't being that careful but we are so obvious looking at all these posts."

"It's because they are all in one place at one time but I don't know how we are going to disprove this," Leo replies.

"Harriet is going to be fuming." My tears are back again.

"It's going to be okay," Leo tries to comfort me but he doesn't sound very convincing.

Chapter Ten

We are heading back to the studio today, me and Leo have had a few days to think about what we are going to do. We have decided to deny everything if Harriet asks us about any of it. None of the photographs show us actually doing anything too bad, it could be just friends messing about, they do not prove that we are together.

We arrive at the studio and Shelly is waiting outside for us, this is never a good sign. I look over at Leo and squeeze his hand. I am so nervous. He looks it too.

"Everything will be fine. We just have to stick to our story."

Leo nods back at me, let's go of my hand and exits the car. I follow him and walk towards Shelly.

"Harriet wants to see you both before you start. I'm sorry but she knows about all the online stuff. We've tried to keep it from her but Jasmin saw it and told her."

"It's okay. I know you and George have tried your best, we are prepared."

Me and Leo make our way to Harriet's office, not daring to talk or even look at each other. We knock on the door and she calls for us to come in. We sit down in front of her.

"Hope you both have had a nice rest over Christmas?"

"Yes, thanks," we both reply.

"Now can you remember the talk we had a little while ago about you two?"

We both nod.

"I have been reading and hearing some things that might suggest that you have ignored my advice and are still together. I am hoping that it is just silly rumours and there is no truth to it. You both know what the consequences are if it is true."

I take a deep breath and reply to her trying to sound confident.

"No, we are not together, we haven't been since you told us we couldn't."

Will she believe me?

"What do you make of all this that has been written about you both?"

"I don't know anything about it."

We had decided to say that we hadn't seen any of it.

"Well, let me show you these articles and social media sites and I want to hear your feelings on it."

She brings it all up on her computer, she is constantly looking at Leo who has said nothing and is sitting with his head down, he is going to give us away.

We go through all the images with a commentary from Harriet the whole time. I don't know how we are going to convince her after looking at everything. Once we have finished, she looks at Leo.

"You're very quiet today, Leo. What have you got to say about this?"

"Nothing," he snaps.

"What do you mean, nothing?" Now Harriet is getting annoyed.

"What do you want me to say, that we are still together and have been all this time, just so you can split the group up. Well, I'm not. We did what you asked and it has been fucking shit this whole time. We are not together and I don't want to be with Jacob ever if this is the crap we would have to put up with."

He stands up pushes his chair away, he is so angry.

"I'm going to work now, got to make all that money, haven't we, Harriet?"

And he walks out of the room.

Harriet watches him leave in shock. She finally looks back at me.

"I hope this is true, Jacob. I don't want to hear any more rumours about the two of you. This will be your last warning."

"We are not together and as you can see Leo is angry about all of these lies and so am I."

"If this is the case then maybe you need to keep your distance from each other for a while to stop any more stories and pictures appearing. Jacob, I really don't want to see any more of these photos."

She stands up from her desk, there is no more to be said. So, I get up and leave.

The rest of the day is horrible. Leo is in a foul mood. He is not talking to anyone, even me. The recording of the new song has not gone well, my voice is just awful and I can't get my part right. It has been a very stressful day; I can't wait to get home.

As we are leaving Harriet calls over to me and Alice, she wants a quick word with us both.

Me and Alice stay to see what Harriet wants, as Leo and Xander leave.

"What was that about today, Jacob? You were not singing well?"

"I don't know."

"You need to get it sorted. I want this album done as quick as possible so we can release it as soon as we can. You can go."

I can't believe her. I hate her so much. I storm away and

when I get outside, I realise Leo has left with Xander. I thought he would have waited for me. I wait in the other car for Alice. When she gets in, she is smiling, at least someone has had some good news.

"Everything okay?" I ask her.

"Yes, thanks. A magazine wants to do an interview on just me and how I feel about being in a group, life as a young woman in the music business. It should be good."

"I'm glad for you, Alice."

"Leo will come around again, he's just so angry with Harriet. He will be fine when you get home."

"I hope so. I don't know what to do, I hate this so much."

"I know you do, you both do. I wish it could be different for you both."

"Thanks."

When I arrive home, I can't wait to give Leo a big hug but when I enter the apartment it is deathly silent. Where's Leo?

"Leo, are you here?" I shout out but it doesn't look like he's been back since we left this morning.

I phone and text him but no answer. I text Xander to see if he knows where he is. Xander texts back to say he came back with Leo and assumed he went home. I'm starting to get worried. I decided to check next door just in case he has gone back to his old apartment. I grab the keys and let myself in. It's quiet in here too but I find him sitting on the bed.

"Here you are. I was worried. Why didn't you pick up your phone?"

He looks over at me, he has been crying. I go over to console him but he moves away from me.

"What's the matter?"

"I don't want to talk about it, can you just go away, Jacob?"

"Come home with me."

"No, how can it be home, it's just full of lies."

"No, it's not, it's the only place that is not full of lies."

"I can't do this any more."

"Leo, please."

"No, Jacob, just go away. I need some space at the minute. I need to think. I can't cope with all the lying and pretending."

"Leo, what are you saying?"

"I don't know what I'm saying. I just need some time."

"Leo, it's okay. We've got through it so far we can keep doing what we have been doing."

"I don't want to keep doing it like this."

"Do you want to break up with me?" *Please say no.*

"No, yes, I don't know. No, I don't."

"Which one is it, Leo?"

"Jacob, please leave."

I can't leave, tears are starting to flow.

"Don't leave me, Leo, I love you so much."

"I love you too, but I can't do this any more."

I can't listen to anything else, I'm scared of what he might say, so I run out of his apartment and back home.

We reach the end of the week and it has been the worst week of my life. Leo has not been home all week, choosing to stay in his old apartment. He has been travelling to and from the studio with Xander in the other car. He has hardly spoken to me and when he has it has only been about work. I've tried to talk to him but he won't let me anywhere near him. He seems so sad not his happy, playful self. I have spoken to Xander to see if Leo has spoken to him about things but he said that he barely talks in the car.

We are all starting to get worried about him, so we suggest

maybe we should go out on Saturday night, he agrees after a lot of persuading.

It's Saturday night, I have made sure I am looking my best for Leo. I am hoping that tonight we may be able to talk about things. We are going to a local club where we are known. They are always amazing at looking after us and it has a VIP area so we will not be interrupted.

We are meeting at Xander's first for a drink before heading out, Alice is already there but no sign of Leo.

"I'm sure he will be here soon," Alice says kindly as I keep looking over at the door.

We have another drink and finally there's a knock on the door, Xander goes to open it and Leo walks in. I'm shocked by his appearance, he is not his normal, well cared for self and it looks like he has had a lot to drink already.

"Are we ready to go then?" Xander asks, looking between me and Leo with concern.

We all nod and he leads the way out to the cars. Leo again gets in the car with Xander. I was hoping he would get in our car. This is not going to be a good night I can't sense it already.

We arrive at the club and we are shown to our table. We order some drinks, Leo wants a large neat vodka, that's not good for him to be on that already.

"What a fucking week this has been," he says as he downs his vodka in one and gestures to the bar for another one.

"Leo, I think you need to slow down, it's still early," I say to him. I'm so worried about him.

"Don't tell me what to do. I've had enough of doing what you want us to do," he shouts back at me.

"Leo don't talk to Jacob like that," Alice snaps back at him.

"I'll talk to him how ever I like."

"No, you can't, Leo, you need to calm down," says Xander.

"Where's my drink?"

He leaves the table, goes to the bar, downs another vodka and asks for a lager then goes on to the dance floor.

As I watch him, Xander asks, "Are you okay? I don't know what's up with him at the moment."

"I'm fine. He's just so angry, but I don't know what to do about it."

As I look over at him on the dance floor, he is jumping around not caring who is in his way. Suddenly, he bumps into another guy and he is not happy with Leo. Leo gets pushed away and Leo pushes back. No! Leo is going to get into a fight. Me and Xander are on our feet at the same time. By the time, we get to the dance floor Leo has thrown a punch at the guy. The staff from the club grab the other guy as we grab Leo.

"What are you doing?" I shout at him, both of us pulling Leo off the dance floor.

"I fucking hate my life," he says fighting to get away from us. "Leave me alone."

"No, not until you have calmed down."

We make our way back to the table, I notice the staff have removed the guy from the club. A little unfair I think to myself as it was all Leo's fault.

"Would you just sit down," Xander shouts at him, forcing him to sit down before letting him go. "What is the matter with you?"

"I hate everyone. I hate my life just leave me alone."

He manages to get up before any of us can grab him and he storms out of the club. Before we can catch up with him, he has jumped into one of the cars and they have sped off into the night.

"He can't be out there alone not in that state. I hope he is going home?"

"Let's get back and see if he's there. If he's not then I will go and see if I can find him," Xander suggests.

We hurry back to the apartments but he is not in his or ours.

"You stay here in case he comes back and I will try and find him," Xander gets ready to leave again.

"I will wait in his place he will go back there not here. I will let you know if he turns up."

"Okay, hopefully, I will see you soon."

Xander leaves and me and Alice make our way back to Leo's apartment.

"Do you want me to stay with you?"

"No, it's okay, there's no point both of us sitting around waiting for him."

"I just thought you might like some company."

"Thanks, but I think I want to be alone."

Alice hugs me, I am so lucky to have these amazing people in my life.

"Thank you."

"Your welcome, let me know when he turns up. Don't worry what time it is I need to know if he's okay or I won't sleep."

"I will," I promise her as she leaves.

Being alone in here feels really strange, we have not spent much time here for so long but it is still full of happy memories.

I settle down on the sofa for what I feel like will be a long night. Half an hour passes and there is no word from Xander that he has found Leo, I'm starting to get really worried. It's now been an hour still nothing, it's not until I have been waiting for nearly two hours that Xander phones.

"I've found him, he's with some of the guys from the band

at a bar. He's okay but he won't come back with me. What do you want me to do?"

I am so relieved that Xander has found him but he's out with the band and the last time he was out with them he almost slept with someone else.

"He definitely won't come back with you?"

"No, he said he is staying where he is."

"Is the car waiting for him outside?"

"Yes, Jim is still outside."

"Leave him there. He won't come by force he's too stubborn. Can you tell Jim to keep an eye on him and get him back here safely when he's ready?"

"Will do."

"Thanks, Xander. You're a really good friend."

"I know. I will phone you in the morning to see if he arrived back okay."

"I will wait here for him to get back. Thanks again."

I hang up the phone and quickly text Alice to let her know what is happening and I sit and wait for him to come back.

I open my eyes. What's the time? I look at my phone and it's seven thirty in the morning. I must have fallen to sleep while I was waiting. I didn't hear Leo come in, did he even come back but then I notice a blanket has been placed over me, I don't remember doing that.

I get up and walk to the bedroom and there he is sleeping in his bed. He must have put the blanket over me, he does still care. I watch him sleep for a bit but decide not to disturb him, he needs his sleep. He would have had a lot to drink last night and I really don't want another fight, so I quietly leave and go home.

I need some more sleep so I decide to go to bed. I'm woken

a couple hours later by a knock on my door. I go to open it and I'm shocked to see Leo there.

"Can I come in to get a few bits?"

"Of course, you can, this is your home. You don't have to ask or knock on the door."

"Thanks, I just need some clothes."

He walks past me and I can smell he has just got out of the shower.

I follow him into the bedroom, he's going through the wardrobe and drawers pulling out some stuff, I watch him for a while.

"Why don't you just come home, then you won't need to take stuff with you."

He looks back at me and my stomach does a flip.

"I can't."

"Why not?"

"You know why. We need our distance."

"But I don't want to keep my distance from you. Please come home."

"Not right now. I need some space. I'm still so angry with everything and I don't want to take it out on you."

"Will you come over later, come for something to eat. You've lost weight, have you been eating?"

"No, not much."

"Please just come over for some food. You don't have to stay if you don't want to."

"Okay."

He picks up his things and heads for the door.

"I will see you later."

"What time do you want me to come over?"

"Seven."

"Okay. See you then," and he leaves.

He seems so sad, I hate seeing him like this.

Right, what am I going to cook him? I rummage through the fridge and the freezer to see what I've got. There is chicken, leeks and pasta. Excellent, I can make him his favourite pasta dish.

As the day goes by, I'm starting to get nervous, it's like it's our first date. The apartment is clean, the food is prepared, the table is set and I am ready, but I still feel strange.

I'm finishing off the pasta sauce when there's a knock at the door. I open it and Leo is there with a bottle of wine in his hand. He smiles, only a small one, but it's the first time I've seen him smile in a while, I smile back at him and let him in.

"Hi," I say, sounding as if we've only just met.

"Hi," he replies, sounding just as nervous as I am. He hands me the wine. "It's still cold."

"Do you want a glass now or wait until the food is ready?"

"I will have a glass now, if that's okay?"

"Of course, it is."

I pour two glasses of the wine and hand one to Leo as I go back to finishing the dinner.

Ten minutes later, we sit down to eat. Leo doesn't speak but just eats his food. I watch him devour the pasta and I wonder when was the last time he ate a proper meal. I let him eat before saying anything to him, he needs his food and not me distracting him by asking him questions.

When he has finished, he takes a sip of wine then looks at me. I've missed his face and those eyes looking at me.

"Thank you, that was really good."

"Your welcome. Are you okay, Leo? You seem so sad, I'm so worried about you."

He looks away. *Don't look away, please look at me.*

"I'm sorry," he replies. "It's this thing with Harriet. I don't want to do anything that will cause any pain or trouble for Alice, Xander and especially you. If we are together and get caught again, all this will end. I don't want that for any of you. I can't be near you because I just want you all the time. I love you so much but I need to keep away so I can control the situation. But I'm not handling it very well. I haven't really been eating, I've just been sat on my own, drinking."

"Leo, you have to look after yourself. I don't know what I would do if anything happened to you."

He drops his head. I reach out for his hand and he lets me hold it.

"I know you want me to come home and I really want to, but I think its best if we don't live together at the moment. I think I'm going to move all my things back next door."

"No, don't leave me."

"I'm not leaving you. I think it's best for us to get some space so we don't do anything stupid out in public. Also, I wouldn't put it past Harriet to do a surprise visit to the apartments to make sure we are not together."

"What makes you say that?"

"Just a feeling. She's not going to let us get away with anything this time. We are making her too much money for her to break up the group. So, she will do anything to keep us apart."

"I don't want you to move out. I love living together, it's our piece of normality when you are here with me."

"I don't want to either, but I think it's for the best."

He gets up from the table and starts gathering some of his things together. He goes into the bedroom and grabs his bags from the wardrobe and starts putting things in it. I can't watch him. I don't want him to go.

"Leo, please stop. Don't go. I want you to stay." I can't stop the tears coming.

He stops and walks over to me. "Jacob, please don't cry. I'm so sorry. I don't want to go, but we need to be apart. I still love you so much. Please don't make it harder than it is."

"Please stay just for tonight. Can I sleep with you one more time?"

He lets out a big sigh but says, "I will stay tonight, but I'm moving out in the morning. You know it's best thing for everyone."

"But what's best for us?"

"Come on, let's have another glass of wine."

He walks back into the living room, pours two more glasses of wine and he sits on the sofa. I join him and he puts his arm around me and I snuggle in so tight not wanting this moment to ever end.

"I can't believe this is our last night together."

"It's not our last night together," Leo replies, "we are still in love and we are still together. Living together makes us feel like any normal couple and this then makes us act like a normal couple outside too and we can't do that."

"But I want to be a normal couple."

"I want to too, but we know we can't, maybe one day."

The next morning, Leo moves out, I am devastated.

Chapter Eleven

Three months have gone by since Leo has moved out, we hardly spend any time together any more. I can count on one hand how many times he has stayed over. When he has it has felt like it always did and I'm so happy. But when he leaves it is horrible and it is getting worse every time, it makes me feel so miserable.

The new album has done amazing, straight in to the number one spot the first week it was released and we have had two number one singles from it. This has made Harriet ecstatic so she has left me and Leo alone but she has made sure that all the staff have been told to keep me and Leo apart as much as they can. We are not allowed to sit next to each other during interviews, we are not allowed to travel in the same cars and we are not allowed to be seen out just the two of us. This is making work unbearable. I can see from watching interviews back how unhappy we both are, we try to put on a happy face but they fail quite often and we just look so miserable most of the times.

Leo has once again started going out with the band and is drinking a lot. He occasionally comes to work in the same clothes he has had on the day before. This is worrying me, is he going home, if not where is he sleeping? We are drifting apart so much.

There has been some good news. Xander has proposed to Shelly and they will be getting married in the summer. They are both so excited and I'm so happy for them, but I think this hasn't helped Leo. I think he still hates the fact that they were allowed to be together and we were not.

Xander and Shelly's wedding is going to be when we are having a break from any recording or touring. I have asked Leo to go to New York for a few days after the wedding. I want to spend some alone time with him. He has said that he would go with me but we haven't confirmed any plans yet. I hope that he does come.

I have been spending most of my time with Alice, Megan and Alice's sister Chloe, who visits Alice regularly. I have trusted Megan and Chloe with letting them know about me and Leo. They are really great company and help a lot when I'm feeling down about him. Alice is not a big drinker and doesn't like going out much so we have been having movie nights, game nights and cooking meals for each other. Some evenings, Xander and Shelly come over to discuss their wedding plans. I'm so thankful to them that they are letting me be involved in some of the planning. It takes my mind off things.

Tonight, everyone is coming over to mine for dinner. I have asked Leo, but I doubt he will come, he never does any more. We are going to help Xander and Shelly with their seating plan for the reception.

Everyone arrives and I'm shocked to see that Leo has come. We sit down to eat and discuss some of the wedding plans, Leo doesn't look at all interested, as usual he looks very down. Xander informs me and Leo that we have a suit fitting at the weekend, we are both in the wedding party. After the meal, we clear the table and get out all the things for the seating plan. Leo moves away and sits on the sofa by himself. I watch him for a while, he's in a world of his own, drinking a glass of wine. I wonder what he's thinking. How amazing this would be if we were planning our wedding, he would be so involved and excited about it. The way things are at the moment I don't think that will ever happen.

Halfway through the evening, I get a text message from Harriet asking for a meeting tomorrow at her office.

"Has anyone else been asked to see Harriet tomorrow?"

Everyone shakes their head. I look over at Leo.

"Have you?" I ask him.

"Yes, I have."

"Do you know what it's about?"

"No, why would I?"

"Have we got it at the same time?"

"Mine's at noon, when's yours?"

"Mines at ten."

"So, no, not at the same time then," he replies sarcastically.

He can be such a dick at the minute, I was only asking.

"What do you think it's about?" I ask Shelly.

"I don't know, sorry. She hasn't told me about any meetings with the two of you."

"Surely it can't be about us being together, nothing new could have come out surely, we are never together any more?"

I look over at Leo and sadness fills me.

"I'm going." Leo stands up and leaves. I watch him leave, I can't cope with his moods.

"I will just have to wait and see what she wants. I hate meetings with Harriet, they are never good news."

Xander pats me on the back.

I'm heading to Harriet's office, wondering what awaits me. When I arrive, I take a deep breath and go inside her building. I'm a little early and she makes me wait. Finally, she calls me in to her office and gestures for me to sit down.

"I'm going to get straight to it. I'm glad to see no more

stories have been published about you and Leo. But I haven't seen any other stories about you dating anyone else."

So, she wants us to be seen going out with other people, probably girls but not with each other, I hate her. She is looking at me waiting for an answer.

"I'm gay. You won't let me date boys so you won't see me out with girls," I reply back a little annoyed.

"I need you to be seen with girls, Jacob, it's what the fans want to see. They want to know that you could be available for them to date too."

"I don't want to date girls. I like boys." I am becoming very angry.

"I need you to at least have a date for Xander and Shelly's wedding. There will be a photographer from a magazine and you need to be seen with a date, a female date. No arguments."

"I don't want to take a date," my voice becoming louder.

"You have to. I am telling you that you have to."

"Are you making Leo take a date and what about Alice, she's single?"

"Yes, I will be talking to him about it later, but I don't think he will protest to much as I have seen him with girls and I have no problem with Alice being single."

This comment makes my blood boil. She is a fucking bitch, how dare she say things like that to me. She can see that I am becoming very angry so she quickly says, "I want you to find a date for the wedding and that's final. Now I have lots of work to do."

That's it, she is dismissing me. I have no say in this. I storm out of her office.

I head back to the apartments. I go to Alice's first. I don't want to go back to mine.

She answers the door and shows me in.

"What did she want?" she asks straight away.

"She wants me to have a date for Xander and Shelly's wedding."

"Can you take whoever you want?"

"No, I have to take a girl because a magazine photographer will be there and Harriet wants us to be with a girl."

"What! She can't make you do that. What did you say?"

"I said I didn't want to. But she wasn't having it, as normal. So, I'm going to have to find a date. Who am I going to take?"

"How about if I talk to Chloe? You both get on well and she knows that you are gay. Maybe you could go with her?"

"That's not very fair on Chloe."

"Let me speak to her and see what she says."

"Okay thanks, but don't force her to do it if she doesn't want to."

"Do you want to stay for lunch?"

"Yes, please. That would be nice. I don't want to go back to mine yet."

We end up spending the day together. Alice speaks to Chloe and she said that she will go to the wedding with me, I'm so grateful to her.

Before I go back to my apartment, I decide to see what Harriet said to Leo. I knock on his door. He opens it and he looks like he is ready to go out and he has a vodka in his hand. It looks like he has already had a few.

"Hi."

"Hi, I'm just going out," he replies.

"I just wanted to ask what Harriet said to you today."

"She told me to get a date for Xander and Shelly's wedding."

"What did you say to her?"

"I said fine, that I would."

"Will it be a real date?"

He looks at me. I wish he would talk to me; I can tell he is not telling me something.

"Look, Jacob, I'm meeting some people. I've got to go."

He downs his drink, takes his glass inside, comes back out shuts the door behind him and walks away. As he is making his way down the corridor, I shout out, "Leo, be careful, won't you. I love you."

"Yeah, see you later."

"Don't forget we've got our suit fitting tomorrow morning."

He waves his hand in acknowledgement and then he's gone.

I hate he's like this towards me now, he never says he loves me any more. I head back to my apartment where I spend another lonely night worrying about Leo.

In the morning, I meet Xander at his before setting off. Leo is meant to be here too but again there is no sign of him, we check his apartment but it looks like he's not been back since yesterday. Where is he? Xander phones him, thankfully he picks up his phone.

"He's going to meet us there," Xander informs me.

"Where is he?"

"He wouldn't say."

We arrive at the shop and as we are sorting everything out, Leo arrives. He stumbles through the door, looking awful. He's still drunk and looks a mess. I pull him to one side.

"What are you doing? I reminded you about this yesterday. You are spoiling it for Xander."

"I'm not. He's fine. I just lost track of time," he says, slurring.

"Leo, you've got to stop this."

"I haven't got to do anything you tell me."

And he pushes me out of the way.

"Xander, your best man is here, where's my suit?" he shouts across the store.

"Leo, you're not the best man, that's my brother, you know that."

"I know but I'm the best man here."

"For God's sake, Leo. You are fucking annoying. Get yourself together or I won't let you be in the wedding at all."

"All right, all right. Let's get this over and done with."

The rest of the appointment is so bad. Leo moans about everything, then once his suit has been fitted, he storms off again.

On our way back to the apartments, I feel I need to apologise to Xander for Leo's behaviour.

"I'm so sorry, Xander."

"Why are you sorry? It's not your fault Leo is acting like a total ass."

"Well, it kind of is. If we didn't start going out together, he wouldn't be like this now."

"It's still not your fault, Jacob. You're going through the same thing and you're not acting like that."

"No, but it's different for him. I knew I was gay. He's still so unsure about himself, he is so confused."

"You can't keep using that as an excuse, he has been with you for a long time, Jacob. He doesn't have to take his problems out on everyone else. And he is being totally vile to you."

"Yes, I know, but I still love him. Not sure he loves me any more though."

"Maybe it's time to put an end to it so you can both move on with your lives."

"I don't want to. He's agreed to come to New York with me for a few days after your wedding. I will see what it's like after that."

"Jacob, you have to look after yourself."

"I know."

The wedding is here. We have been staying at the country house for a few days and we have had so much fun. I haven't laughed like this in so long. Leo hasn't joined us yet, but I think this is why I've had such a good time, he's not here for me to worry about or bring me down.

Leo isn't here because he has been looking for a house to buy in London. He hasn't told me he is house hunting but he mentioned it to Xander and he told me. I haven't spoken to or seen Leo since I left London. I'm still hoping he will come to New York with me, maybe we will be able to sort things out then.

It's the evening before the wedding day, the girls have gone to have a spa night and the boys have enjoyed a meal and a few drinks. Leo has just arrived and he's not with any one, I wonder who he is going to bring to the wedding tomorrow. He joins us at the table and to my surprise he sits next to me.

"Hi," he says quietly.

"Hi, what have you been up to?"

He looks guilty and he drops his head. "I've been looking for a house to buy."

"Really, you're moving out of the apartments. Have you found anywhere?"

"Haven't found anything I love yet." As he answers, he looks deep into my eyes.

As I stare back at his brown eyes, I think, *You have found something you love, but you're letting it go.*

"I'm sure something will turn up. Are you looking forward to tomorrow?"

"Yes, I'm sure it will be great." He sounds so sad.

"Right, I'm having one more drink as a single man then I'm going to bed," announces Xander.

We all cheer at him and order another round of drinks. I look over to Leo and I always wished one day we would have a wedding, but that dream is slowly disappearing.

Xander goes up to his room with his brother Max in tow. Slowly, everyone starts to leave. I'm about to get up but Leo touches my arm, I look at him.

"Can you stay a little longer? I want to talk to you while no one is around."

"Okay."

I sit back down, order another drink wondering what Leo wants to talk about. Finally, the last few people leave and we are alone.

"What do you want Leo?"

"I want to talk about us."

"Really, why now? I've been trying to talk to you for months."

"Things are so different now. I have been seeing someone else. She's coming to the wedding tomorrow, but I wanted to tell you first."

Fuck. I knew something was going on. This is it it's over.

"So, what you are ending it between us at Xander and Shelly's wedding. How could you?"

"I don't know."

"Well, you need to know, you can't be with us both. You either love me or her." I am so angry and upset that he is doing this today.

"You can't be mad, you've got a date for tomorrow too."

How dare he bring this around on to me.

"I don't have a date. I'm here with Chloe. She knows I'm gay. We won't be pretending to be together, we are just friends. I don't want to be with a girl, I'm gay and I have a boyfriend, you. I just want to be with you Leo."

"I know I'm sorry."

"You have to make your mind up, Leo. Either you're with me or you're not. I can't be messed around like this any more. You need to let me know before we leave here as we have the New York trip booked and there's no point going if you don't want to be with me."

I stand up and walk out as I can't talk to him. I don't look back so I don't know what his reaction is.

I haven't had a very good night's sleep. The argument I had with Leo last night kept going around my head mingled with images of him and a mysterious girl on their wedding day. I get myself ready and head down to Alice and Chloe's room. Alice has already gone to join Shelly as she is one of the bridesmaids. Chloe looks lovely in a pale green dress. She is the image of Alice but thankfully not as tall as her sister, so she doesn't make me look too short.

We make our way down to the ballroom where the ceremony will be taking place. The first person I notice when we arrive is Leo; he is looking really good in his suit. Suddenly, a girl approaches him and puts her arm through his and he smiles at her the way he used to smile at me. Chloe notices what I'm looking at and she puts her arm through mine and asks, "Are you okay?"

"I'm going to have to be."

We walk over to them and when Leo spots me and Chloe he

releases the girl's arm from his.

"Hi," I say to him, "you look great."

"He does, doesn't he. He's so handsome," the girl he's with says to us.

Leo looks at me embarrassed.

"This is Sarah. Sarah, this is Jacob and Alice's sister, Chloe."

"Hello," me and Chloe both say without smiling at her.

Sarah gives me a strange look and doesn't smile either, she just turns back to Leo and hangs off his arm.

Then a photographer is calling for us, so we can't speak any more which I'm glad about I can't face this Sarah, she's not taking my man away from me.

After a few photographs, Xander appears and he is looking a little nervous. Me and Leo go and join him for more photographs, the photographer makes me and Leo stand next to each other. I can feel his body touching mine and I can smell his aftershave, it's not the one he normally wears but he still smells amazing. I'm sure Harriet wouldn't be happy if she saw us being photographed together and just as I'm thinking this thought Harriet appears out of nowhere. She pulls the photographer to one side and says something to him. From then on me and Leo are no longer photographed stood next to each other.

After waiting for a while, it is time for everyone to take their seats, me and Leo join Xander, Max and a school friend of Xander's Scott at the front. Xander has become very nervous now that the time has come to actually get married but as soon as the music starts and the doors open and Shelly appears at the top of the aisle on her dad's arm the nervous look on his face disappears and a huge smile appears. I look at Leo, who looks back at me and smiles my stomach does a flip, that hasn't happened in a while.

The ceremony was lovely. We've had more photographs taken and now we are making our way to our table for the reception. I notice that the seating plan has been changed. I was meant to be sitting next to Leo but he has been moved to the other side of the table and Chloe and Sarah have been added on. I'm not happy that I'm sitting opposite Leo and Sarah. I have to spend the whole reception having to watch them be together, I don't think I can take it. After a few hours, the torture is over. I have tried to ignore them but it has been hard. The meal was very delicious and the speeches were funny and emotional and now the staff have asked us to leave the room while they move everything around to set up the evening party. I need to escape from here I can't watch Sarah draping herself all over Leo for one more minute. I leave Chloe with Alice and tell them I will be back in a bit. I walk out of the room and as I do I spot Leo watching me leave and he is ignoring what Sarah is saying to him.

I decide I need some fresh air so I make my way out to the gardens. It's a warm sunny day with a light breeze blowing through the trees and shrubs. I have been walking around for about five minutes there is no one around and I am enjoying the quiet surroundings when I hear footsteps on the gravel path behind me. I turn around and Leo is walking towards me, he grabs my hand and pulls me behind one of the trees, as he does he pushes me against it and starts kissing me.

"What are you doing?" I try to say against his kisses.

"I want you, Jacob, I want to go to New York with you."

"What about Sarah, she seems to really like you?"

"Don't talk about her just kiss me."

I can't help myself, I try not to but I miss him so much, so I kiss him back.

When we finally stop, I look into his eyes my favourite part of him and hope that he is serious.

"Do you mean it, Leo? Do you really still want to be with me? Do you really want to come to New York?"

"Yes, I do."

"I'm so glad to hear that."

"Can we meet up later?"

"Yes, of course."

"I will wait for Sarah to go to her room and I will come to yours."

"I look forward to it. You had better go back in we don't want to be caught missing for too long."

He kisses me again and runs back inside. I stay in the garden for a little longer. I hope he really did mean what he just said. I'm also glad to hear they have separate rooms, it means they are not sleeping together, yet.

The evening has been so much fun, Xander and Shelly look so happy and in love with each other. I hope one day me and Leo can show the world how much we love each other. Xander and Shelly make their way to the honeymoon suite which signals the end of the celebrations. Sarah has spent the whole evening right next to Leo so I've not been able to speak to him but he did say he would meet me later. I decide to go up to my room before the others, I need to get away from Sarah, I really don't like her. I smile at Leo as I leave and he smiles back and gives me a wink. I can't wait for him to come up it's been to long since we've had sex.

I don't expect him for a while, so I have a drink whilst waiting but time starts going by and I've been waiting two hours and he is still not here. After another hour, I decide to go to bed maybe he will be along in a bit. I eventually fall to sleep.

As I wake up in the morning with no sign of Leo, I realise that he has done it again. He's let me down. I'm so angry with myself for believing him. I throw on some clothes and make my way down to breakfast. There he is with Sarah stood talking to Alice. I walk over to them, not caring who sees me.

"Morning, can I talk to you?" I grab Leo's arm and pull him away. Alice gives me a look to say what are you doing?

"Jacob, what are you doing? There are loads of people around." Leo is trying to get free of my grip.

"I don't care, what happened last night? You said you were going to come to my room."

"I was. I tried but I couldn't get away from Sarah, she kept wanting to dance and drink. She didn't want to go back to her room."

"Why didn't you say you wanted to go back to your room?"

"I did but she wanted to come with me."

"You have to tell her you don't want to be with her, Leo. It's not fair on her."

"I know, I will but it's complicated."

"Why is it complicated?"

"It just is."

I'm not happy with that answer but I decide I need to calm down, so I ask him, "What are you doing later, once everyone has gone? I'm staying at Mum and Dad's. Would you like to come and stay for a bit?"

"Maybe, I still want to stay in London for a while to see if I can find a house."

"How about in a few weeks then? I will phone you next week to see when you can come up to us."

"I will try. If not, I will see you for our trip."

"Great, I will speak to you next week." I lean in and whisper, "I love you."

He smiles at me and walks back over to Sarah and Alice.

Alice looks between me and Leo and makes her way over to me.

"What was all that about?"

I tell her everything that has happened between me and Leo since he arrived. She looks concerned.

"Be careful, Jacob, make sure he doesn't hurt you again. I wasn't going to say anything but I was watching Leo and Sarah yesterday and they seem happy together."

Before we can talk more Xander and Shelly appear to lots of cheers. They make their way around the room talking to their guests before we all sit down for breakfast. Leo sits on a different table with Sarah away from me and this gives me an opportunity to see what they are like together without me being around them. Alice is right, they do look happy together, I haven't seen him smile like that for a while. But he has agreed to come to New York with me so he still has feelings for me.

After breakfast, we wave off Xander and Shelly, they are heading to Paris for their honeymoon and we all make our way off in different directions. We will see each other in the New Year to start recording again and to plan our tour for next summer.

Chapter Twelve

I have been staying at Mum and Dad's and I am loving being at home. The only down side is that I have asked Leo to come and stay with us a few times and he has said that he couldn't. He has bought a house in London and he moves in to it a couple of days before we go to New York so he hasn't got the time to come and stay here.

I have decided that I am going to buy a house near Mum and Dad, I don't want to have a place in London just yet. I can stay in the apartment for now when I have to go back. I have been looking at a few places near here but I have decided I want a place in Hale. I have viewed a few properties and there is one that I love and I am seriously thinking of buying it. It is rather large just for me, but hopefully, one day Leo will share it with me. It is a lot of money too and Mum and Dad have advised me to take some time to think about it before making my final decision. I would like to have decided before I go to America in two weeks. I have asked Leo to come and see the house with me but he is so busy with his own house, he has decorators in and is sorting out furniture and everything else for the move, so he is unable to come and see it.

I am on my way to look at it one more time and then make my final decision. I walk into the house again and I still love it like I did the first time. It has four large rooms plus the kitchen and utility room downstairs, six bedrooms upstairs and four bathrooms. It is light and airy and I love all the space. I need to do some work to it before I can move in. I would like to turn two of the rooms downstairs into a recording studio and a gym but keep the lay out everywhere else the same, just redecorate and put in a new kitchen and bathrooms. I just love it and I can see myself living here and making so many memories hopefully with Leo. I decide there and then that I want it. I put in an offer and it is accepted straight away. I am so excited I can't wait to tell Leo and wish he could come and see it. I also can't wait to see his new house too.

I phone Leo to tell him the news but it goes straight to answer phone.

I leave a message, *Hi Leo. Just wanted to let you know that I have bought that house I was telling you about. I can't wait for you to see it.*

I wait all day for him to phone me back but he doesn't. I text him again on his moving day to wish him good luck with the move and I ask him to call me to talk about the New York trip. He phones me back but not until late at night.

"Hi, Leo, how did the move go?"

"Good, thanks. We are all moved in."

"We?"

There is silence on the other end.

"Leo you just said 'we are all moved in'."

"I just meant that I had some of the band helping me move."

He's lying. I can always tell when he's not telling me the truth. He quickly changes the subject.

"What time is your flight on Friday?"

"It's in the morning, so I will be there before you arrive. I will meet you at the apartment. You have the address, don't you and there will keys left for you at the desk in the foyer?"

We made the decision to fly separately from different airports just to be sure we are not seen together.

"Yes, I have, so I will see you there. I've got to go I still have lots to do."

"Oh, okay." I'm a little shocked by how little he has to say to me.

"Bye."

"Bye," I say back just as he is hanging up the phone.

I have arrived in New York and I am settled into the apartment we have hired for the few days we are here. Leo should be here in about an hour. He texted me to say he had landed and was heading for the taxi. I can't wait to see him and spend some alone time just me and him, we haven't done that for so long. I'm sat scrolling through my phone when I hear keys in the door, he's here. I jump up and go and greet him. As he walks in I just stand there and admire him, I'm so glad that he is here.

"Hi," he smiles at me, it's as if the old Leo has come back.

"I'm so glad you're here."

I walk over to him, put my arms around his waist and kiss him. He returns my hug and kiss and everything feels right in the world again.

"Do you want anything to eat or drink?" I say letting him go.

"No, I want to take you to bed."

Straight to the point but that's okay because that's what I want to do too.

I grab his hand and pull him into the apartment. He turns me around pulls me into him and he kisses me so hard, our tongues exploring each other's. He pulls off my t-shirt and throws it on the floor. I start to undo the buttons on his shirt as he continues to kiss my lips and down my neck. I take off his shirt and nip at his skin over his toned chest. Then I'm on my knees and I undo his zip on his trousers, his hands are in my hair then on my shoulders as he moans out loud. We don't make it to the bedroom, we have no control and have sex in the middle of the apartment.

"I've missed you so much."

"I've missed you too. I'm sorry about what's been happening, how I've been acting."

"It's okay. But we've wasted so much time."

We spend the rest of the evening just being together.

The next two days are perfect. We have ventured out the apartment to do some sightseeing but we have been very careful. We have made sure we have gone out with baseball caps and sunglasses so that we are not instantly noticeable. It has been so wonderful to walk around together without anyone knowing who we are. On the evenings, we have spent it eating, drinking and making love just how it was when we were living together. I don't want it to end.

It's the final night and we are in bed, my head is on Leo's chest. I'm looking through my phone when a headline pops up on my search that makes me catch my breath, 'Leo and girlfriend move in together'. I click on it and there are photographs of Leo and Sarah moving into what I assume is the house Leo has just bought. There are also photos of them both on nights out and in many of them they are kissing. I sit bolt upright and look at Leo.

"What's wrong?"

I show him my phone. "This."

I get out of bed pull on some tracksuit bottoms and a t-shirt and storm out of the bedroom.

I hear him follow me.

"What the fuck, Leo. Are you living with her?"

He doesn't say anything.

"So, you are definitely with her now."

He still doesn't say anything.

"Fucking say something. Where does she think you are now? Leo!" I shout.

"She thinks I've met up with some of the band to do some recording."

"So, you are with her, is she living with you?"

"Kind of. She comes and goes."

"I can't believe what I'm hearing. I hate you. I fucking hate you so much."

"Jacob, please, you've got to understand."

"I understand. You just want to be seen as everyone else wants you to be and not who you really are."

"Jacob, don't be like this. I need to be with Sarah."

"Don't you say her name to me. I'm not fucking sharing you."

"Jacob."

"That's it, Leo. I can't do this any more. We're finished. You can go and live your life with her. Don't come to me any more. I hate you."

"Jacob, please." I can see he is upset and close to tears but I don't care, I keep going I am so angry.

"No, Leo. I've taken your shit for too long, no more. I'm glad we are going home tomorrow and that I won't see you for a while I need to get you out of my system."

"Jacob."

I can't look at him. I can't believe what he has done and that it is over. I run into the bedroom, lock the door behind me and bury my head in the pillows on the bed and cry, they don't stop coming.

When I wake up, I have calmed down, to be honest I knew this was coming but I was just hoping in my heart that it never would. I need to talk to Leo, I can't leave it like this I need to clear the air. I pack, get ready and leave the bedroom. Leo is still sleeping on the sofa. I go over and kneel down beside him. I gently touch his face to wake him. He opens his eyes and I wonder if I will ever see his amazing eyes so close again, I take them and his whole face in to my memory.

"I have to go now," I say to him.

"Okay, I'm so sorry that it ended like this. I didn't mean to hurt you so much."

"I know you didn't and I knew in my heart that it was coming. I'm sorry I got so mad, I don't hate you."

"Don't be sorry it's not your fault, you have always been honest and open with me from the start and I haven't."

"I love you and I always will."

"I love you too. Thanks for everything."

"Thank you too. I had an amazing time with you. I just wish things could have been different for us both."

We both lean into each other and we kiss for one last time, it is full of love and emotion.

After I stand up, I grab my bags and walk towards the door.

"See you soon," I say as I open the door. I look back one last time and I'm filled with heartache. He waves out to me and I have to go as I can fill tears filling my eyes.

My house is finally finished and I am moving in today. I love my house but I thought that decorating it would have been a much happier process than it was. I was hoping Leo would have been here helping me make decisions and deciding on things that we both like together but that never happened. I haven't got much more stuff to move but Mum and Dad are helping me out. I think they just want to be with me. They have both been extremely worried since I told them that me and Leo had split up. It has been tough these past few months, I haven't spoken to him in all that time.

There have been lots of articles about him recently. Everyone seems to love the fact that he is with her. In some of the articles my name is thrown in and a couple of them have even put in some photographs of us when we were together but most are about how happy they both are. I don't know what it is going to be like when we go back to work.

To take my mind off of everything, I have been concentrating on making my own music and songs especially now I have my own studio. I can write my own stuff and maybe one day venture out on my own.

I'm finally moved in. We decided to have a take away to celebrate the new house before Mum and Dad head back home.

"Are you sure you are going to be okay in this big house by yourself?" Mum asks, she is so worried.

"Yes, I'm sure. I'm going to be fine."

"You don't have to stay here; we love having you home."

"I know you do, Mum, but you and Dad need your own space and so do I. I'm going to continue writing and recording my own songs. It will be great."

"If you are sure, but we are not too far away so just come home if you feel lonely."

"I will," I promise her.

Mum and Dad eventually leave. I sit in my living room and suddenly I feel really alone. I'm not sure now if I am going to be okay. I am really missing Leo. He should be here with me, this was to be his house too. I was making a home for the both of us. I go to my drinks cabinet and pour myself a vodka. I don't normally drink vodka but Leo always did and it reminds me of him and I need that at the moment. I take my drink up to my bedroom and go into my closet, go over to the chest of drawers and open the bottom drawer. In it are some of Leo's clothes that had got mixed up with my things and I didn't want to give them back to him. I pull out a pair of tracksuit bottoms and a t-shirt and change into them. I then go into the bathroom and find the aftershave he wore when we were together and spray some on myself and it feels like he is here, it is very comforting. I'm missing him so much tonight. I reach for my phone and pull up his name on my contacts I really need to hear his voice. I'm about to press the dial button when I change my mind. I can't phone him he has his new life now. Instead, I head towards the studio and sit at the piano and let all my feelings flood out into songs. I'm in there until the early hours of the morning and I have the bases for a few good songs. They are all very sad and would have to be changed slightly if I ever wanted to record them because they are obviously written about Leo but they are a good start to my own music.

We were meant to travel back to London to start working on our next album and to organise our tour, but the world shut down so we cannot do any of that at the moment. We don't know when we will be able to go back and record and we have postponed the tour until 2022.

We have had a few online meetings to discuss the new album and throw around a few ideas for songs and we have decided to keep these up, so we can carry on writing songs. Then when we can go back to the studio everything will be ready.

Leo looks happy every time I see him on the calls so everything must be going good with him and her, but this then makes me feel really miserable.

Since we have been in lockdown, I have been so down. I miss Leo terribly and many nights I have been wearing Leo's clothes and aftershave, pouring myself a vodka and spending hours and hours in the studio writing sad love songs. We still haven't spoken to each other only on the work calls and then everyone else is there. I have found myself a few more times going to call him but I stop myself.

We are finally allowed to meet up with other people so I have decided to invite Xander, Alice and Leo to mine for the weekend to do some song writing. I can't wait to see them in person, it's just not the same on the online calls. They are arriving this evening. I'm not sure how I'm going to feel about seeing Leo here in the house I wanted to share with him. I have got the spare rooms ready for them to stay the night, lots of food and drink in. I'm hoping it will be a bit of a party for us to celebrate being back together again.

Alice arrives first, she is so excited to be here. She gives me the biggest hug and she can't wait to look around the house. I show her to the living room and tell her to get herself a drink as the door goes for the second time. I open it and there he is. My stomach does its usual flip. He is looking amazing. It looks like he has been working out a lot. His body is usually so good but it now looks so toned and defined.

"Hi, come in."

"Thanks. It's great to see you. How have you been?"

"I've been okay. You're looking great."

"Not much else to do but to work out."

"Alice is here already, come in to the living room."

I notice him looking around as we walk through to the living room.

"You have a great place."

"Thanks, I like it."

I would love it more if you were here with me, I think to myself.

As we walk into the living room, Alice runs over and gives Leo a big hug just as she had given me. I feel a pang of jealousy as I would have loved to give him a hug just as big.

We are having a drink when the door goes for the third time. I answer it to Xander and he also gives me a big hug and we make our way to the others; everyone gets a hug from Xander. Everyone is looking so happy why can't I feel like that.

I open a bottle of champagne and pour everyone a glass and hand them round.

"I would like to make a toast. To UsFour back together again. I can't wait to make more great songs with you all. Cheers."

We all clink our glasses and they all shout, "Cheers."

"Would you like something to eat first? I put out some snacks in the kitchen or do you want to go to the studio to start some writing."

"I want the tour first," Alice says excitedly.

"Okay, let me show you around."

I show them the downstairs first, the gym, the studio, kitchen and the office. At one point, Leo brushes so close to me that I can smell his aftershave, I miss his smell. It's not the same one I wear which used to belong to him but it is still intoxicating. I then show them upstairs and point out the rooms in which they will be staying in. When the tour is over, we head back downstairs and into the kitchen for another drink and some snacks.

"Your house is lovely, Jacob," Alice says.

"Thanks, sometimes it feels very big for just me but it's great to have you all here. It feels like how I thought it would do, a house full of the people I love."

I look over at Leo and smile at him and he smiles back. Alice reaches over and hugs me tight.

We spend hours just drinking, eating and catching up on life. Thankfully, Leo hasn't mentioned anything about her, a few times I think he was going to but it seemed like he stopped himself.

It's getting late so we decide to go into the studio to start to write some songs, everyone has lots of ideas. As we are talking about these, I notice Leo looking at some papers that I forgot to put away. It is the songs I had been writing. I go over and take them from him, I don't want him to read any of these.

"I forgot to put these away."

"They're good," he lowers his voice so Alice and Xander can't hear. "Are they about me?"

"Some of them. I have been writing a lot lately," I reply.

"Can we use any of them for the group?"

"No, these are my personal songs. I doubt they will ever get recorded."

"You should record them, they are very good."

He moves in closer and whispers, "You're wearing my old aftershave. You didn't use to wear that before."

"It's your old bottle that got mixed up with my things, I

didn't want to waste it."

I don't want to tell him that I always wear it so I can smell him every day.

I put my songs in a drawer and we go back to writing. After a few more hours and a lot more to drink we decide to leave it for this evening, we have made some good progress.

We make our way back to the living room, where I pour everyone another drink. I pour myself a vodka which I notice Leo watching me do.

"Would you like a vodka?" I ask him.

"Since when have your drunk vodka, you used to hate it?"

"Since we split up I have found a taste for it."

I pour him one and hand it to him. I put my glass out to cheers him and he clinks his glass against mine and we both down it in one. Leo looks at me in shock.

"Another?"

He nods and I pour us both another.

"Jacob, do you mind if I go up to bed?" Alice asks.

"Of course not. Do you remember which one is your room?"

"Yes. Thanks for tonight it's been great. See you in the morning." Alice leaves to go upstairs.

"I think I might go up too," Xander says, "being a married man has made me a bit boring, I'm afraid, me and Shelly are usually in bed long before now. See you in the morning."

"See you in the morning," me and Leo both say to Xander.

We are then alone. We haven't been alone since we were in New York.

"Are you okay, Jacob. You don't seem yourself any more?"

"I'm a bit lonely to be honest. At least you have someone to keep you company and to be with. I'm not able to find anybody new as I'm not allowed to let the world know I'm gay, so I don't know how I'm ever going to find someone."

"I'm sorry, Jacob. I didn't know you were so down."

"How would you? We never talk. You were the one I told everything to, but now I have no one."

I pour us another drink and we both drink it in silence.

"Are you happy, Leo?" I finally ask.

"Sometimes and sometimes I'm not."

"Are you happy with her?"

"Her name is Sarah, Jacob, you know that. Yes, I am, but sometimes I really miss talking to you. I can't always talk to Sarah about certain things that I could always with you."

I pour us another drink, I'm feeling quite drunk now and I can see Leo is getting drunk too.

"Can I see some more of your songs that you have written? I really liked the ones I did see."

"I don't know. They are very raw."

"That's when they are true."

"All right."

I grab the bottle of vodka and walk down to the studio, Leo follows.

When we are in the studio, I pull out all the songs I have started writing and hand them to Leo. He reads through the songs as I sip my drink and watch him. He keeps going back to one song but I can't see which one it is. Eventually, he hands me that piece of paper and it is the song called 'Lost Love', it's all about how I felt when we split up.

"Can you sing me this song?"

"It's not finished."

"Please."

I sit at my piano, he pours us both another vodka and sits next to me on the piano stall. I feel his leg touch mine and I feel a tingle run through my body.

I begin to play and sing the song, I can feel his eyes on me, then he puts his hand on my leg and this makes me stop abruptly. I stand up from the piano and look at him.

"What are you doing?" I ask him.

"I'm sorry, the song is so sad, I just wanted to comfort you."

"You can't do that any more, Leo. We are not together."

"You are just so sad."

"Yes, Leo, I am sad because the love of my life left me and I don't know what to do with myself being in this house all alone. This was meant to be your house too, I wanted to share it with you. I wanted this to be our home. But you left me to live with her."

"Jacob, I'm sorry."

"I'm going to bed. I will see you in the morning."

I walk away from him, if I stay any longer something will happen between us. I will not be that person who he cheats on her with.

I make my way up to my bedroom and I can hear him coming up the stairs behind me. I don't dare turn around, I have had a lot to drink and my defences are weakened and if I look in to his eyes they will just disappear completely. I make it to my room, go inside and close the door quickly before he reaches me. As I'm undressing there's a quiet knock on my door. I ignore it but then there's another one and I hear Leo's voice saying my name very quietly. I can't help myself I go to the door and open it.

"Can I come in?"

I nod and move aside so he can come in. He walks in and I see him looking at the clothes flung over the chair in the corner of my room. I notice that it's all his clothes that I have been wearing. It's too late he's making his way over to them and picking them up. He looks over at me, "These are all my clothes."

"Yes," what else can I say.

"Why are they here?"

"They got mixed up with my clothes."

"Have you been wearing them and my aftershave too? I can smell it on them all?"

"Yes, I wear them when I'm missing you."

"Oh, Jacob."

He walks over to me and he stands so close, I can feel his breath on me.

"I can't do this, Leo, it's not right. What about Sarah?"

"Jacob, please."

His hands are on my waist like he used to do and I'm weakened. He leans in and kisses me.

"Leo, we can't."

"*Shhh!* We can."

He runs his hand down my bare back as he kisses my neck and I moan in pleasure. I haven't been touched for so long and I didn't realise how much I had missed it. He kisses me again and he starts to undo my trousers.

"Leo, we have to stop," I say to him not meaning it at all.

He looks at me with those eyes and I find myself pulling of his t-shirt and undoing his trousers. He takes my hand and leads me to the bed. We lay down and he pulls off my trousers before he takes off his own. I can't take my eyes off his naked body, I have missed it. We continue to explore each other's mouth with our tongue's and I can feel the excitement building as he pushes his body against mine. He flips me over and kisses down my back and I'm lost to him and all guilt gone.

I wake up the next morning and my head is aching, why did I

drink so much vodka last night it always gives me a bad head. What happened last night I can't remember much after we stopped writing. I turn over and there he is on the far side of my bed. What have we done? I can't believe we ended up in bed together. And why is he so far away from me, when we used to sleep together he would always snuggle up so close to sleep, but that's not the point he can't be in here. He needs to get up before Alice and Xander find out.

"Leo, Leo, wake up."

I see him stirring, "Leo, wake up."

He opens his eyes and looks at me in shock.

"What am I doing here?"

"We slept together, you've got to get out of here before the others see you."

"What. No, I can't have slept with you. What will Sarah say if she finds out?"

"Well, you have and she won't find out."

He jumps out of bed grabbing his clothes from all over the room and throwing them back on. I watch him and I can see he is very agitated.

"Are you okay?" I ask him.

"No, I'm not fucking okay. This was a huge mistake. I shouldn't have come here."

"What do you mean this was a huge mistake, thanks a lot."

"Sorry but it was a mistake. I shouldn't be sleeping with anyone else."

"I'm not just anyone, I'm not a random person you've just met."

"I can't do this, Jacob. I've got to go."

"Don't go. Look no one knows what happened and won't it look more suspicious if you disappear early. We still have more writing to do. Just stay a few more hours."

"Okay," he says as he pulls open the bedroom door quietly to check no one is around and he leaves without looking back.

What have I done? I can't keep doing this. When we are together it just too easy to go back to him.

We spend the rest of the day in the studio, we finish writing another two songs. Leo has been avoiding me all day and Alice and Xander keep giving us looks. They know something has happened but they have not said anything. After we finish for the day we all say goodbye, we did make really good progress this weekend and the album is nearly finished, so once we get back to the studio we should be able to record the album in a short time. The less time I spend with Leo the better for the both of us.

Once everyone has left, the house is empty once more and again the heaviness fills me.

Chapter Thirteen

I'm back in London. Only myself and Alice are living in the apartments now, it's very strange here without Leo and Xander. I don't want to buy a place in London so I'm just going to stay here for the time being.

Over the last few months, I have been thinking a lot about what I am going to do in the future. After I slept with Leo over the summer, I've decided that I can't be around him any more, the more I see him the more I want him and I need to move on with my life. So, I have made the decision that I'm going to leave the group and do my own thing. I need to talk to Alice and Xander about this first before anyone else as I need to know how they feel about it as it could change their lives too. I have asked them both to come over for a drink later to talk to them.

They have both arrived, I offer them a drink and ask them to sit down.

"What's wrong, Jacob, you seem really serious?" Alice asks.

"I need to talk to you both about something I have been thinking about for a while. I think you both know that something happened between me and Leo in the summer when you were at my house."

"We did think something had happened, Leo was acting totally different the next day," Xander says.

"Yes, it did, and Leo totally freaked out about it. It is becoming very difficult for me to be around him so I have made the decision that I want to leave the group. I want to do my own thing and also be free in my personal life."

Alice and Xander look at each other then look back at me.

Alice speaks first. "I don't want you to leave, but I totally understand why you would want to. To be honest, I have been thinking about going to do something different. I've always wanted to do some theatre. Maybe we all should take a break from the group to pursue our own things for a while."

"I would love to try some acting and me and Shelly are thinking about having a baby."

"That's great, Xander. You will make an amazing dad. Thanks, guys, for the support. I was so worried that if I left, it would ruin everything for you both."

"No, honestly, it's fine with me, and Xander seems to be on board too."

"What about Leo and Harriet? I'm not sure if they will feel just as happy as we do about this decision?" Xander says.

"I think I'm going to talk to George first before we say anything to Harriet, but I don't know what to do about Leo, I don't think I can tell him."

"Do you want us to tell him?" Alice asks.

"Would you do that?"

"Yes, of course. I'm sure it will be fine."

"Thanks, that would be great."

We spend the rest of the evening talking about all the things that we want to do but have never been able to whilst we are in the group. Xander and Alice have said they are going to try and talk to Leo tomorrow. I hope he is going to be okay about it.

The next day I am so nervous. I don't know when they are going to tell Leo, but I've texted George asking to speak to him in the next couple of days. He hasn't replied back yet.

I've just sat down for some lunch when there is a loud, hard knock on my door. I go and answer it and Leo is standing there looking fuming.

"What do you think you are doing?" he shouts as he pushes past me and storms into the living room. I follow him in.

"I guess Alice and Xander have spoken to you then?"

"Yes, why do you want to leave?" He's mad.

"I need to get away from you and have my own life. Move on like you have. I can't do that being in the group, I'm not allowed."

"But I don't want the group to break up, what will I do?" His voice has changed from angry to worried.

"Are you worried about what to do after the group?"

"Yes, and I would miss you all."

"I'm sorry, Leo, but I just can't stay in the group any more. Xander and Alice want to do different things too. I'm sure you will be fine."

"Well, I'm not happy about it and Harriet won't be either. We've still got contracts. She won't let you break them." He's angry again.

"Yes, we do have contracts but there is only six months left on them, we were all going to renew them for another couple of years but we won't now."

"This is crap." And he storms back out of the apartment.

This was not the reaction I was expecting from him. I thought he would be happy to go and live his own life with Sarah and do his own thing. I stand staring at the door where Leo has just left. I wish we could have been allowed to be together none of this would be happening. Me and Leo would be happily together and the group would have carried on for many more years. I hate that I'm upsetting Leo but it is time I think about myself. Ever since we have met all I have done is put him first but he moved on and so must I.

Two days later, George invites me out for lunch so we can talk. I arrive at the restaurant and I am shown to his table. As I arrive, he stands up and shakes my hand and asks me to sit. We order our food and drinks and he looks at me, ready to hear what I have to say.

"So, what is this all about, Jacob?"

"I want to leave the group. I've spoken to Alice and Xander and they are happy for us to go our own way once our contracts have ended."

"What about Leo?"

"He's not happy about it, but if three of us want to do it, unfortunately, he doesn't have much choice."

"Why do you want to leave?"

"I'm not happy. I can't be around Leo now that he is with someone else. I'm not allowed to have a personal life because I'm not able to be my true self. I just want some freedom."

"I totally understand, Jacob, but I'm not sure Harriet is going to let you all go in six months, even if your contracts are up."

"If we don't sign new ones, she can't do anything about it, can she? What do you think she will say?"

"I don't know. I think she will find a way to make you all stay longer. You make her too much money, she won't let you go without a fight. You will have to talk to her about it and see what says. Shall I organise a meeting with her for next week?"

"Yes, that would be great, but could you not say why we want a meeting with her, we would like to tell her ourselves."

"Okay, I won't say I know why."

"Thanks, but there is another reason why I wanted to talk to you today."

"What is it?"

"After the group splits, I want to do a solo album. I have started to write some of my own songs for it. I would also like you to be my manager."

"Are you sure?" He looks surprised.

"Yes, I am. You have been there for me and the rest of us right from the beginning and you supported me and Leo when the other management team didn't. I would really love to work with you."

"Are you positive that you don't want someone with more experience? I haven't worked in the music industry for that long."

"No, I couldn't work with another Harriet. I want my freedom to be myself in both my music and my personal life and I think you are the best person to help me with that."

"Well, if you are really sure, then I would be honoured."

"Excellent. I can't wait to start working on things with you."

I tell George all about the songs I have written and about what I see in my future. He seems really impressed by what I have been doing.

As we leave, he promises that he will speak to Harriet later today and arrange the meeting. He will let me know as soon as it is sorted.

That evening, George phones me. "Hi, Jacob. I have spoken to Harriet. She wants the meeting with you all at ten tomorrow morning."

"So soon?"

"Yes, I think she knows something is going on."

"How?"

"You've never asked her for a meeting before."

"No, I suppose we haven't. Thanks, George, do want me to tell the others or will you phone them?"

"I will phone them. Do you want a car to take you and Alice to the office or will you drive?"

"No, it's fine. I will drive us both. Will you be at the meeting tomorrow?"

"Yes, she's asked for all the management team to be there."

"Okay, I will see you tomorrow."

"Jacob, don't mention anything about you asking me to work with you after. I don't think Harriet will be too pleased."

"Yes, sure."

"See you tomorrow."

"Bye." I hang up the phone and I come over so nervous. What will Leo be like in the meeting? Will he fight us all the way? What will Harriet be like? I am not going to sleep well tonight.

The next morning, Alice and I are driving to Harriet's office we are both feeling really anxious. Wondering what she is going to say. Will she be her vile, horrid self or will she understand why we want to do this?

Xander and Leo are already there, Leo is sitting away from Xander and doesn't acknowledge us when we arrive. When Harriet calls us in, he storms into the room sits in a seat on the furthest side of the table and looks very miserable.

We all take a seat around the table too. George smiles at me as we sit, he can tell I am worried. Jasmin is sat next to Harriet and Shelly is sat on another table ready to take notes.

"Good morning, everyone. Great to see you all after such a long break. Now George informs me that you all wanted a meeting to discuss something. He said he doesn't know what it is regarding, but I don't believe him for a second." She looks around at George; she is not happy with him.

"Now who is going to tell me what this is about?"

I look at the others and as it was my decision first, I feel I should do the talking. I look at George and he nods his head as if to say everything is going to be all right.

"Well, we have decided that once our contracts are finished, we do not want to continue as the group."

"Not all of us have decided that," Leo interrupts.

"Not all of us, no, but Alice, Xander and myself have. We would like to explore different things that we can't do when we are in the group."

Harriet is staring at us all, looking from one person to the next, but she is not giving anything away.

We all sit in silence waiting for her reaction, finally she responds, "You have only six months left on your contracts but since we have lost a year and you have not fulfilled everything that you had promised your fans you would do, I don't think you will be able to leave in six months."

I knew she would bring up the fans, making us feel guilty and that will work on us, we don't want to let down our fans.

"You said you would do another album and a tour and I'm holding you to that. The tour has been rearranged for next summer and you cannot pull out of that. Places have been booked, fans know that it is happening and they have bought tickets. You all need to think about that."

Again, there is silence. I look over at Alice and Xander. Xander speaks up, "Can we leave the room to discuss somethings?"

"Yes, that's fine," she replies.

Xander stands and Alice and myself follow him but Leo

stays seated. Alice looks at him, annoyed with his behaviour.

"Leo, you have to come too," Alice snaps at him.

He huffs and follows us out of the room.

"What do you think?" Xander asks.

"I don't mind finishing the album. I think it's the best one we have done. It would also be unfair to the fans if we don't follow it up with the tour. But after that, I don't want to do any more," I say to them all, hoping they are thinking the same thing.

"I agree with Jacob," Alice states.

"Me too," Xander agrees.

"What about you, Leo? What do you think?" I ask him.

"I don't have much choice, do I, you've all decided my future for me." He sounds heart broken.

Alice goes over to Leo and puts her arm around him.

"Leo, we are not doing this to hurt you. We all just feel we need to do other things that we really want to do. I'm sure there are things you would like to do too?"

Leo looks over at me, but I can't look back at him so I turn away.

"It's fine. I will be okay."

"So, we agree to do the album and the tour then go our own way," Xander says.

We all nod in agreement and it suddenly seems all very sad. I love all these people so much they are my family. I feel the need to hug every one of them. They must feel the same as Alice pulls Xander into a hug with Leo and I join them. We stay like this for a while and when we finally move away we all have tears in our eyes.

"One day we will get back together; this isn't goodbye, it's see you later," I say to them all.

They all smile at me and we make our way back into the

room. We sit back around the table.

"So, have you made your decision?" Harriet asks.

"Yes. We have agreed to do the album and the tour but that's it. After the tour we would like to go our own ways."

"And you all agree to this?"

She looks at Leo and he nods as does Alice and Xander.

"Fine, if that is your choice. I will get Shelly to write up new contracts with that information on it, get you to sign them and then we can get back to work."

We all get up to leave but as I do Harriet says, "Jacob, can I have a word with you alone before you leave?"

Why does she want to talk to me? I give Alice the car keys and tell her I will be there soon. They all look at me as they are leaving. I look back at them and shrug my shoulders. Harriet even asks Jasmin, George and Shelly to leave as well.

"Jacob, please sit down. I want to ask you something."

I sit back down and wait for her to start talking.

"I want to ask you if you have had any thoughts about what you are going to do after you have left the group?"

"Yes, I have."

"Can I ask what they are?"

"Why do you want to know?" I don't really want to tell her anything.

"If you are deciding to go solo, I think that would be a great idea. You are the best vocal in the group which makes you the best for doing this on your own."

I'm shocked. I don't know what to say. What is she after? She normally hates me.

"I would like to keep you on here. I would like to work with you as a solo artist. What do you think?"

What! No way would I work with her, not after what she put

me through. She wouldn't let me do what I wanted to do and she certainly wouldn't let me have freedom in my personal life. But I have to be careful how I say no I still have to work with her for a while yet.

"That's great, thanks, Harriet, but I think I want to have a clean break from everything."

"Think about it before saying no. You would be very well paid if you stayed with us."

"I will think about it." *But it's a definite no,* I think to myself.

I get up and leave. I'm in shock; does she really think I would stay with her? I get back to the car.

"What did she say?" Alice asks as soon I'm in my seat.

"She wants me to stay signed on to her as a solo artist."

"She doesn't, what did you say?"

"I told her I wanted a clean break, but she told me to think about it."

"You're not thinking about it, are you?"

"No, I'm not. Not after how she treated me and Leo and anyway, I've already asked George to work with me."

"I really don't believe her; she seriously can't think you would stay with her."

"I know."

What a year. We finished the album and again it went straight into number one and it has been our biggest selling album yet. We have had numerous number one singles from it and so many awards given to us. Tour has been amazing. We have sold out every event and the fans have been fantastic.

We announced that we are having a break at the beginning of the year and we were expecting a lot of backlash because of it, but it never came. The fans have been so supportive towards us.

We are so thankful to them.

I have told Harriet that I am going to work with George and not her. She was not pleased with either me or George. But I'm happy with my decision.

The stage is set. The lighting is dark except for four spotlights shining down on four glittering microphone stands marking the place where we will stand for the final time. We hug each other tightly, not wanting to let go.

The music starts up and we step onto the stage, and I hear the roar of the crowd for the final time as we make our way to our microphone stands, I can't believe that this is it. Five years down the line, one broken relationship, a lot of happiness and a lot more heart break has come to this point. We all go through the motions of the concert but I can tell that we are all in a world of our own. It then suddenly comes to an end and it was so emotional for us all. We can't stop hugging each other and don't want to leave the stage. Finally, with tears streaming down our faces, we wave one more time to our fans and leave the stage.

Back stage we are having a small get together for the team and our families to celebrate the end of an era.

It's a very strange feeling. I am standing at the edge of the room just looking around at everyone. Xander and Shelly are stood talking to George and his wife. Alice is with her family laughing at something her dad has just said. Leo is with Sarah and his brother, deep in conversation. All the management, the song writers, the band and lots more people who have been with us for a long time are in this room.

I feel so much love for most of these people here, they are my family. It is going to be strange, some of these people I may never see again. Not seeing Alice, Xander and Leo everyday will be the hardest of all. And that makes me feel really sad.

I look over at Leo and wonder if we will ever be in the same room again. We hardly speak any more. When we have been at work, Sarah has been there with him and it feels like she has been keeping him away from me. I don't know if Leo has ever told her about us but she doesn't like me to be near him. I keep looking at him, taking in every detail of him as I don't know if I will ever see him again. As I'm looking at him he turns and notices me, he gives me a small smile which I return back. I wonder how he is feeling. He goes to take a step in my direction but as he does Sarah grabs his arm and moves him away to the other side of the room to talk to someone else.

As I continue watching him, Mum and Dad make their way over to me they have been talking to Xander's parents. Mum stands next to me and puts her arm through mine.

"Are you okay, love?"

"I think so, just taking it all in."

"You have been watching Leo a lot I've noticed."

"I know but I don't know when I will ever see him again."

Tears fill my eyes and Mum pulls me into a hug.

"Oh, sweetheart. It will be okay. You are free now. You can start a new life, find someone new to love. Someone who will love you back the way you deserve."

"I know. I hope I can."

It's time to say goodbye. I hug everyone then it's just the four of us left. We hug each other, we are all crying and we promise we will meet up soon. I hug Leo last and as I do, I whisper in his ear, "Thank you for everything. I had an amazing time with you."

"Me too," he replies, and I take in his deep brown eyes and his touch for the last time. "Good luck with everything."

"You too," I say back as I let him go.

We have one final group hug and leave the room to make our own way. I hope we have made the right decision. I hope everyone gets what they desire.

Part Two

Chapter Fourteen

I am in London. It has been two weeks since the tour has finished and we went our separate ways. I have to empty the old apartment as I won't ever be coming back here again. There's not much to pack as I haven't been here for a while and I took most things with me on tour. There are a few clothes left in the wardrobe so I throw all those into a bag. As I empty the wardrobe, I notice at the back is the box of Christmas decoration from mine and Leo's one and only Christmas spent here together. I pull out the box, I don't want these to be thrown away so I put it with the stuff I am taking. There are few random bits in the bedroom drawers so I pack them. In the bathroom, I clear out the cupboard under the sink, there are still a few things of Leo's in there. I don't know if I should pack them, I decide not to. In the living room there are a few things around that I pack into the box. In a drawer there is a pile of magazines and papers that I need to sort through, most of it is rubbish but as I pick up one magazine something falls on the floor. I pick it up and my stomach flips, it's a photograph of me and Leo. I look back in the drawer and there's another one. I forgot about these. We look so happy in them. One is of us sat on the sofa having a drink. Alice or Xander must have taken this. The other is a selfie of us in bed. We are smiling as if nothing could ever change or hurt us. These are the only photos of just the two of us together in private so I carefully pack these into the box. I pack a few more things from the living room. Only the kitchen left to do, there is only two things I want from there as the rest was already here when I moved in. I go to the cupboard where the mugs are kept and take out two of them. They are the ones that me and Leo used all the time they have our initials on. I pack these carefully too.

That's it everything packed but I'm not ready to leave just yet, I'm feeling too emotional. I sit on the sofa, look around and think about everything that happened here. This is the place where we had lots of our firsts as a couple, it is the place that we lived together, it is the place we shared all our hopes and dreams for the future. This apartment will always have a special spot in my heart. Thinking of everything I did with Leo makes my heart ache and I feel the tears rising. I try to hold them back but they just begin to fall. Trying to get over Leo is still so hard and this is a piece of us that I am now leaving. I finally pull myself together. There's just one more thing I want to do before I leave. I grab my keys, leave my apartment and head next door to Leo's. I go in and I know he hasn't lived here for a long time now but I want to see it one more time, there are lots of memories here too. I wonder around the apartment taking all this in. I take the key off my keyring and leave it on the table. I will never forget this place but it is time to go.

I gather the box and my bag from my apartment, leave my key on the table there, take one more look around and leave.

As I get into my car, I can't help having one last cry for the life that I am leaving behind.

I'm home and need to sort out the things I have brought back from London. I place the two mugs at the back of a cupboard in the kitchen. I take the box with the photographs and the Christmas decorations in upstairs to my bedroom and decide that I need to put Leo out of my life so I can move on. I gather all his clothes that I had been wearing and what is left of his aftershave and place them in the box with the other things. Then put the box at the back of my wardrobe in my closet so I can no longer see it. A new start for me.

A week later, George is at my house to talk about our next move. After a quick catch up, we go into the studio and I show and sing him some of the songs I have been working on.

"I am loving all these, they are great. Now we need to decide which ones will work best together on the album. Are there any songs that you feel must definitely go on the album then we can work around that?"

"I don't really mind and I know some of them will need more work done to them to make them fit into an album. There is only one that I want on there and not to be changed and that's 'Lost Love'."

"I thought you would say that one. Is it about Leo? You sang it with so much passion."

"Yes, it is. Do you think it is obvious that it's about Leo?"

"Yes, but only to people who knew about your relationship. To the outside world, it won't. Now I've got a writer to work with you just to help finalise some of the songs. She has worked with some big names before, so I think she will be a great help to you."

"Who is she? Would she be willing to come here to write as I don't want to go back to London just yet?"

"Her name is Mia and I'm sure she won't mind coming here, but you may have to travel down to London at times."

"When can I meet her?"

"I will arrange for her to come up here, we can go out for a meal. Is that okay with you?"

"Yes, great, just let me know when. Do you want another cup of tea? There's one more thing I want to talk to you about."

"Yes please, just a quick one then I need to go."

I take George back to the kitchen and make him a tea.

"When do you think I should announce that I am gay? I really want to move on and I don't feel I can until I have told people about my true self."

"That is something only you can decide. You know that you don't have to do a big announcement, it really isn't anyone else's business about your sexuality."

"I know but I want to do some kind of announcement, so it is out in the open."

"It is your choice, but please will you let Leo know before you do anything? As it will affect him after too."

"I was hoping to be able to do it without speaking to Leo."

"Is that really fair on him? You know he will get press attention once you say anything, what with past stories of the two of you."

"Okay, I will phone him and let him know."

"Will you let me know before you do it too just so I can be aware of the press you are likely to get?"

"Of course, I will."

"All right. I have to go now. I will sort out dinner and let you know when Mia is free to meet up."

"Great and I will let you know when I've heard from Leo."

I wish that George was our manager from the beginning things would have been so different.

I need to phone Leo as I want to do the announcement as soon as possible. I'm not looking forward to speaking to him. I don't think he will be happy about me saying anything. Well, there's no time like the present. I find his number in my contacts and press the dial button. My stomach is full of butterflies, I'm so nervous to talk to him. The phone rings and rings but he doesn't answer, it goes to answerphone. He must be busy I will phone him again later.

I try two more times throughout the day but every time it goes to answer phone.

On the fourth time, I leave a message, *Hi Leo, it's Jacob. I need to talk to you about something really important. Can you please phone me back straight away?*

A week goes by and he has still not got back to me. I have phoned a few more times and left messages each time but nothing from him. I don't want to make the announcement without him knowing but he's not leaving me much choice. Before I do it, I will send him an email explaining what I'm going to do. I go into my office and sit in front of the computer. I pull up his email address and I stare at the blank screen. I finally start to write.

Hi, Leo

I have tried to phone you and I have left you messages but for some reason you are either not getting them or choosing to ignore them.

I need to tell you something and now this is the only way to let you know what I am planning to do.

I want to do an announcement that I am gay. I know it's no one's business about my sexuality but I feel I need to do this to move forward with my life.

I wanted you to know as George says that you are bound to get press attention from it too and I'm sure they will bring up our past and I want you to be prepared for it.

You don't have to worry about me saying anything about you because I won't.

I'm sorry I have to tell you this way but you needed to know. Hope you are okay?
Love Jacob.

I read it back and I think it sounds okay. I debate with myself whether to keep love in it. I delete it then put it back in but I decide to keep it in. I hover over the send button for a while, then press it. He needs to know one way or the other. I don't even know if he will see it.

A few days later, I finally notice that he has replied. I hope he is okay with it and I wonder what he has said. I open the email and I'm shocked by what I see. There is only one word written.

Fine.

Is that it? That is all he has to say about it. He is infuriating. He now knows. I'm free to make my announcement.

I text George to let him know that Leo knows and I tell him that I am going to do it tonight. He texts back wishing me well. I then send a quick text to Alice and Xander. They know that I am going to do it because I spoke to them both about it but I just want to give them the heads up that it is happening today as I'm sure they will get asked about it.

I make my final phone call to Mum and Dad asking them to come over tonight for dinner. I want to tell them in person and I want them here for support.

Mum and Dad are on their way. I have cooked some dinner for them. When they arrive I feel much calmer. I didn't realise how tense I was feeling. We sit down for food and Mum is giving me the look like she did on the day I told them I was gay. She knows something is up.

"What's up, love?"

"I had an email back from Leo today."

"What did it say?" asks Dad.

"He just put 'fine', nothing else."

"What? He never." They both look at me stunned.

"So, what are you going to do now?"

"I'm going to do it tonight. That's why I want you both here."

"Do you want us to stay once you have done it?" I am so grateful that Mum has asked as I think I am going to need their support through this, I don't know what the reaction will be.

"Yes, please. Could you stay the night too as I'm sure the press will get hold of the news overnight and it might be everywhere tomorrow."

"Of course, we will," Dad answers.

Once we have eaten, Mum and Dad make themselves busy in the kitchen and I take this opportunity to do my post. I choose to put a rainbow background and just write the words,

Time for the truth
I'm gay.

I look at it and I have mixed emotions and just as I am faltering about posting it and deleting it, Mum and Dad come and sit by me.

"If you don't want to do it, you don't have to. You will always have our support whatever you decide." Mum reaches over and hugs me.

"Thanks, I'm so lucky to have you two." As I say this, I press post. I do it again on all my other social sites. I feel the weight of the world has just been lifted.

Dad gets up and goes to the drinks cabinet. "What does everyone want, do you want a vodka, Jacob? That's what you drink now, isn't it?"

"No, thanks, Dad. I think we should have some champagne in celebration. There's some in the wine cooler."

Dad goes into the kitchen to get the drinks and he comes back with three glasses of champagne. As we drink, my phone starts to light up with reactions to my posts. I am so relieved most of them are positive and supportive replies from my fans. There are obviously some not so nice ones and some really vile comments, I delete these and block them from my sites. By the time, we make our way up to bed there have been thousands of comments and likes to my posts. What will it be like in the morning?

I wake up and the first thing I do is turn my phone and the television on. I put the news on and on the headline bar rolling across the bottom of the screen is my name. 'UsFour singer Jacob Adams announces on social media that he is gay.' I can't believe I've made the morning news. I then check my phone, I am glad I turned it off last night so I could get some sleep, as it has gone mad during the night. I have had loads of texts of support from people I used to work with in the group. My social media sites have gone insane. I am no longer able to read all the comments as there is just too many. I am so pleased that it has been such a positive response.

This week has been mental. Press have been camped outside my house. Mum and dad have not been able to leave, which I'm secretly glad about as I really need their support right now. The phone hasn't stopped ringing. My emails are full of press asking for interviews. Alice and Xander have been bombarded with press whenever they go out, asking them questions about it but all they have said is that they are really happy that I am free to live my life as I have always wanted too. I love them both so much. With Leo it has been a different story. I have seen reports of him not being very happy with the press being around him and Sarah and asking them questions. One showed him pushing a photographer over when he got in his and Sarah's way. Many of the articles written about me and Leo have resurfaced and he has been denying them very loudly on social media. I understand why but it is still hurtful.

George managed to fight his way through the photographers at the house to visit us. He advised us just to stay inside for now and that it will calm down soon. He showed me the statement he is going to release to the press to make sure that I was happy with it. Hopefully this should quiet them down a bit.

Jacob would like to let everyone know that he is very grateful for all the support that he has been shown from his family, friends and fans about the recent announcement about him being gay. He hopes that his strength to be open about his sexuality will give others the encouragement to do the same. He also asks that the media now let him live his life the way he wants to. He also asks the press to give his fellow group members the space to do the same.

The statement was released yesterday and since then the press have moved themselves from the front of the house and everything has quietened down slightly. Mum and Dad have managed to go home and I now feel ready to move on.

I have informed George that I want to meet up with Mia as soon as possible and get back into the studio to get the album recorded. He has promised to organise that straight away.

Everything is falling into place, the only thing I now worry about is Leo. He has gone silent on social media and Alice and Xander have tried to speak to him but he won't answer his phone to them, I just hope he is okay.

I finally met Mia and we are getting along well. She is so much fun. She reminds me so much of Alice with her zest for life.

She has been coming up to Manchester to do most of the writing, but on occasions I have travelled back to London. I have met some of her friends on nights out and I finally feel that I am moving on with my life and that I'm happy again.

The others are moving on too. Alice has a part in Moulin Rouge and is loving acting. I must make time to go and see her play but I have been so busy. Xander is taking a break and enjoying life. He wants to do a film but will wait until the right part comes along. Neither of them have seen or spoken to Leo. It seems he has cut us all out of his life. Shelly has seen him a couple of times going in for meetings with Harriet, but he never speaks to her. I can't believe he decided to stay with Harriet after everything that happened between us all. We all need to meet up soon it would be great to see everyone but we are just so busy.

Me, George and Mia have held auditions for a band to work with me as we are nearly ready to go into the studio to record soon. We have found some great musicians and I am so pleased with my new team. I can't thank George enough for all his help and support.

I am going to have to move down to London to do the recording. I'm not really looking forward to that. I'm so happy living in my home and don't want to leave it. I'm just going to rent an apartment near the studio and work as hard as I can to nail the album quickly so I don't have to be there for too long.

Three weeks later and we have all the songs written with a rough idea of the music side, there will have to be some changes once we start recording, but overall I am happy.

I have to leave Manchester and go to London. I hate going there as it brings back memories of the group and Leo and I have been trying so hard lately to not let him in to my thoughts and I have been doing really well but moving away I think will bring them to the surface again.

I move into the new apartment. It is only a short drive to the studio. There's nothing special about it and I have only brought a few things with me as I don't plan to be here much, hopefully only to sleep.

The first week of recording goes great, everyone is working really well together. We have managed to lay down a few songs and I am really elated with them. To celebrate we decide to have an evening out. I try to make an effort with myself tonight. I put on some decent clothes, do my hair properly and I think I'm looking good. Maybe it's time I start putting myself out there and looking for someone new. For some reason though I am feeling really anxious about going out tonight. It's a very strange feeling, so I have a bottle of lager before I leave just to settle my nerves. My phone goes, it is Jim to tell me he is here to take me to the club, I text him back to tell him I will right down. I decided to keep Jim on as my driver as what he witnessed in the car between me and Leo at times and he never uttered a word to anyone. I felt I needed him in my life.

When I arrive, Mia is already there with some of her friends that I've met previously but there is one guy that I haven't met before. He is very handsome, very tall, short blond hair and a beautiful smile. My stomach does a flip. I haven't had that feeling in a very long time. Mia hugs me when I reach their table.

"Hi, you know everyone else, but this is Ryan."

"Hi, I'm Jacob."

"Yes, I know who you are. Nice to meet you finally. Mia doesn't stop talking about you."

"Is that right, I hope everything is good?"

"Most of it."

I laugh and he gives me a smile that melts me.

"Would you like a drink?" he asks.

"Yes, please. I will have a lager, thanks."

As he walks over to the bar, I watch him, he has a great ass. Mia whispers in my ear, "He's gay."

"Really, well, that's good news."

"I thought you would like him."

Ryan comes back and he hands me my drink. I smile at him and I see him blush slightly. I sit at the table and he sits next to me, more of our party joins us throughout the night but my attention is mainly on Ryan. We talk for hours. I haven't talked to someone like this since Leo. Thinking of Leo makes me feel guilty that I am doing something wrong talking to another man but that's stupid I'm not cheating on him. I'm moving on and I try to remove these thoughts from my mind.

It's the end of the night and I have had a great time. I really like Ryan and I think he likes me too. He has been flirting a bit and that makes me feel really good. I'm not sure whether I want anything to happen between us just yet but I would definitely like to talk to him again.

We are leaving and if I want to get in contact with him this is my chance.

"It's been great to meet you. I had a lovely time, thanks."

"I did too," he replies

"Could I take your number?"

"Yes, sure, I'd like to hear from you again."

I hand him my phone and he enters his number in it. He hands it back with a smile.

"I will text you."

"Okay great, I look forward to hearing from you."

I go to bed and for the first time since Leo and I dream of another man.

Chapter Fifteen

The album is finished and ready for release in the New Year. I am so pleased with it. I hope everyone will like it too.

I have been talking to Ryan a lot over the last couple of months and we are getting on really well and I think I could be with him. I want to ask him out on a proper date but as I have never been on a date before, as me and Leo were never able to, I am nervous about doing it. Maybe I should ask him to come to Manchester and we could go out here at least I would feel more comfortable at home.

I've said goodbye to everyone I've been working with and we have a break before we release the album so they are all going home for Christmas. I can't wait to get back home. Mum and Dad have been sorting the house out for me for me whilst I was away and I am so looking forward to seeing them both, they will be waiting for me when I arrive.

I pull into the gates and it's great to see my home again. I've missed being here. I walk in the door and Mum runs towards me, hugs me then holds me out to look at me. She smiles, "Hi, love, you look very happy, London did you good."

"Hi, Mum. It's good to see you."

"The house is cleaned and stocked for you. Your dad has been doing a few jobs around the place too."

"Thanks, Mum. You both didn't have to do that."

"I know but we wanted to. Come see your dad he's making a cup of tea."

I follow her into the kitchen, Dad gives me a big hug too.

"Great to have you back."

"I'm glad to be back. I had a good time in London but it's not the same as being here."

Dad hands me a cup of tea and we go and sit in the living room.

"So, tell us what has made you so happy," Mum asks.

"The album is finished and it's great, so we are on schedule to release it after Christmas."

"And?"

"And I've met someone."

"Tell us about him. He's obviously made you happy."

"His name is Ryan. I met him through a friend of Mia's. He makes me laugh. We've not spent much time together, but we've spoken lots on the phone. I've just been too busy to meet up with him."

"Do you like him?"

"Yes, I do but…"

"But what, what's the matter?"

"I don't know. I've never been on a date or dated someone openly. So, I'm just a bit nervous about it all."

"I'm sure you will be fine. It was always going to be hard the first time after Leo."

"I want to ask him here to go on a date but I'm not sure."

"You will be fine, Jacob, you sound like you get on well and I am sure he will understand how you are feeling if you talk to him about it. Invite him up for a meal out somewhere quiet but make sure he knows you want him to stay in a hotel."

"Yes, I might do. Now tell me what you two have been up too?"

I spend a lovely day with them both and after they have gone home, I make the decision to text Ryan and ask him on a date.

Hi Ryan. I was wondering if you would like to come to Manchester. We could go out to dinner?

I don't wait long for his reply.

That would be great. Are you free this weekend?

Yes, I am. I will book a table somewhere for us to eat.

Great I will book a hotel room and maybe we could meet for breakfast the next day.

I'm relieved that he wants to come here and that he is going to stay in a hotel, I don't need to talk about why I don't want him here in my house yet.

I would like that.

Okay, I will see you Saturday.

I will let you know the name of the restaurant and what time to meet.

Okay, great x

I stare at the x on his final text. What will it be like to kiss him? I have only ever kissed Leo and that was amazing. I hope I feel the same way about Ryan.

Saturday evening is here. I am so nervous that I keep pacing around the house. I have to calm down. I decide I need a drink to help. A lager is not going to cut it today so I pour myself a vodka, I haven't had one in ages. I down it in one and I feel it run through me and it has helped a bit so I pour another one and take it upstairs. I don't know what to wear tonight and I look through my wardrobe I spot the jacket and shirt that Leo always loved me to wear and those guilty feelings come back again. I pull them off the hangers, screw them up in a ball and throw them in to the corner of my wardrobe where the other stuff of Leo's is. He is not going to ruin this for me. I decide on a pair of black jeans, a burgundy shirt and a black jacket over the top. I look in the mirror I think I'm looking okay but I'm still a nervous wreck. I down the rest of my drink and Jim has arrived to drive me to the restaurant.

When the car pulls up, I have to give myself a minute before I leave the car just to settle my nerves. I take a deep breath and get out. I am the first to arrive. I'm shown to our table and I order a bottle of champagne and wait.

I am facing the door so I can see when he walks in. I am waiting five minutes when he arrives. I had forgotten how handsome he is. I watch him talk to the man at the entrance and he is directed to where I am sat. He reaches the table and smiles at me and suddenly, all my nerves have disappeared.

"Hi," I say.

"Hi,"

"Champagne?"

He nods and as he sits down, I hand him a glass.

"It's great to see you."

"Yes, you too." He sounds a little nervous which I'm surprised about, he doesn't normally come across like that.

"Shall we order?"

We order our food and another bottle of champagne and as the evening goes on, we become more comfortable in each other's company; we talk and laugh so much, we are being quite loud and some people look over at us but I don't care. It's been such a long time since I've laughed this much. It's been a great night but unfortunately, it's time to go and I'm sad about the evening ending. I've enjoyed it so much. This is what it's like to have a proper relationship in the open.

Ryan pays the bill and we make our way out of the restaurant but as soon as I walk out the door, there is a rush of people. Photographers suddenly swarm us, taking photographs of both of us. There are loads of them, how did they know we were here. I look at Ryan and he is looking rather worried. I wasn't expecting this but I'm used to it. I'm not happy about it but I'm more concerned for Ryan. I spot where Jim is parked, I grab Ryan's hand. "Come on," I shout as I pull him through the crowd as quick as I can.

We finally reach the car. I fling open the door. "Get in," I cry as I shove him into the car and climb in next to him.

Jim waits until I have slammed the door and drives off down the road as the photographer's chase after us.

I look over at Ryan. "Are you okay?"

"Yes, that was mad."

"I'm sorry. I don't know how they knew we were there."

"It's okay, could you drop me at the hotel?"

"You're not going to the hotel, they will be following us, you won't get any peace there. Come back to mine."

He nods. I'm secretly glad he's not going back to the hotel I don't want the evening to end yet.

We arrive back at my house and I show him in.

"You've got a lovely house," he comments as he follows me into the kitchen.

"Thanks. Do you want a drink?"

"Yes, that would be great, thanks."

"What would you like?"

"Do you have any vodka?"

Another vodka drinker, like Leo. I hope that's not a bad sign.

"Yes, sure, it's in the living room, follow me."

I pour him and myself one and we sit on the sofa next to each other.

"That was crazy outside the restaurant."

"I'm sorry about that. I'm used to it but I still get surprised by it sometimes. Just to warn you now you've been photographed with me you will probably end up on social media and in magazines. I would totally understand if you don't want to be with me because of it."

"Don't be silly. I really like you and if it means I have to put up with a bit of publicity to do that then I don't mind."

"Are you sure it can get too much sometimes?"

"Yes, I'm really sure."

"I'm glad to hear that. I really like you too."

I put my glass on the table, I put my hand on the side of his face and kiss him for the first time. It's soft and gentle not like when I kissed Leo, they were full of passion. Maybe these will become passionate in time. I look at him after I kiss him and he smiles at me.

"I've wanted to do that all night," he says.

"Really?"

"Yes," and he kisses me again.

I can feel myself becoming excited with every kiss but I'm not sure if I'm ready to do anything else with him yet, so I stop kissing him and get us another drink.

He goes to kiss me again, but I feel I should say something before he wants to take it further.

"Ryan, I really want to keep kissing you, but I don't want to go any further tonight. I'm just not ready. I can't tell you why, but I have my reasons and I feel like I need to wait. I hope that's okay?"

He looks a little disappointed, but if he likes me then he will understand. He nods and kisses me once more.

"I better get going, I will call a taxi."

"You don't have to go. You can stay here. I have the spare rooms set up, you can stay in one of those. Then we can have breakfast together in the morning and maybe do something together afterwards."

"I would like that," he replies.

We have a few more drinks and then make our way up to bed. I show Ryan the room next to mine, I kiss him again and then go into my room. I'm having conflicting feelings again. I really like Ryan, he makes me feel happy but it feels so different. When I was Leo it was so exciting, hot and all I wanted to do was make love to him all the time but with Ryan I want to keep him at arm's length. I don't want him in my bed. Will I ever want to? I go to bed and have a restless night with dreams filled of Leo and Ryan.

I do not feel rested and I don't know what to do about Ryan. I've realised that my feelings for Leo are still there and I'm not sure if I can let anyone else in if they are there. I will see how today goes and if I still feel like this, I don't think I should see Ryan any more it doesn't seem fair. I throw on some clothes and make my way downstairs. As I come to the bottom, I hear noises coming for the kitchen. *What's going on?*

As I step into the kitchen, Ryan is there making breakfast and he is looking hot. He's got his jeans on, his shirt is undone so I can see glimpses of his body, his feet are bare and his hair is messy from sleep, now there's the feeling I was looking for. I stand in the doorway and watch him until he notices me.

"Good morning," I say to him with a cheeky grin on my face.

"Morning," he says, looking a little embarrassed. "I was up and didn't want to wake you so I thought I would make us some breakfast. I hope that's okay?"

"Yes, that's great."

I walk over to him and stand really close, I feel him take an intake of breath. I'm glad I affect him this way. I look at him. He is so tall. I move my hand up to his cheek and run it down to his chin and gently turn his head towards me and I kiss him and this time I feel the passion as he kisses me back. When I stop, he gives me one of his drop-dead gorgeous smiles.

"I've done some eggs, bacon and avocado, I hope that is okay?"

"Yes, that's one of my favourites actually."

"Good."

"I will get some drinks and lay the table. What would you like?"

"Orange juice, please."

I pour him a glass of juice and I put the kettle on for a cup of tea for myself. I go to the cupboard to get a mug and my eye catches mine and Leo's mugs at the back I turn them around so I cannot see our initials and grab a different one.

We enjoy a lovely breakfast together. As we are eating, I catch him glancing at me but every time I catch his eye he looks away, is he feeling a bit shy?

We finish breakfast and then tidy up the kitchen and I feel like having a bit of fun with him so I make sure I touch him at every opportunity, just little brushes on his arm or his back. It reminds me of the first night at the apartment in London with Leo. I've forgotten how thrilling this sort of thing feels I hope Ryan is feeling it too.

"Do you mind if I have a shower?" Ryan asks.

"No, of course not, there's towels in the wardrobe in the room you were in."

"Okay, thanks."

He makes his way upstairs. I'm left in the kitchen wanting more. I have wound myself up, so I follow him upstairs. I stand outside his room. What am I going do, jump on him in the shower, what would he think? I stand there for a few more minutes and I make a decision. I open the door and walk in. I can hear the shower running, I take off my clothes and walk into the bathroom. He has his back to the door so I stand and look at him for a second. His body is amazing and very tanned just that sight has me excited. I take a step towards the shower and walk in. I run my hand down his back and he jumps at my touch. He turns to face me.

"Hi."

"Hi, I fancied a shower too so I thought I would join you. Is that okay?"

"Oh yes, definitely."

He kisses me so passionately that all the guilty thoughts and worries about Leo disappear as he pulls me into his arms.

Two days later, and Ryan has gone back to London but we had a wonderful weekend. It feels so great to be with someone again and even more so because we are able to go out and do things that couples should be able to do. We went out for a walk in the countryside then for lunch at the local pub. We had a few fans come up to us and ask for photographs. Ryan took it really well, he stood back and let me take photos with them. Luckily, no press has bothered us during the rest of the weekend.

I'm just lazing around the house when I have a phone call from George.

"Hi, Jacob."

"Hi, George. How are you?"

"I'm good, thanks. I'm just phoning to let you know that photographs of you and Ryan have been put online. There are also some on that website about you and Leo and they don't like that you two are together."

"Really? Okay, thanks for letting me know. I was expecting it and I had warned Ryan that it might happen. I will phone him to let him know."

"That would be good. I'm sure more will turn up throughout the week. You may want to warn him that he may get the press following him in London."

"Yes, will do. Hopefully, they won't find out who he is for a while and not know where to find him."

"I will keep you informed if anything else comes up."

"Thanks, George. Have a good break and I will see you in the New Year."

"You too."

As soon as George hangs up, I phone Ryan.

"Hello. You can't be missing me already?"

"Only that ass of yours."

He laughs and that makes me smile.

"I'm phoning to let you know photographs of us have been put online."

"What, already?" He doesn't sound very happy about it.
"I'm sorry, they work fast to get their stories out."
"I can't believe they are online already."
"I'm sorry. Ryan, it will be okay."
"I have to go."
And he hangs up the phone.
What the fuck? What is his problem? Surely he realised what would happen by going out with me? I told him that would happen he seemed fine with it at the weekend. Was he just using me for sex or does he really like me and just didn't realise what he was getting into?

Later, I'm working out in my gym and the phone rings, it's Ryan. I'm busy and I don't want to talk to him at the minute, so I let it go to answer phone. I'm surprised as he actually leaves a message. I will listen to it later.

I finish my workout, take a shower then I listen to his message, *Hi, Jacob, I'm so sorry about earlier. I just freaked out about it all. I will phone you again later.*

Yes, you did freak out. If you can't cope with this sort of thing, it's probably best if you are not with me. I'm not hiding another relationship. I'm not phoning him back. I will wait until he phones me again.

I've gone to bed early, after a weekend of late nights, I need some sleep. Just as I am about to turn off the light, Ryan phones again, this time I answer it.

"Hello."
"Hi."
"What do you want, Ryan?"
"I want to apologise for how I reacted earlier. It threw me

how quick the photographs came out. I didn't think they would be interested."

"I told you they would be. Unfortunately, you are dating someone who is famous and there will always be people who will pay money to get stories on us. If you can't handle it, then I'm sorry, but I don't think we can be together. I can't hide another relationship."

Shit, I shouldn't have said that.

"What do you mean? Who else have you had a relationship with?"

"No one," I say quickly. "It's just whilst in the group, I wasn't allowed to date anyone as they wouldn't let me say I was gay. I suppose you wouldn't know that."

"No, I didn't. I'm sorry. Look, I do like you. I just think it's going to take some getting used to."

"You never get used to it. You just learn to live with it."

"How do you do it?"

"The fans are fine. I don't mind them coming up to me for photos they just want them for themselves. It's the press I can't stand. They try and get you all the time. You just need to know how to deal with it."

"When are you free next?" he asks.

"Not this weekend but the one after that I am, why?"

"Would you like to come and stay with me?"

"Are you sure? If we are seen at your place, you will get press attention there."

"Yes, I'm sure."

"Okay, then I would like to come and stay with you."

"Great."

"I will see you Saturday afternoon."

"Yes, see you then."

Chapter Sixteen

I am on my way to stay with Ryan. He has booked a restaurant for us to go out for dinner later tonight. I hope he will be okay if the press finds out. If we don't get bothered by them, then we might go to a club after. I'm actually really looking forward to this weekend.

I arrive at Ryan's apartment. It's a lovely place but I realise that it's only around the corner from where Leo lives. I didn't realise this and it has thrown me a bit.

Ryan welcomes me in and shows me to his bedroom and where I can put my things. He leaves me to unpack and I feel a little strange being in another man's house. I don't know if it's because I'm so close to Leo. I need to shake this feeling off or it will ruin the weekend and I don't want that. I need to do something to distract my thoughts. I text Ryan saying I need his help with something. He arrives only seconds later.

"What's the matter?"

"Nothing." I walk over to him, put my hands on his hips and pull him in so I can kiss him. He kisses me back. I run my hands across his chest and down to his jeans putting my hand inside them. He is taken aback a bit by my forwardness. I continue to move my hand and I can feel he is relaxing and starting to get excited. He continues to kiss me more and more passionately and then he is on his knees undoing my jeans. This is just what I need to get any thought of Leo out of my head.

The car is here to take us to the restaurant. We jump into to it, Ryan keeps looking at me.

"Are you okay?" I ask him.

"Yes, that was an amazing afternoon."

"I thought so too, it was just what I needed."

"Thanks for coming down this weekend."

"That's okay."

We are shown to our table, we ordered our food and drink. We are enjoying our meal when half way through I notice a couple coming through the door of the restaurant. I glance at them briefly but don't take much notice of them but as they move through the restaurant, I look at them again and my stomach does a flip. Oh no, it's Leo and Sarah. Some other people are looking at them too. Please don't let them see me and Ryan, it may cause a scene.

Ryan notices I've stopped eating.

"What's the matter?"

"Nothing, it's fine."

He glances over to where I was looking and spots Leo and Sarah.

"Hey, isn't that who you were in the group with, what's his name?"

"Leo."

"Yes, none of you talk to him now, do you?"

"He doesn't talk to us."

"What happened between you all?"

"Nothing."

I don't look at them any more, they have been seated on the other side of the restaurant and luckily haven't seen us. I continue with my food but Ryan keeps looking at me. I eat quickly, I need to get out of here.

"Do you want another drink?" Ryan asks.

"No, I'm good, thanks. Could we go?"

"You want to go now?"

"Yes, I do."

"But why? I thought we could move to the bar and have another drink. Do you want to say hi to Leo? Maybe they could join us after they have eaten?"

"No!"

"Okay. What's the matter?"

"Nothing."

I look over to where they are sat and as I do, Leo notices me. Oh no, now he's seen me. He says something to Sarah and she looks over at us and doesn't look happy. Leo gets up from their table. He's coming over.

"Hi," he says as he reaches our table.

"Hi," I reply with a shaky voice.

He looks at Ryan.

"Hi, I'm Leo." He holds out his hand. I just stare at him. Fuck, he is looking good.

"Hi, I'm Ryan. I'm Jacob's boyfriend." He shakes Leo's hand.

"Nice to meet you." He looks at me and his eyes are on me. *Don't look at me, Leo, please.* He gives me one of his smiles, the one that he used to use when he wanted to do something to me.

"How are you doing?" he asks.

"I'm good. You?"

"Yes, not too bad. I've been trying to write some songs. How about you?"

"I've just finished an album. We are releasing it in January."

"Wow, that's great. I will look out for it. Well, it was great to see you. Better get back."

I notice Sarah glaring at us.

"Nice to meet you, Ryan."

"Yes, you too. We are going to have a drink at the bar if you want to join us after your meal?"

Leo looks at me and I discreetly shake my head at him. He looks slightly disappointed but says, "No, but thanks. We are not staying long."

He walks back over to their table and I let out the breath that I hadn't realised I had been holding. I look back over at them and Sarah's is giving Leo a hard time. His face has dropped and doesn't look happy. I look back at Ryan and he is staring at me, he's been watching me watching Leo.

"Do you want to go?"

"Yes, please."

"Okay, let's go."

We pay the bill and leave the restaurant. I glance one more time at Leo, he catches me looking and gives me a small smile as I leave. As we walk out the door, there are a few photographers there, I'm just about to rush away when Ryan grabs my hand and holds onto it and walks slowly through them. They are all shouting questions at me,

"Who's your man, Jacob?"

"Where did you meet him?"

"What about Leo?"

"Did you meet Leo inside?"

"How long have you been dating?"

I just want to get away but Ryan seems to be walking very slow, what is he playing at? I look at him and he is smiling. What is going on?

We finally get back to the waiting car, he makes me get in first and follows me in.

"Do you want to go somewhere for another drink?"

"No, can we go back to yours?"

"Fine."

What is the matter with him, surely he doesn't want to be out when photographers know we are here? I certainly don't and seeing Leo has shaken me.

We arrive back at Ryan's. He lets me in. He pours us both a drink. He is staring at me.

"What's going on with you and Leo?"

"What? Nothing."

"You totally changed when you saw him."

"It was just strange to see him. We haven't spoken for so long."

"He's who you were talking about the other day?"

"What do you mean?"

"When you let it slip about not wanting to hide another relationship. You two were together?"

I don't say anything.

"How serious was it? I would say from your reaction tonight that it was really serious and he broke your heart. Did you love him?"

I still don't say anything, I just down my drink.

"Jacob, talk to me. Do you still love him? He still has something for you, that was obvious tonight."

"He doesn't, he's with her," I snap. *Shit, don't say anything.*

"Wow, shit, you still have feelings for him."

Looking at Ryan, I feel that I need to tell him the truth if we are ever going to move forward. If I'm ever going to move forward. He stands waiting for me to answer him.

"Yes. We were together and it was very serious. We lived together, but our management wouldn't let us be together so we had to have our relationship in secret. Only a few people knew about us. We then got found out, photographs of us were taken and articles were written saying that we were together. Leo couldn't handle the secrets any more and we slowly grew apart. He started seeing Sarah and we split up. We slept together once when they were together and we both felt so guilty that we hardly spoke to one another after that. That's was when I decided to leave the group. It has been hard for me to get over him I loved him so much. Then I meet you and you make me happy again and I feel like I've got my life back. Yes, at times I miss him, we went through so much together, but I'm happy with you now."

Ryan is still looking at me.

"Say something. Sorry, I didn't tell you."

"Do you still want to be with him?"

"No, I don't"

"Are you sure?"

"Yes, I like being with you."

"Good, now let's forget about him and enjoy the rest of the weekend."

He walks over to me and kisses me. "Let's go to bed."

I follow him to the bedroom and I try and focus on him but always in the back of my mind is Leo.

The rest of the weekend goes by in a slight daze. I tried to be happy with everything we did, but I found it difficult. When we were out, I kept looking around to see if I could get another glance of Leo. I don't think Ryan noticed. He seemed happy enough. He even wanted to be in photographs that fans wanted to take of me.

But I'm glad to be home finally. I spend the evening looking up interviews and articles on Leo to see how he is doing. From the photographs he doesn't seem very happy when he is with

Sarah. I go to phone him. I want to talk to him but I can't do that, so I text Ryan instead and thank him for the weekend.

It's the New Year and I'm back in London to start promoting the album. I am staying in a hotel this time as I'm not going to be here very long. Ryan did ask me if I wanted to stay with him but I didn't feel ready for that. We have been dating for two months now, some of the time it's good, it's mostly okay and other times it feels like he is only with me because of who I am. Since I told him about Leo, he is constantly asking about our relationship and it makes me feel uncomfortable and brings my feelings for Leo right back to the surface again. Another thing that is really annoying me is that he is always wanting to get into photographs with me and then spends the next week searching online to find the article or fans social media to see us there. He then tells me all about it. I want to give him a chance as I do enjoy his company when he's not being an ass and we do get on well and the sex is good, admittedly it's not me and Leo good but I do like it with him.

I'm in the hotel room just going over some notes on an interview I will be doing later today, when my phone starts to ring, it's Ryan.

"Hello."

"Hey, what are you doing?"

"I'm preparing for an interview I've got later today."

"Can I see you?"

"Yes, sure, why don't you come to the hotel after I am done and we can have dinner?"

"Could I come to the interview with you?"

Why would he want to come to that?

"I don't think so."

"Come on, please, I've never seen you at work. I won't get in the way; I will stay in the background. Are you singing?"

"Yes, I am, why?" I really don't want him to come to the interview.

"I would just like to see you sing live, I never have. Please can I come?"

I don't answer him, what can I say. If I say no, he will be in mood for days and if I let him come with me that would definitely make our relationship official.

"Jacob, are you still there, you've gone very quiet?"

"Yes, I'm here. Do you really want to come?"

"Yes, and after I will take you out for dinner to celebrate the official release of the album."

I give in. "Okay, but you have to stay out of the way."

"Great I will. What time shall I get to you?"

"Two-thirty."

"Great, see you later."

I hang up the phone. What have I done? I so didn't want him to come, but I seriously could not put up with the pouting and moodiness he would have if I didn't. I just hope he keeps his word and stays out of the way.

Two-thirty comes around too quickly and we take the car to the television studio. Ryan seems very excited and he is making me unusually nervous.

When we arrive George is there waiting, he looks between me and Ryan.

"I didn't know you were bringing Ryan?"

I roll my eyes at George when Ryan isn't looking as if to say I didn't want to.

"Yes, he really wanted to see me work. I hope that's okay?"

Hoping George will say that he is not allowed and he will have to wait in the car but George says, "Yes, that's fine. I will show you both to the green room. They are going to take some photographs of you getting ready first before you do the interview."

We both follow George and I can see Ryan getting even more excited by it all, he's acting like a kid. He needs to calm down.

We only wait a short while before they ask me to go down to make up and to have a few photos taken. I get up to follow the television assistant and I see Ryan rising from his seat to come too.

"You can stay here. I won't be long," I say to Ryan.

The television assistant asks, "Is this your boyfriend?"

I nod at her.

"Great, you can come along too. I think they would like him in the photographs as well. Showing how supportive he is of you, it will make a great article."

Shit, that's what I didn't want. I give Ryan a look of disgust but he doesn't see me. He is already off with the assistant, chatting away.

As I am having my hair and makeup done, they start taking the photographs, they ask Ryan to sit in positions so that he can be seen in the background of all the shots. I'm not very happy about it and wonder why he suddenly wants to be in photographs with me all the time. He hated it the first time it happened. Then it occurs to me it started after we saw Leo in the restaurant and I told him everything. Is he purposely getting in them in case Leo sees them and to let him know he's with me now? I have got to ask him about this.

The interview goes well and so does my first ever solo

performance. It was the most nerve-wrecking thing I've ever done as I didn't have the support of Leo, Alice and Xander on stage with me to help get me through it. I got asked about Ryan, apparently, everyone knows who he is now. I just told them that we are together but nothing else.

After, I say bye to George. I will be seeing him in a couple of days to do some more interviews in London, then we are off to promote the album around the UK for a few weeks.

Back in the car Ryan seems very pleased with himself.

"How do you think that went? I thought you were amazing. Your voice is so good."

"I think it went okay."

"It was better than okay." He reaches over to kiss me, I let him kiss me but I move away so he can't get into it too much, I not in the mood for that with him. He doesn't seem to notice.

"I've booked us a table for dinner in a restaurant near the hotel. I hope that's okay?"

"Yes, that's fine."

"What's the matter? You don't seem very happy."

"It's nothing, I'm fine."

I'm not really so I just sit there in silence as we make our way to the restaurant.

We arrive and Ryan gets out first then holds out his hand to help me out the back of the car. I look at him confused but as I get out, I realise that there are a few press photographers waiting. I look at Ryan feeling annoyed but he just smiles back and holds my hand. As we pass them he waves out to them, he holds my hand even tighter and pulls me closer to him. What is he doing, has he planned for these photographers to be here? I am so mad that I can't enjoy the evening. I quickly eat my food, I only have one drink and as soon as we've finished I want to leave.

Again, as we leave, more photographers are there and once again Ryan is very touchy with me as if posing for the cameras.

"Do you want to go for a drink somewhere else?" he asks.

"No, I'm going back to the hotel."

"Great, we can have a drink there."

Does he not realise that I am so angry at the minute?

In the hotel room, he phones down for a bottle of vodka, two glasses and ice. I haven't spoken a word to him and I don't know if drinking vodka is going to be a good thing.

The drink arrives and he pours us both a glass, he hands it to me and I down it in one and pour another. He's looking at me, has he finally noticed that I am pissed off. I down my drink again.

"Take it easy, you will be drunk in no time if you keep doing that."

I down another one. *Don't you tell me what to do.* With every drink I feel more confident to confront him about today. I do one more and he is looking at me really worried. I can't hold it in any longer.

"What the fuck was today about?"

"What do you mean?"

"You know what I mean. Wanting to come to the interview, letting them take photos of you when you said you would just stay out of the way. Then the photographers at the restaurant, they knew we were going to be there."

"Now don't be mad."

"I'm not mad, I'm fucking fuming."

"I thought it would be good publicity for you to be seen happy with your boyfriend, help with the album sales. I did let one photographer know we would be at that restaurant but not the others."

"Get out," I shout.

He's shocked by my outburst.

"Get the fuck out."

"What, why?"

"I can't talk to you. Get out of here, Ryan. I can't believe what you just did. This is my life, I don't need you to do any of this for me, I can do it myself. Now get out."

"I was just trying to help."

"I don't need your help."

"Jacob, I'm sorry."

"I don't want to hear it, just go."

"Fine," and he storms out.

Who does he think he is, how dare he do that?

I don't hear from Ryan for a week after our argument and I don't want to contact him either. I'm still so mad. So many articles have come out about the two of us this week after his little stunt and it has taken the publicity away from the album release and it is not doing as well as we hoped. This has prompted George to arrange more interviews and to do a one-off intimate concert for the fans and press in London after we have travelled the UK to promote it. I'm not particularly happy about having to come back to London for it but needs must now.

I'm packing up the hotel room when there is a knock at the door. I open it and Ryan is standing there.

"What do you want?"

"Can we talk?"

Standing aside, I let him in.

"I'm really sorry about what I did. I totally get why you were so angry. I shouldn't have done it, I thought it would help."

"Well, it never, it has made things worse. I now need to promote the album more, so I will be travelling more."

He pulls one of his pouting faces.

"You're upset I'm away for longer, well I'm fuming about it and I have to come back to London to do a concert too."

This seems to pull him out of his sulk, the news that I'm coming back to London.

"I'm sorry. I will miss you when you're away, but I'm happy you're coming back to London. Can I see you when you are here?"

"I don't know. I don't know if I can trust you any more."

"You can, I won't do anything like that again."

"Okay, I will see how I feel when I get back here and I will call you."

"That's great."

He moves in to kiss me but I don't let him.

"Why can't I kiss you? I'm not going to see you for a month, I will miss you."

He goes to kiss me again and this time I do let him. I hope he is telling the truth and that he won't do anything like this again.

Chapter Seventeen

Everything is great; after the UK tour and the concert in London, the album went to number one and stayed there for four weeks. The first single from it 'Lost Love' went straight to number one. The one-off concert was actually amazing, the fans were astonishing, singing every word to all the songs. It made me feel so proud.

Me and Ryan are okay. I wish it felt more like when I was with Leo, but I don't think it ever will. When I was away, he was so moody it made me not want to talk to him when he phoned but as soon as I was back, he was happy again. There have been no more stunts as far as I know. Although, photographers are still following us around and I'm still asked about him all the time, but I suppose that's to be expected.

To celebrate all the success of the album, I am throwing a party at my house. Xander and Shelly are coming. Alice is too and she is bringing her new boyfriend Oliver. I cannot wait to see them and catch up. I have been so busy that I haven't been able to speak to them properly in ages. I have been so excited about seeing them but every time I mention it to Ryan, he gets in a mood and doesn't speak to me for hours. I really wanted to invite Leo but with Ryan's reaction to the others coming I didn't think that would be a good idea. I have also invited some people who I worked closely with during the time in the group and all the new team. Mum and Dad are also coming. It will be the first time they all get to meet Ryan. I hope they all get on and like each other.

The caterers have been here for the last few hours and the bar staff have just arrived to set up the bar in the garden. Hopefully the weather stays nice enough to spend the time out there.

I don't know what to wear; I look through my entire wardrobe and there's nothing that makes me feel really good. I then spot the box at the back of the closet. The box with Leo's things in it and on top is the shirt and jacket that I threw in there, the one Leo always loved me in. I grab it out of the corner. This is what I'm going to wear, I always felt so hot wearing this. Leo always wanted me in this, so I hope it will have the same effect on Ryan. I run it down to the laundry room to freshen it up as its been rolled up in a ball for a while.

Back upstairs, I put the shirt and jeans on, leaving the top few buttons undone to show off my chest; this is what made Leo go wild, the fact he could see so much skin. I put the jacket on over the top. Looking in the mirror, the reflection takes me back to very happy times.

Just before the party is about to start, Ryan arrives. I open the door, I'm hoping he notices how I'm looking but he just kisses my cheek and walks past me. He goes straight upstairs. I follow him up to my bedroom.

"Good journey?"

"Not too bad." He doesn't sound very happy. "How's your day been?"

"Busy getting everything ready."

He still hasn't looked at me.

"I'm going to take a shower and get changed." He throws his t-shirt off and walks into the bathroom.

"Okay, I will see you downstairs," I call after him.

Disappointed, I go back downstairs.

Mum and Dad arrive first, they both give me a big hug.

"Hi, love, how are you doing?"

"I'm good, looking forward to seeing everyone."

"Well, where is he?"

"He's just upstairs changing. He has just driven from London so he wanted a shower. I'm sure he will be down soon. Why don't you get yourself a drink? The bar is in the garden. I will bring him out when he comes down."

"All right, we will see you in a bit." Mum kisses me on the cheek and they make their way outside.

A few more people arrive and I wonder what's keeping Ryan. I go to see where he is, but the door goes again. Xander and Shelly have arrived.

"It's so good to see you both. Shelly, you are looking stunning."

I give them both a huge hug.

"We have some news…" Xander blurts out.

But before they can tell me, the door goes again.

"Go and get a drink at the bar, I will catch up with you in a bit," I shout back to them as I answer the door.

I open it and its Alice, who as soon as she sees me screams and jumps into my arms.

"It's so good to see you, Alice."

"Hey you, you're looking good." *At least someone thinks so.* "This is Oliver."

"Hi, Oliver, great to meet you. I'm Jacob." I hold out my hand for him to shake, which he does.

"Hi, Jacob, nice to finally meet you. I've heard so much about you." I smile at him, he seems nice.

"Alice, you look very happy. You must be doing something

right, Oliver. Go and get yourselves a drink in the garden. Xander and Shelly are already out there."

"Yes, they're here. Come on, Oliver, let me introduce you to them. Hey, Jacob, where's Ryan? We need to meet him to see if he's good enough for you."

"He's upstairs, he will be down soon."

"Okay," she says as she drags Oliver off towards the garden. She seems so happy.

I have a moment without any guest arriving, so I run upstairs to see where Ryan is. I walk into the bedroom and he is just sat in the chair on his phone.

"What are you doing?"

"Just waiting."

"What for?"

"People to stop arriving."

"Why?"

"So I can have you all to myself so you don't keep running off to see people."

What? Why does he want to do that? I can't put up with his games today.

"Will you come down now please? I would like you to meet my mum and dad and some friends that are here already."

I turn to leave.

"Jacob, wait."

He walks over and grabs my arm, a little bit too tight, and pulls me into him. He puts his other hand on my face and kisses me. It's not a loving kiss, its hard and forced it's like he's saying you're mine and don't forget it. I don't like it. I pull away.

"I've got to go, are you coming?"

I leave and he follows me but as we reach the bottom of the stairs, he grabs hold of my hand and won't let it go as we walk into the garden. He's holding my hand very tight and I try to release it, but he won't let me. I spot Mum and Dad sat at a table, so we make our way over to them.

Mum is giving me a look, so I force a smile on to my face. Ryan's actions have shaken me.

"Ryan, this is my mum and dad."

He plasters a smile on his face and finally lets go of my hand to hold it out to my dad. I shake my hand as he actually hurt it slightly. "Hi, Ron, Lisa."

I'm not happy by the way he addresses them.

"Hello, Ryan," they both say as my dad shakes his hand.

"I'm going to get a drink," he says.

"Oh, okay."

He walks over to the bar. He didn't even bother to ask if I wanted one.

"Are you okay, Jacob?" Dad asks.

"Yes, I'm fine."

They both know that I'm not.

Then I see Alice waving for me to come over.

"Go and see your friends." Dad pats me on my back.

Alice is stood with Xander, Shelly and Oliver, I make my way over to them and just like the last time they were here, I have a prang of jealousy at how happy they all look. I thought I was happy, but I don't think I am, not compared to these four.

"You don't have a drink, Jacob?" Xander says as I stand next to them.

"I will get one in a minute."

"I will get you one. What would you like?"

"A vodka, please." He smiles, giving me a knowing look. I watch him walk over to the bar, Ryan is stood there. Xander orders the drink and I can see Ryan say something to him.

Xander walks back over and hands me my drink.

"Thanks. What did Ryan say to you?"

"That was Ryan? I didn't recognise him, sorry. I've only seen a few pictures of him."

"Yes."

"Why wasn't he getting you a drink?"

"I don't know. What did he say?"

"He asked who I was. When I told him, he didn't want to talk any more."

Oh shit, what is his problem today? He was rude to Mum and Dad and now Xander.

"Hey, I recognise that outfit you are wearing," Alice screeches. "That was your outfit from our first photoshoot, that's the one Leo really likes you in. Shit, sorry."

"It's okay, Alice. Yes, it is, I was hoping it would have the same effect on Ryan. Obviously not."

"Is everything okay with you two?" Alice asks.

"I don't know, it's not the same as it was with Leo, and I don't know what his problem is tonight. Anyway, I don't want to talk about him, tell me everything."

I look at Xander and Shelly who have the biggest smiles on their faces.

"Well, we have some big news..." Shelly begins to say.

"What is it?" Alice screeches again, interrupting them.

"We are pregnant. We are having a baby in October."

Me and Alice both scream and pull them into a huge group hug.

"That's amazing news. Why didn't you tell us before?" I say.

"We wouldn't have had that reaction if we had told you over the phone."

Just as we are all laughing, Ryan appears at my side and tries to grab my hand, but I pull it away before he can get a hold of it. The atmosphere changes. I look up at him and he has a sombre look on his face and as he couldn't grab my hand, he wraps his arm around my shoulders, pulling me into him and holding me there as tight as he can. I try and wriggle free but this just makes him hold me tighter.

"This is Ryan. Ryan, this is Alice and her boyfriend Oliver." He nods at them.

"This is Xander and Shelly. They have just told us they are expecting their first baby in October."

"Oh really, better you than me."

I look at him with disgust. *What's the matter with him?*

"Don't you want children then?" Xander asks him, he's not looking too impressed by him.

"Oh my god, no. Major benefit to being gay. No kids."

What! He doesn't want children? I know we've never discussed it, but this is massive news to me.

"Jacob wants children though," Alice adds, she's not happy with him either.

He looks at me. "Really, you do?"

I nod and he releases his grip from me slightly, so I take this opportunity to move out of it and move closer to Alice. She gives me a look.

"He wants to get married too. Do you?" Alice continues. I wish she would stop.

"No, I don't want to be tied down. Being gay, there's no pressure to get married and start a family."

They all look at me. I need to get away.

"Excuse me, I just have to go and check on something."

I walk away and I can feel that they are still looking at me. I need to escape to compose myself for a second. I walk past Mum and Dad, but I can't look at them either.

"Jacob," I hear Mum call as I get to the house, but I keep going. I run up the stairs into my bedroom and sit on the bed. Why does this happen to me? First, Leo wasn't allowed to be with me and, now, Ryan doesn't want to settle down with me. I hear a small knock on the door.

"Jacob, it's me. Can I come in?" I hear Alice's voice and am glad it's her.

"Yes."

She opens the door and comes and sits next to me.

"Are you okay?"

"No, not really. I know we hadn't discussed settling down and I don't want to yet, but I just hoped one day he would want to."

"Why are you with him? He doesn't seem right for you."

"Sometimes, we have a great time together, but other times we are just so different."

"You don't have to be with him."

"I know, but it's hard to find someone. I wish I could be as happy as you and Xander are. I'm so jealous of the both of you. I was the last time you were here, you both are so happy and I'm not." I start crying, Alice pulls me in for a hug.

"I'm sorry you're not happy, Jacob. I wish I could make it better for you. Do you still miss Leo?"

"Yes, every day."

She holds me even tighter and lets me cry. Eventually, I pull myself together and she lets me go.

"It will be okay."

"I hope so."

"Come on, pull yourself together and let's get back downstairs. I bet everyone is wondering where their host is. We need to get celebrating the amazing success of this album of yours."

"Thanks, Alice." I wipe the tears away, give her a smile and she kisses my cheek.

Arriving back downstairs, everyone has arrived and they are saying hi and wishing me congratulations. I see Alice talking to Mum and Dad and then to Xander and Shelly. I finally make it back to them, there is no sign of Ryan. Xander has gone to the bar and is asking the staff to hand out champagne to everyone. He then stands on a chair and taps his glass to get everyone's attention. Mum and Dad make their way over to me and Mum puts her arm around me and whispers, "Are you okay?"

"I am now."

Xander is calling for silence.

"I just want to say that I am extremely proud of this wonderful person. He has been through some fucking shit—sorry, Mr and Mrs Adams." Mum and Dad laugh at him. "But he has kept going and he has produced this amazing album. Let's hope we get to hear lots more of Jacob's amazing song writing in the future. Will you all raise a glass to Jacob?"

Everyone raises their glass and shouts, "Jacob."

I can feel my cheeks burning with embarrassment.

"Well, I don't know about all of you, but I would like to hear this number one song sang in the place it was written," Xander finally adds.

"No, you don't," I say back to him.

"Yes, we do," a few other people shout.

"Okay, okay. Follow me to the studio then. You won't all fit in so you will have to crowd around the door."

As I make my way back to the house, I spot Ryan going inside and upstairs. He can stay up there for all I care.

I sit at the piano and wait for everyone to squeeze around. Mum, Dad, Xander, Shelly, Alice and Oliver are closest to me. I know this is going to be hard as the song is about Leo and my emotions are all over the place. As I start playing and singing 'Lost Love', I can't help the tears falling, I look around and Mum, Alice and Shelly are crying too. I get through the song and the three of them surround me with a hug.

"Come on, let the boy breathe," I hear Dad say, he even sounds a little choked up. Everyone else is clapping and cheering.

The party from then on is so much fun. I don't see Ryan for the rest of the evening, but I don't care as I'm having the best time with everyone else.

At the end of the evening when everyone else has gone, it's just Mum, Dad, Xander, Shelly, Alice and Oliver. They are all staying here tonight. We all collapse in the living room for one final drink before going to bed.

"What happened to Ryan?" Shelly asks.

"I don't know. I saw him go upstairs when we all went into the studio, but I haven't seen him since."

"He's not right for you, love."

"I know, Mum. I realised that tonight."

"There's something you need to know," Oliver says, looking at me. Alice looks at him.

"When I was getting a drink at the bar, I overheard him telling someone that he is going to do an interview with a magazine about your relationship."

"What!"

Dad looks at me and says, "You had better talk to him, Jacob, before it goes too far. Does he know about Leo?" I nod. "You don't want him to bring that up."

"Why is he doing that? He knows I wouldn't like it."

"You better talk to George too," Xander adds.

"I can't, he's away. That's why he wasn't here tonight. I will talk to Ryan first to see what he's got to say about it and persuade him not to do it. I will go and find him now. You all know where you're sleeping. I will see you in the morning."

In my bedroom, Ryan is sat in the chair again.

"Oh, you've remembered me then?"

"You were the one who walked off."

"Yes, you were too busy with everyone else to worry about me." I don't like the tone of his voice.

"Ryan, they are my best friends and I hadn't seen them in ages."

"Still."

"Look, this isn't working, we both want different things. I want to settle down and have children one day and you don't."

"I thought you were having a good time?" he snaps.

"Yes, sometimes. But I want more."

He's up on his feet, marching towards me. He pins me against the wall.

"You mean you want Leo," he says in my face. I manage to get around him.

"No, that's not what I'm saying."

"Yes, it is. You've been different since we saw him that night. Keeping me distant, not wanting to show me off, not wanting to be with me."

He's walking towards me again, he's so close. I really don't like how he is being tonight.

"That's not true. You were the one who was pushing the photographers on us. It felt like you were just using me to get fame for yourself."

He doesn't say anything. He doesn't deny it.

"And this interview you've been asked to do; I don't want you to do it."

He grabs my arms tight. Fuck, that hurts. "How do you know about that?" His voice is so angry.

I try and release my arm, but he is holding me so tight.

"You were overheard telling someone." He lets me go and walks away.

"I will do what I want, Jacob, you can't stop me."

"I can, Ryan."

He walks back over to me and I back away, but my legs hit the table against the wall.

"I'm doing the interview. They have offered me a lot of money to do it."

He pushes me, I'm not expecting it and I bash into the table and fall to the floor.

"Is that all I am to you? A way to make money for yourself?"

I am so angry. I pull myself off the floor. "Don't do the interview, please," I add more gently.

"I am and you can't stop me," he yells back at me.

I've had enough, he has to get out of my house.

"Get out of here. I can't look at you any more."

He goes to grab me again, but I'm ready for him this time and I manage to move out the way.

"And don't you fucking touch me like that again, now get out."

He lunges for me once more and I'm too slow this time and he grabs my jacket, pulling me towards him.

"Gladly, but don't expect me to come crawling back when you feel lonely and want someone to fuck you," he spits in my face. He raises his hand about to hit me when the door bursts open and Xander, Oliver and Dad come rushing in.

Xander storms over to him and pushes him away from me.

"It's time you left," Xander commands.

Ryan picks up his bag and pushes past Oliver and Dad who are standing by the door. He doesn't get past Dad quick enough. Dad grabs him by his shirt. "Don't you ever touch my son like that again." And we are momentarily shocked into silence as Dad punches Ryan in the jaw, knocking him off balance.

Ryan regains himself. "You will pay for that, Jacob." He scowls as he leaves the room.

We all stare at Dad, not believing what he had just done.

"Dad, you shouldn't have done that," I say, shocked.

"I'm sorry, but no one is touching you like he was. I hope I haven't made things worse."

"That was great, Mr Adams," Xander calls out as he comes over to me and holds me as I'm shaking so much.

"It's okay, Jacob, he's gone. Don't worry, we will get this sorted. I will phone George in the morning to see what he says."

"Thanks."

"Do you want a drink?"

I nod and Xander guides me back downstairs where Mum, Alice and Shelly are, looking worried. Dad pours a large vodka and hands it to me.

"Here, son, that should calm you down."

"Thanks, I'm so glad you are here. I don't know what would have happened if I was on my own."

They are all looking at me.

"I'm fine."

"I'm sorry, I'm going to have to go to bed, I'm exhausted," Shelly says standing up and it's then I notice she has a little baby belly showing that wasn't noticeable when she was stood up earlier.

"Oh, Shelly, I'm so sorry, this couldn't have been good for you or the baby."

I get up, hug her and kiss her cheek.

"It's okay, Jacob, I'm fine, I'm just a bit tired."

"Xander, please take your wife up to bed. You have to cherish her more than ever now." I hug Xander.

"Good night, all."

"Night," we all say back.

"Well, I'm taking your dad to bed. He's had too much excitement for one day. Are you sure you are okay?"

"Yes, I'm fine. Goodnight, love you." I give Mum and Dad a hug.

It's then just me, Alice and Oliver. I know I can open up and be honest with Alice.

"Alice, Ryan was horrible up there. He was just about to hit me before they came in and he's been grabbing me tight all night and it has really shaken me." I can see the shock on her face. "Would you stay with me tonight? I really don't want to be on my own?"

I turn to Oliver. "But only if you don't mind?"

Alice looks at Oliver and he nods at her.

"Be with your friend, Alice, he needs you more than I do. Could you just show me where I'm sleeping again?"

"Thanks, Oliver."

I show him to his room and me and Alice head to my bedroom.

"Thanks for doing this. I was so scared. He was so angry he grabbed and squeezed my arms, pushed me against the wall and knocked me into the table. It was horrible."

"We thought something was up when we heard a crash. That's when they came up."

"I'm so glad you were all here, I can't imagine the state I may have been in if you hadn't been."

She pulls me in for a hug.

"Come on, let's get you to bed, you need some sleep. You've had a lot of vodka and you know that gives you a bad head."

I nod.

We get into bed but sleep doesn't come. The evening's events keep going around in my head and what am I going to do about Ryan? I start to feel really down.

I'm awake before Alice, having hardly any sleep. I quietly get out of bed and tiptoe into my closet. I sit in the corner and reach in the wardrobe and pull out the box hidden at the back. I slide it in front of me. I remove the Christmas decorations and put them back in the wardrobe. I then start going through the things in there. I take out the clothes and fold them neatly and put them back into the drawer where they used to be kept, leaving out a pair of tracksuit bottoms and a hoodie. I want to wear them today. I take out the aftershave and breathe in the scent, I close my eyes and I image that Leo is here with me. I put it to one side and finally I take out the two photographs I found at the old apartment. I sit looking at them for I don't know how long, tears streaming down my face. I see a movement out the corner of my eye, I look over and Alice has found me. She comes and sits by me, I put my head on her shoulder as she holds my hand. We sit in silence for a long time.

I finally sit up.

"What am I going to do, Alice? I still love him so much. I can't move on."

"You will one day, you just have to find the right person to move on with."

"I don't think I can. I just can't get him out of my head or my heart."

"He was your first love, your soul mate. It's going to take a long time to get over that."

"But Leo has managed it, why can't I?"

"I'm sure you will one day. Just take your time, don't rush into anything like you did with Ryan."

I hug her. "I miss you being around. I love you."

"I love you too. Now I better get back to my boyfriend, make sure he's okay."

"I'm sorry and say sorry to Oliver. What must he think?"

"He will be fine." She kisses my cheek and leaves.

I'm left sitting in my closet alone again. I hate feeling alone, I can feel a fog coming over me. I need to move, so I get into the shower to see if this will help not only with the immense sadness but the major hangover I have from drinking too much yesterday. The shower doesn't help, so I get dressed into Leo's clothes, spray on some of his aftershave and make my way downstairs. The time is getting on and everyone is up. Mum and Dad are cooking breakfast while everyone else is sitting at the kitchen table talking happily, but this stops as soon as I walk in. I give them all a small smile and go to make myself a cup of tea.

"Morning, love. How are you?" Mum asks.

"I'm okay," I lie.

I reach to the back of the mug cupboard and pull out the cup with 'J' written on it as this was the cup Leo always used. I used the one with the 'L' on. Leo found it cute to use each other's cups. This makes me smile as I remember the day he decided to do it when he was making breakfast in bed for me one Sunday morning. As I go to walk back to the table with my tea, I realise no one is talking, they have been watching me as I was in a daydream about Leo.

"What?" I say to them all.

"Are you sure you are all right?" Xander asks this time.

"Yes," I lie again.

"I phoned George earlier."

"Oh my god, what did he say? I bet he's pissed off with me disturbing his holiday."

"I don't think so, he told me he is back today anyway and he will come and speak to you tomorrow."

The morning goes by in a haze and everyone has to leave.

"Take care, Jacob. You will have to come and stay with us really soon. We can show you the nursery." Shelly hugs me.

"You take care of her, Xander, she has our precious cargo on board now."

"I will, don't worry, and we will definitely have to organise for you to come and stay."

"I would love that." I hug Xander.

I wave them off and it is time for Alice to leave.

"You have to come and see my play. I'm not having the 'I'm too busy' line any more. Come in a few weeks?"

"Okay, I will. I'm in London in a few weeks, so I will come and see it then."

"I will hold you to that."

"It was lovely to meet you, Oliver. I'm really sorry for stealing her last night."

"It's okay. Hopefully see you in a couple of weeks?"

"Yes, definitely."

Once they have gone, I go back into the kitchen. Mum and Dad are still there.

"Why don't you come home with us, love?" Mum suggests.

"No, I'm going to stay here. George will be here tomorrow to sort this Ryan mess out. I'm so sorry about him."

"It's all right, we just want you to be happy and you're not."

"No, I'm not. I thought I was, but it turns out I wasn't."

Mum pulls me into her arms. "I'm so sorry, Jacob. What can I do to help? We hate seeing you like this."

"There's nothing you or Dad can do. I just need time."

"Do you want us to stay?" Dad asks.

"No, you get going. I'm sure you've got things to do."

"No, you are our first priority."

"It's okay, you go. I'm going to have a relaxing day. I might even do some writing. I will see how I feel."

"If you are sure. But phone us if you want us to come back and you can always come and stay with us."

"Thanks."

Once they have gone, I don't want to do anything. The fog that I have been trying to fight back all day is slowly engulfing me, so I take myself back to bed and that's where I stay until I'm woken by the door bell ringing over and over.

Chapter Eighteen

I drag myself out of bed. The doorbell is still ringing. I hurry downstairs almost falling over. I open the door and George is standing there.

"Hi, George, what are you doing here so early?"

"Jacob, it's two in the afternoon, what time do you think it is?"

"What, really?"

"Yes. Are you okay? You don't look good."

"Yes, I'm fine."

I can't believe I have been in bed for nearly twenty-four hours. What happened to me?

"Come on in. You put the kettle on, and I will sort myself out. Give me ten minutes."

I show George into the kitchen and I run back upstairs.

Looking in the mirror I can see what George means, but I look how I feel. Crap. And I don't care. I change my clothes, throw some water on my face and go back downstairs.

George is sat in the living room, waiting.

"You don't look much better," he says.

"I'm fine."

Why can't I tell anyone I'm not fine?

"Now, Xander told me about Ryan and what he is planning on doing. Why did you have to tell him about Leo?"

"He kind of guessed when we ran into him at a restaurant."

"You didn't need to confirm it."

"I know, but I wanted to be totally honest with him."

"Well, I wished you hadn't. If it was just an interview about the two of you, it wouldn't be so bad but he knows more than he should."

"Let him do the interview. I don't care any more."

"I will not let him do that. He will bring up Leo and how do you think that will make Leo feel?"

"I wouldn't be happy if it upset Leo."

"That's what I thought."

"He will do this interview. We won't be able to stop him. They are paying him a lot of money."

"Then we will have to think of some other way to persuade him not to."

"The only way that he may not do it is if I pay him not to say anything about Leo. Get him to sign something, pay him money and if he breaks the deal, we will sue him for everything he's got. I don't care what he says about me, but I don't want him to upset Leo."

"That might be the last resort. I will get him in for a meeting and talk to him first. To see if we can resolve this without money."

"I don't think we will be able to. I believe he was only with me for the fame and money."

"If that is true, I'm so sorry for you, Jacob. You liked him."

"I did, I was stupid to fall for it, especially at the beginning when he acted like he wasn't happy having the photographs taken of him. It was just a decoy to get me to stay with him."

"You weren't stupid, you were lonely."

"Well, I'm back there again so what was the point?"

"How was the party?" He's trying to change the subject.

"It was good. It was great to see Alice and Xander. They've

both asked me to go and stay with them."

"Maybe you should."

"Yes, maybe."

"Think about it. I'm going back to London to sort this mess out. I will contact you as soon as I know what is happening."

He gets up to leave.

"Take care of yourself, Jacob, please."

After George leaves, I feel so tired and miserable, I take myself back to bed.

That's where I stay for three days, only getting up to get a cup of tea, a very small amount of food and to use the bathroom.

On the fourth day, I decide to turn my phone back on. It was off as I really didn't want to speak with anyone. When it comes back to life, it is full of messages and missed calls from Mum, Dad, George, Xander and Alice.

Mum and Dad have only phoned once, so I phone them back straight away; I don't want them to come around.

"Jacob, are you okay?" Mum sounds panicked.

"Hi, Mum. Yes, I'm fine. Why?"

"You didn't answer mine or your dad's call."

"My phone has been playing up and I have had it off as I've been writing." They will believe that as I always turn my phone off if I'm writing.

"Are you sure that's all it has been?"

"Yes."

"Do you want to come over for dinner tonight?"

"Thanks, but I can't. George said he is coming over tonight to talk to me about Ryan."

"Okay, love. We will pop in at the weekend."

"I might go to London at the weekend to see Xander and Alice, so I won't be here."

"That will be nice. Give them our love and we will see you when you get back."

"Okay bye."

"Bye, love you."

I hang up the phone. I hate lying to Mum. She will definitely know something is wrong, she always does.

I then phone George, he said on a text he has some news about Ryan.

"Hi, George."

"Where have you been? I've been trying to phone you for days."

"My phone is playing up."

"We better get you a new one," he says, not sounding convinced by my excuse.

"What's happening with Ryan?"

"You were right about him. He will not drop the interview."

"Will he mention Leo?"

"Yes, he said he is going to tell them everything."

"No! He won't hurt Leo. I will pay him whatever he wants, George. I'm going to phone him and pay him anything."

"Don't you phone him."

"I am, I will talk to you later."

"No, Jacob," I hear him say as I hang up the phone.

I am fuming; he will not do this to Leo. I get his number up and press call. It doesn't take long for him to answer.

"Hello, Jacob. What do you want?"

"I need to talk to you about this interview."

"I've already told your people I'm still doing it."

"Okay. Do the interview, I don't care what you say about me, but please, please don't mention Leo."

"You're begging me now. I was right, you do still have

feelings for him."

"I will pay you whatever you want not to say anything about him."

He goes silent on the other end.

"Ryan, please."

"Fine, but how much are we talking?"

"Whatever you want. But if I do pay you, you must sign an agreement saying that you won't say anything ever about him and me being together."

Silence again.

"Ryan, please."

"Fine, get your manager to call me and I want the money tomorrow, as I'm doing the interview in two days, and if the money is not in my account by then, then I will tell them everything."

"Fine, how much do you want?"

"A million."

"What, you can't be serious?"

"I know you can afford that. The price for love, Jacob. Surely, Leo's happiness is worth that?"

What can I do?

"Fine, I will sort it with George. But if I give you that money, you sign the agreement and I don't ever want to hear from you again."

"Fine."

I hang up. How did I ever think I liked him? I need a drink.

I get out of bed and go downstairs pour myself a vodka and down it in one, I pour myself another before I phone George back.

"George, he's not going to say anything as long as I pay him by tomorrow."

"How much does he want?"

"A million, but he will sign an agreement to never say anything ever."

"Jacob, you can't pay him that much, it's ridiculous."

"I will. I will for Leo."

"I thought you were over Leo?"

"No, I'm not, and I never will be."

"Well, if that's what you want to do, I can't stop you. I will get it sorted and hopefully this mess can be put behind you."

"Thanks, bye."

"Bye, take care."

After he hangs up, I look at the messages from Xander and Alice. I can't talk to them today. I'm exhausted. I take the bottle of vodka upstairs and get back into bed. I lay there drinking and looking up images of Leo on my phone.

I don't know what's going on, I can hear someone shouting my name and pushing me. *Get off. Leave me alone, I'm sleeping.*

"Jacob, Jacob," I hear someone shout.

"Jacob, wake up, please."

I don't want to wake up, leave me alone. Someone is lifting me off the bed. *Where am I going? Who's moving me? Put me down, I want to sleep.*

I'm put down, but now I'm cold. *Where am I? No, I'm wet. Where am I?*

Slowly, I come around and realise that I'm sat fully clothed in the shower. There is someone sat with me.

"Leo," I whisper.

I hear distant voices.

"He's coming around."

"Thank goodness."

"Jacob, can you hear me?"

That doesn't sound like Leo.

"Leo, is that you?"

"No, Jacob, it's Xander."

I open my eyes and look at him, he's soaking wet. He sees my eyes are open and he pulls me into his arms and hugs me tight but before I reach his chest, I can see he is crying.

"What's the matter?" I say to him before he holds me tight. I can hear other voices clearer.

"Xander, is he okay? Jacob, it's Mum and Dad. Can you hear us?"

Eventually, the water stops and a fluffy towel is wrapped around me. Xander stands up and pulls me to my feet. I can't stand and fall into him. He puts his arm around me and helps me out of the shower. Once out, someone grabs my other arm. I look around and it's Dad.

"Dad, what's going on?"

"Come on, son, let's get you sorted."

Everything is becoming clearer; there are two other people in the room, they are standing very close to each other. I think it's Mum and Alice.

"Mum, Alice," I call out.

Someone walks up to me, it is Mum.

"Mum, why are you all here?"

"Don't worry about that now, love, we need to get you dry."

"Let's get him to the chair. Lisa, can you grab him some clothes? I will get him changed and back into bed," I hear Xander say.

I feel myself being moved around then lowered on to the chair.

"Go and make some tea for us all, I will sort him out." I hear them leave the room.

I'm cold and wet and I don't like it, but I just sit here staring into space, I feel awful. Xander kneels down in front of me. I look at him.

"Jacob, can you hear me? Jacob, it's Xander."

"Xander, why are you here?"

"You've given us quite a shock. No one was able to contact you. What has happened to you? We found you in bed with empty bottles of vodka and lager next to you and you were unresponsive."

"I don't know."

Xander starts drying me.

"Who knows what might have happened to you if Alice wasn't so worried, she made me come up here with her. We knocked at the front door for ages. Then Alice thought you might have gone to your mum and dad's, so she phoned them. They said you told them you were coming to London to see us. That's when we all got really worried. Your mum and dad rushed over and let us in and this is how we found you."

"I don't remember what happened."

"Don't worry now, let's get you into some dry clothes and back to bed. Then you better eat and drink something. When was the last time you had anything?"

"I don't remember."

Xander helps me change my clothes. These are Leo's clothes Xander has got for me. I bet he doesn't know.

"These are Leo's clothes."

"You know that but you don't know what you've done for the last five days." He laughs and hugs me so tight.

I hear movement coming back into the room and I look around and finally can see everyone clearly. Mum looks like I've just died, Dad doesn't look much better and it's Alice and she is crying. They have tea and a plate of something but I can't see what it is.

Xander helps me back to bed, Mum fusses with the covers whilst not taking her eyes off me. Dad hands me a cup of tea and Alice sits on the bottom of the bed.

Dad asks Xander, "Does he remember anything?"

"No, he doesn't know what's happened. Although, he knows the clothes he's wearing belong to Leo."

"Jacob, who was the last person you spoke to? Was it your mum and dad the other day?" Alice asks.

"I don't know, maybe."

"Can I look at your phone to see?"

I nod. Alice finds my phone, she opens it and a tear runs down her face. Everyone is looking at her.

"What is it?" Xander asks her.

"It's all images of Leo. That must have been the last thing he was looking at."

"Oh, Jacob." Now Mum is crying and Dad hugs her. What is happening, everyone is upset and I don't know why.

"He spoke to George after you, Lisa. Then Ryan straight after, then George again and that's it. Jacob, what happened between you, George and Ryan?"

"I'm sorry, I don't know."

"I will phone George. He might be able to shed some light on everything." Xander leaves the room.

Xander isn't gone long. He storms back into the room.

"What did you do, Jacob?" He sounds mad.

"What happened?" Alice asks.

"He told Ryan he would pay him a million pound not to say anything about Leo in that interview he's giving, but that he can say anything about him he doesn't care."

They all look at me in shock.

"Jacob, what have you done?" Mum ask softly.

Suddenly, some things start coming back to me. I start to cry realising everything that has gone wrong. Mum comes to sit next to me and hugs me until I calm down. I then tell them everything that I can remember over the last few days. When I'm finished, Mum and Alice are crying again. Dad and Xander just look angry.

"Did George say if he had spoken to Ryan?" I ask Xander.

"Yes, he has and he has been to see him and signed the agreement and he has the money."

"Good, at least Leo will be protected now. I'm tired, do you mind if I sleep?"

"You need to drink that cup of tea and eat that sandwich then you can go back to sleep," Mum says.

"I'm not hungry."

"I don't care, you need to eat it."

She has that look on her face and I'm not going to get away without eating at least some of it. So, I try my best and I drink the tea. When Mum is happy that I've at least ate something, I lay down and close my eyes. I hear them all leave the room.

I spend the next two days in bed, drifting in and out of sleep. Mum keeps coming up brining me food and drink and I start feeling stronger. I can see the worry on her face.

"I'm so sorry, Mum."

"It's okay, love. You just get strong again."

She hugs me and kisses my cheek. I feel so guilty, the stronger I get the more that comes back to me and I can't believe I put them through that.

The third day of being in bed I feel much better so I get up. I need a shower. I take my time letting the hot water wash over my body and it's the best I felt in ages. I grab some clean clothes. I still want to wear Leo's clothes as they bring me comfort. Looking in the mirror I do not look myself, I've lost weight and I'm very pale but I feel a bit better in my head.

It's time to venture down stairs. As I make my way down, I can hear voices coming from the kitchen as I walk in they all turn and look at me.

"Jacob, love, you're up?"

"Hi."

Mum comes over to hug me and I hug her back.

"And you've had a shower."

"Yes, I thought it was time."

"Would you like something to eat?"

"Yes, please."

"What would you like?"

"Can I have avocado and egg on toast please, but not too much."

"Of course, you can, sweetheart. You sit down. Your dad will make you a cup of tea."

Dad gets up from the table to put the kettle on as he passes me, he pats me on the back and gives me a big smile. I sit at the table Xander and Alice are looking at me with worry on their faces.

"I'm so sorry."

"It's okay," Xander replies.

"Thanks for staying."

"You're welcome. We've all been really worried about you. Shelly and George drove up to see you, but you were sleeping so much and they couldn't stay long, they didn't get to speak to you."

"I'm sorry. Shelly shouldn't be running up here because of me."

"She wanted to come and she brought some things for me and Alice. She couldn't stay because it is so busy at work, and she didn't think you would want Harriet to know why she needed time off."

"How was George. Was he mad?"

"No, he's not mad. He's worried like the rest of us. He told us to tell you not to worry about anything. You don't have to do anything until you are ready."

"We were going to release another song soon, but I don't think I can do it any more."

"You will eventually, just not yet. He also said for you to stay away from social media too. Just for now until you are feeling better."

I nod but wonder why he wants me to stay away from it. What's on there he doesn't want me to see, is it about Leo or Ryan?

Mum puts my breakfast in front of me, but I've suddenly lost my appetite but I force some of the food down.

I spend the day with them all, but I just sit and listen and watch what's going on around me. All the time going around in my head is what is online they don't want me to see.

Finally, they all say they are going to bed. I go up to my room and Mum makes sure I'm okay before she goes to bed. I wait for an hour, to make sure they are sleeping, and I quietly make my way back downstairs. In the living room, I pour myself a vodka from a new bottle in the cabinet, take out my phone and start searching. I search Leo first, but nothing new comes up. I spend a little time looking at his beautiful face, but that's not what

I'm looking for. I then type in Ryan's name and up comes the interview, he's done it then. This is definitely what they didn't want me to see. Before I read it, I need another drink, I get up and pour another glass and grab the bottle and bring it back to the sofa with me. I read the interview and keep drinking. The interview is worse than I thought it would be, so I drink more. He has told them everything, I drink another glass. He has even brought up our sex life which I'm most upset about, that's private. I drink more. One thing I'm glad about is that he has kept to his agreement and Leo is not mentioned. I have another glass.

"Jacob, Jacob," Xander is shouting and shaking me. "What have you done?"

He continues to shake me and I can hear someone running down the stairs.

"What's happened, Xander, why are you shouting?" I hear Alice say.

"Oh no, Jacob, not again. I will get Lisa and Ron."

"Jacob, wake up," Xander is still shouting at me.

I open my eyes and look at his face, he looks angry. I close them again as my head is pounding. I hear more running coming down the stairs.

"Jacob, no," I hear Mum cry out.

"Get him some water, Alice, please," Xander says.

I try and open my eyes again, but I can't move. I can hear them talking, but I just can't reply.

"What happened, what made him do it again?" I hear Mum say.

"I don't know, he seemed a bit better yesterday," Xander replies. "He's got his phone in his hand. What has he been looking at?"

I feel my phone being taken out of my hand.

"He's found the interview. Look." Xander must be showing them the phone.

"What's happened?" Alice must have just come back into the room.

"He saw Ryan's interview. He must have waited until we were sleeping and come down. I knew I shouldn't have said anything about not looking on social media. I bet it was playing on his mind all day."

Xander tries to give me some water, but I push his hand away.

"Jacob, you need to drink this. It will make you feel better."

I let him pour some water into my mouth. I try and open my eyes again. I manage to keep them open to see all their faces and they are full of concern. Why am I doing this to myself? I need to stop. I take some more water from Xander. Dad comes and sits by me.

"Jacob, look at me." I try and focus on Dad.

"This has got to stop. You will end up in hospital or worse kill yourself. Do you want that to happen?"

I try and shake my head, but it hurts too much.

"Now we are going to sober you up and you are coming home with us. Alice and Xander have to get back to their lives, they can't keep staying here. You can't be here either, you need a break from everything. There will be no more drinking and you are not having you phone back until you are better." He sounds very serious. "Now drink the rest of that water. You need help. We will find someone for you to talk to about everything and get you sorted. We want our Jacob back and at the moment he's not here."

I drink the rest of the water and I feel so bad, I keep putting them through all this bad stuff they don't deserve it.

The last few months have been hard but I am now doing so much better. I have been staying at Mum and Dad's they have been my rock. Once I was back at their house, Dad cleared the house of any alcohol and took my phone away and made sure I had all the help I needed so I could get better. I spent the first few days in bed but after that they helped me recovered.

Alice has been visiting lots, sometimes Oliver comes with her. It is so great to have her back in my life so much. I did miss her.

Xander and Shelly have visited a couple of times, but with the baby due soon they didn't want to travel too far. I speak to Xander on the phone all the time though.

I have been seeing a therapist, he has helped me through a lot of my issues. Having someone neutral to talk things through, from worries I have about my career, my relationship with Leo and my feelings about him now and the toxic relationship I had with Ryan has really helped and I'm starting to feel like myself again.

A few weeks ago, my therapist said that he thought I was ready to move back home if I wanted to. I don't know if I feel ready to be on my own yet. So, I spoke to Alice about it and she suggested I move in with her for a while, to give my mum and dad a break and to have a bit of independence but still have my support bubble of her and Xander around if I need it. I talked to mum and dad and my therapist about doing it and they thought it would be a good step forward.

So, I did, I moved in with Alice.

I have been here for two weeks. I've been fine most of the time, especially when Alice is home, but at first when she was at work or out with Oliver and I found myself alone, I worried I would relapse but Xander is always at the end of a phone or would come around to Alice's to talk me around.

To stop this from happening this week, I have been trying to keep myself busy. I have finally seen Alice's play and she is superb in it. I have been around to Xander and Shelly's for dinner and to see the nursery, it is so cute. I have even tried to write, but I seem to have writer's block and nothing seems to come.

It's two days before Xander and Shelly's baby's due date. We are all on tender hooks waiting for news. Tonight, Alice is out to dinner with Oliver and she is staying at his. So, I am going to order a takeaway for my dinner and have an early night. I don't like it when Alice doesn't come home all night, so it's best if I just sleep.

I've eaten and I'm lying in bed about to scroll through my phone which I don't really want to do but having no one to talk to makes me think of things. I'm just about to search Leo's name when it rings. It's Xander, my heart skips a beat.

"Hello."

"Jacob, it's happening. Shelly's gone into labour. We are at the hospital. Can you and Alice come?" He sounds frantic.

"Calm down, Xander. Alice isn't here, she's out with Oliver. I will make my way there and I will phone her to let her know. I will be as quick as I can."

"Okay, please hurry. I'm freaking out."

I laugh at him. He is usually so calm.

"Xander, it's going to be okay. Go back to Shelly and look after her. I will be there soon."

"Okay, bye." He hangs up the phone.

I jump straight out of bed, throw on some clothes and run downstairs. I phone for a taxi and wait by the door, wishing for it to be here quickly. As I'm waiting, I phone Alice, it just rings and goes to answer phone. That's not like her, she always has her phone on so I can get hold of her when I need to. I rush back into the house, she left Oliver's number for me just in case. I grab it and go back out to wait for the taxi.

"Where is it?" I say out aloud.

I phone Oliver's phone that also goes to answer phone. *What is going on, where are they both?* I phone Alice's phone again and all I get is the answer phone, I leave a message.

Where are you both? Shelly has gone into labour. They are at the hospital. I'm on my way now. I will have to see you there.

Just as I hang up the phone, the taxi arrives. I run down the path and jump in it. If I'm in this state, how on earth is Xander feeling?

I arrive at the hospital quicker than I thought which is a miracle. I jump out of the taxi and run into the hospital, trying not to bump into anyone. I search the signs for the maternity ward and follow them until I find the reception desk.

A smiley receptionist is sat there drinking her coffee. I rush over, I'm out of breath and I have to stop for a second before I can talk.

She laughs at me and says, "Now calm down. Who are you looking for?"

She must be so used to seeing panicking partners and I'm acting as if it is my baby coming.

"I'm looking for Shelly Davidson."

"You must be Jacob. Xander was very insistent that I know

that you were coming." She laughs again. "Let me show you where they are."

I follow her along the corridor to their room.

"They are in here."

"Are you sure I can go in?"

"Do you want me to go in and let them know you are here?"

I nod. I don't want to just barge in if Shelly doesn't want me in there. She goes in and I hear her telling them that I have arrived.

She comes back out. "Xander wants you in there."

"Thanks."

I take a deep breath. I need to calm down so I'm able to keep Xander calm. When I feel a bit more composed, I go in. As soon as Xander sees me, he rushes over and throws his arms around me. I try and comfort him the best I can with my arms pinned to my side. I look over to Shelly and she smiles at me and rolls her eyes at Xander. He finally lets me go.

"You're here. Thank god. Where's Alice?"

Before I answer him, I walk over to Shelly, she seems much calmer than Xander does. I kiss her on her cheek.

"How are you?"

"Better than he is, he's been in a right state. I'm glad you are here, you might be able to do something with him as I'm a bit busy."

I laugh at her but then she goes quiet and start to do deep breathing. Xander rushes over and holds her hand.

"Okay baby, just breathe, breathe."

I stand back and let them have their space. Once the contraction is over, and Shelly recovers a bit, she asks, "Where is Alice? I could really do with another female in here with me."

"I don't know. I've phoned her and Oliver but they both go

to answer phone. I've left her a message, but I will try them again," as I see Shelly's pleading face.

I phone Alice and Oliver but once again it goes to answer phone. I shake my head in answer to their looks.

Two hours pass, Shelly is being a superstar, Xander not so much. I haven't been able to calm him down very much. There is still no word from Alice.

A midwife comes in to see Shelly as she feels the baby will be here soon, she wants to examine her so I leave the room to give them some privacy. Whilst outside, I phone Alice and leave her a very annoyed message.

Where the hell are you? The baby will be here soon. Shelly really needed you here. You are going to miss it.

The midwife comes out of the room and smiles at me. "It won't be long now."

"Can I go back in?"

She nods and I go back into the room.

"She said Shelly is ready to push and the baby will be here really soon." Xander looks like he's about to pass out.

"Xander, you and Shelly are going to be fine. Just calm down and make sure Shelly has you by her side. I'm going to wait outside. This is your time now."

He gives me an unconvincing nod and goes back to Shelly. I go over to Shelly, kiss her forehead and give her a hug.

"I will see you both once your precious baby is here."

I leave the room and wait on the chair placed outside the room. Another hour goes by, still no sign of the baby or Alice. Another half an hour and I hear running down the corridor, I look around to see who it is. It's Alice and Oliver, they are finally here.

"Where have you been?"

"I will tell you later. I'm so sorry I had my phone off."

Just as they are explaining, the door opens and a beaming Xander pokes his head out. We all turn and stare at him.

"Come and meet our daughter."

"A girl?" Alice and I scream at the same time.

He nods and goes back in.

We both rush in behind Xander. As we enter the room, there is a bundle in Shelly's arms. We go over quietly and peer into the blankets and there is the smallest face I have ever seen, she is beautiful. Shelly looks exhausted but happy. Xander has finally calmed down and is grinning like a Cheshire cat.

"Congratulations, you two. She is beautiful."

I go over and hug Xander and he starts crying, I hug him tighter.

He pulls himself together and I let him go.

Alice asks, "Does she have a name yet?"

"Yes. Let us introduce you to Molly," Xander replies.

"Molly. That's a lovely name," Alice replies and she starts to cry, Oliver puts his arm around her and pulls her close to him.

"Jacob, would you like to hold her?" Shelly asks.

"Really? Yes, I would love to."

Shelly places her in my arms. I look at Molly and there's a wave of love surging through me, one I've never felt before.

"Hi, Molly. I'm your Uncle Jacob. I will always be there for you."

I look up and everyone is looking at me.

"What?"

"You better be," Xander says back to me. And I know what he is thinking and at that moment I know what I have done to myself over the last months has finally ended. With this little miracle in my arms, my life is once again worth living. I kiss her on her head.

"Thank you," I whisper to her.

I catch Alice out of the corner of my eye. I can see she is desperate to hold Molly. So, I carefully place her into Alice's arms.

"Where were you two, anyway?" Xander asks Alice and Oliver.

"Well, we have some news of our own."

"What is it?"

"We had our phones off because Oliver asked me to marry him and I said yes."

"Oh my god. Congratulations," I say as I go over to hug her gently, minding little Molly in her arms. I then hug Oliver.

Looking at my best friends all starting new chapters in their lives and being so happy, I am genuinely happy for them all and not with one bit of jealously, like I had before.

Chapter Nineteen

What a six months I have had. After Xander and Shelly had their baby, I stayed at Alice's until Christmas. I stayed to help out Xander and Shelly for a bit, even if it was just to cook them some food and I loved seeing Molly everyday; she is the most precious thing ever. I love her so much.

Alice and Oliver started their wedding planning and they have been letting me help with that. Wedding planning is so much fun. Alice asked me if it was okay if she invited Leo and Sarah, I wasn't sure about it but thought that it would be unfair if I said no.

I spent Christmas with my mum and dad and it was a quiet affair, but once the New Year came, I felt that it was time to start getting my life back on track. I moved back home and it feels so great to be back in my own space. George and I spoke and we released two new singles from the album and they both did really well. For that, I had to go back onto social media to promote them. I was a little nervous to go back on as I didn't want anything to trigger bad things. I still don't use it anywhere as much as I did.

I do still think about Leo. I don't think I will ever stop but now it all brings me comfort, not sadness like it used to. I have framed the two photographs of us and placed one in my bedroom and one in the studio they inspire me and it makes me happy to see them.

I still see my therapist but not as often. I sometimes need to get things off my chest as I never want to back to the dark place I was in. I am the happiest I have been in a very long time.

It's the wedding weekend. I am a mix of emotions. I feel excited for Alice and Oliver. I have got to know Oliver really well whilst I was staying with Alice and we have become good friends. He makes Alice so happy. I'm also feeling quite nervous because I will be seeing Leo again and the last time I saw him at the restaurant, everything stated snowballing and I ended up in my depression. I hope everything will be fine this time.

The wedding is being held at a hotel in London, so I have driven down early to stay here and help them with any preparations. We have the whole hotel to ourselves for the weekend and lots of people are staying so it should be one hell of a party.

Xander and Shelly are arriving later and they are bringing Molly, she is becoming such a little character. Alice has got her a little bridesmaids dress to match Shelly and Chloe's and she is going to look so adorable in it.

Mum and Dad have also been invited and they are also driving down tonight to stay the weekend.

Alice told me that Leo and Sarah have not booked a room so we are assuming that they are only going to be here for the wedding tomorrow.

Tonight, we have had a lovely meal together and there is so much excitement and anticipation for the big day.

Waking up this morning, my stomach is full of butterflies but for some reason it's not nerves, it's excitement I'm feeling about seeing Leo. I'm a little taken aback by the twist in my feelings. I shouldn't be feeling like this, he is going to be with her and she won't let me anywhere near him if she can help it, but I truly can't wait to see him in the flesh again.

I start to get myself ready. I have bought a new navy-blue suit. The trousers are tight around my ass and the jacket is fitted into my waist. I have been working out so much and my body has never looked so good. I have paired the suit with a white shirt and a navy tie. My hair has grown out a bit and I'm loving it longer. I look in the mirror and looking back at me is someone I haven't seen in many years. If Leo was still with me then he would not be able to control himself. I don't understand where all these feelings for Leo are suddenly coming from. I need to shake them off.

I make my way down to the room where the ceremony is taking place, as I walk in my breath is taken away it looks so magical. Mum and Dad are already waiting for me, so I take a seat next to them. Not long after, Xander joins us. We wheel Molly's pram to the side and luckily, she is sleeping and we all hope she stays like that. She looks like an angel in her dress.

The room fills up with guests, I keep looking around trying to catch my first glimpse of Leo. Finally, I sense him before I see him, I turn around and there he is walking down the aisle towards an empty seat. He is looking so good and so alone. Where is she? She must be here, surely he wouldn't be alone. Alice didn't say he was coming alone. Suddenly, he looks up and our eyes meet and I'm transported back to the first time I saw those eyes back at our audition. My stomach is doing somersaults and there's movement in my trousers. This is ridiculous. He gives me a small smile. I smile back and the feelings I have are overwhelming. Shit I want him so much. I have to stop this, that is never going to happen, get a grip. I turn back around adjusting my trousers and trying to control myself. I notice Xander watching me staring at Leo.

"What?" I say to him, a little annoyed by the smirk on his face.

"You okay there? You look a little flushed."

Oh no, it's showing on my face.

"Yes, I'm fine."

"Just remember, he's not single and you don't want to bring those feelings back to the surface. You can't be with him and you don't want to go back to that dark place, do you?"

"I know," I snap back. I don't need him to remind me I can't have him.

Just as he's about to say something else the music starts and the room quietens. Oliver arrives at the front of the room with his best man. He looks a little nervous but nowhere near as nervous as Xander was at his wedding.

The music changes and we are asked to stand. The doors open and in walks Alice and what a sight. She looks absolutely beautiful in her long elegant dress. Followed by her two bridesmaids, Shelly and Chloe. She makes her way down the aisle and I can't help tear up with happiness for them both. I look back to see if I can see Leo, he is a few rows back and he is definitely on his own, I wonder where she is?

The ceremony is wonderful you can hear how much they mean to each other from their vows they had written.

The photographs are now being taken. The photographer asks for the four of us to get a group photo. We haven't had one of these taken for so long. Me and Xander make our way over to Alice and I look around waiting for Leo to appear. Suddenly, he moves out from a group of people and for the first time in a long time we are all back together. Alice hugs Leo and thanks him for coming. Xander hugs him and tells him it is great to see him.

Then he is stood in front of me. I can see those amazing eyes looking me up and down but he won't look into my eyes. I should speak first.

"Hi," I finally say.

His eyes are then on mine and wow there's that feeling that makes me want to get lost in his eyes forever.

"Hi," he replies.

We can't say anything else as the photographer is fed up of waiting for us, he makes us stand in a row for our photo. I'm just disappointed that Leo stands next to Xander. Once the photograph is taken Leo moves back into the crowd before I can talk to him. I don't see him again until we are sat down for the meal. He is not sat at our table. He is sitting with some of the people we used to work with in the group. I notice an empty space next to him so obviously Alice didn't know Sarah wasn't coming either. I wonder if everything is okay?

After the meal and the speeches, I ask Xander and Shelly if they would like me to take Molly for a while so they can have some time on their own to enjoy the evening.

"Really you would do that?" Xander's face lights up.

"Yes, you deserve to enjoy yourself. I will take her somewhere quiet, feed her and get her off to sleep."

"Thank you that would be lovely but only if you are sure?" Shelly replies.

"Yes, of course. Have fun."

I gather up Molly's bag, lift her out of her highchair. As I do she kicks out happily.

"Come on, Molly Moo, let's let Mummy and Daddy have some fun. See you in a bit."

"Her pram is just outside," Xander informs me.

I carry Molly out of the room, throw the bag into the pram

and take her into one of the quiet side rooms.

We have a little play, then I feed her and she starts to yawn so I lay her in her pram and wheel her around the room until she falls to sleep. Once she is sleeping, I park her up and I settle into one of the big comfy chairs in the room. I'm sat enjoying the quiet when I hear the door open, thinking it is Xander or Shelly coming to check on Molly I don't worry about looking over.

"Hi." It's a voice I was not expecting to hear, my eyes shoot over to the door and standing there is Leo with two glasses of champagne in his hands.

"Can I come in?"

"Yes, but keep your voice down I don't want her to wake up yet."

He makes his way over to me and sits in the chair next to me and hands me a glass.

"Thanks, but I can't have that."

"Why not, you used to love champagne?"

"There was a lot I used to love." Shit that came out a bit harsh. I see Leo's face drop.

"Sorry, that was unkind."

"It's okay, but really why can't you have the champagne?"

I don't know if I want to tell him what happened to me.

"Jacob, is everything okay?" He looks concerned.

"It is now but it wasn't."

"What happened?"

Should I tell him, he seems genuinely concerned about me, but do I really want to let him in. I'm not looking at him because if I do, I may just spill everything once I look into his eyes. I'm looking over at Molly still sleeping soundly when I feel his hand on mine. It sends a shock right to my heart. I look down at his hand on top of mine a touch that feels so familiar. I look up into his eyes and I can see he is pleading me to tell him what has happened.

"Jacob, tell me what happened to you please."

That's it, he has me broken, I start to tear up. He notices and squeezes my hand.

"Well, back in May I had a breakdown, actually it started before that."

I don't want to tell him it was when I saw him but I can tell by the look on his face he knows I don't want to tell him something, he can still read me like a book.

"Actually, it started when I saw you in that restaurant and Ryan became obsessed with showing you that he was with me."

He looks shocked.

"I was able to keep some control over it at first but I was drinking much more than I ever did. Then I had a party in May to celebrate the album and I found out that Ryan was going to do an interview on our relationship and I didn't want him to do it because he knew about you and me. When I confronted him about it, asking him not to do it, he became violent. If it wasn't for Xander, Oliver and Dad, I don't know what would have happened. He also knew I still had feelings for you even if I didn't think I did."

"I would have killed him if I was there. How dare he touch you like that."

"But if you were there then he wouldn't have been, would he?" I can't help adding.

"After that I paid him a lot of money to not speak about you. I just wanted to protect to you. It was then I realised I was missing you so much that I went into a depression. I slept all the time and I didn't want to see anyone. I then drank so much that when they finally found me they couldn't bring me around and I couldn't remember how I got in the situation."

I look at him and I can see he is so upset.

"It happened twice in the space of a couple of days where I drank myself into unconsciousness. So I had to move back with Mum and Dad. They helped me get better. I see a therapist and Xander and Alice have been my support all the way through it. So since then I haven't had anything to drink."

"Jacob, I don't know what to say. I'm so sorry I hurt you so much."

"You don't have to apologise. It wasn't you that made me drink until I nearly killed myself."

"How are you now?"

"I'm great now. Since little Molly was born, she has been my reason for living. I'm so happy."

"I'm so glad."

He stops but I can tell he wants to ask something else. I don't say anything I just wait and we sit in silence for a while.

I see him take a deep breath.

"And how do you feel about me now?"

There it is the question I could see was causing that battle in his head.

"I'm not sure. I obviously can't be with you. Which I now accept. I have things in my house of yours that once brought me sadness but now give me comfort and peace."

I laugh at Leo the emotions that just passed over his face was funny. When I said that it made me sad his face dropped then when I said it comforts me it lit up again.

"What?" he asks.

"Nothing," I answer smiling at him.

"So, you still have feelings for me?"

"I may do but I have them under control as there is no point having them as I can't have you because you are with Sarah. And to be honest I don't know if I could go back again."

His face drops again and he looks away. What is going on with him?

"Are you okay?"

He glances at me and see he has tears in his eyes.

"Leo, what's up? What's happened?"

He's now crying and he hangs his head. I get up, kneel in front of him. I put one hand on his leg and lift his head gently with my other one. I reach up and brush away his tears rolling down his face.

"Leo, it's your turn to talk to me."

"I'm sorry about everything."

"I'm okay it wasn't all about you, a lot of it was Ryan and it was mostly my shit that I couldn't deal with."

"But it all started with me," he cries. I rub his leg to calm him down.

"I need to tell you something," he says through his tears.

"When me and you grew apart." I roll my eyes at him. "Sorry when I pulled away from you. Do you remember that meeting we had with Harriet before Xander's wedding about having to have dates?"

I nod I remember like it was yesterday.

"Well, she asked me to do something else."

"What did she make you do?"

"She had a contract drawn up and wanted me to agree to it."

"What was the contract for?" I'm very confused.

"You know that she wanted us to be seen with girls for the publicity?"

I nod still none the wiser.

"Well, she knew that we were still together and how much I

loved you. She was not happy at all, especially as you had refused to get a date for the wedding before me."

"She knew we were still together?"

"Yes."

"What did she make you do, Leo?"

"She said if I signed a contract to be in a relationship with a girl, then she would leave you alone and not pressurise you into having girlfriends and she would give you some freedom to live your own life and be with whoever you wanted."

"What? Please tell me you didn't sign it?"

Just as he is about to answer, the door opens. We both flip our heads around to see Xander coming in. When he sees us together, me on my knees, he stops dead and looks between us both.

"I've come to check on Molly. Jacob, can I speak to you?"

I stand up and walk over to him. He grabs my arm gently and pulls me out of the room.

"What do you think you are doing?"

"I'm not doing anything, he came and found me. We are just talking."

"It doesn't look like nothing."

"He was upset I was just comforting him."

"What are you talking about?"

"I told him about my breakdown."

"What, why?"

"He offered me a drink and he asked why I wasn't drinking any more."

"You could have made something up. Do you want to end up back where you were?"

"You know I don't want to ever go back there."

"But…"

"But nothing, Xander. We are just talking. Molly is fine, she is still sleeping. Why don't you go back and enjoy the party?"

I turn and walk away from him and back to Leo.

He's sat with his head in his hands.

When he hears me come back in, he looks up. I go and sit next to him again.

"What did Xander want?"

"He doesn't think I should be talking to you. He's worried seeing you will bring back all my feelings and I might go back to how I was."

"Are they coming back?" he asks with what looks like hope in his eyes, surely not.

"Leo, did you sign that contract?"

"Yes."

"What, why?"

"I did it for you. I wanted you to be free in your life. So, I gave up mine." He's crying again.

"You did that for me. I thought you just fell out of love with me. But I was never allowed to be free."

"Jacob, I never fell out of love with you. I was just so unhappy that we couldn't have a relationship out in the open, so I pulled away and Harriet saw this and took an opportunity to sort it permanently. I was so mad with her when you were not allowed to say who you really were, but by then it was too late, I had signed it."

"Leo. So, your relationship with Sarah is not real?"

"No, not really. I did try to make it work as I didn't have much choice. I was miserable most of the time. I missed you so much. That's why I was so upset about the group splitting up. I knew after I wouldn't be able to see you ever again."

I can't believe what he is telling me.

"What about when you came to New York and to my house?"

"I shouldn't have done either. I was breaking my contract and luckily no one found out, but I just needed to spend time with you."

I'm shocked I don't know what to say.

"When I saw you at the restaurant with Ryan, I was so jealous that you had moved on, but talking to you I could see that you still had feelings for me because of the way you were acting. From then on, I followed you online, even though in my contract I wasn't meant to. I just needed to know how you were doing to see if you were happy. I was so proud of your music and how well your album did. I could tell lots of the songs were about me, and I couldn't believe the song you wrote for me was your first single you released. I then saw the photographs of you and Ryan, and you didn't look very happy. Many times, I wanted to phone you to make sure you were okay, but again I wasn't allowed to."

"Leo."

"I saw that interview he did about the two of you. I couldn't believe that you had allowed that. Then you disappeared from all social media and there were no new photographs of you for so long and I wondered what had happened to you. When your new singles came out, I was so relieved to see you had come back on social media, but you hardly posted anything during the promotion and after you stopped again and this worried me. Then, I got the invitation to Alice's wedding, and I couldn't believe I would finally be able to see you to make sure you were okay."

I'm totally in shock by his confession. I don't know how to respond so I just say, "So, why haven't you brought Sarah today?"

"The contract is nearly over, it was five years and it has nearly been that. I told her because of that I didn't think we needed to be seen together any more. She wasn't happy about it; I think she thought we had a real relationship. Anyway, I wanted to see you on my own."

I want to hug him for doing all that for me, but I don't know if I should. I look at him and he looks back at me and I know that look.

We are both on our feet, stood inches away from each other.

"You are looking so good," he whispers.

Then I'm back in his arms. It feels so good. I take in his touch and his scent, it's different but still intoxicating. As we are stood together, I hear Molly stirring in her pram. I don't want to but I need to move away.

I let him go and walk over to Molly. Leo follows me and as I go to pick her up, he is stood right beside me and I can feel the electricity between the two of us.

"Who's this then?"

"This is Molly. My life saver."

Leo runs his hand up and down my arm in comfort.

"Hi, Molly, I'm Leo."

She gives him a huge smile.

"She's beautiful."

"Do you want to hold her? She does squirm a lot though."

"Yes, please."

I hand Molly over to him, she's kicking her legs about which shows she is very happy. As he holds her, he smiles and makes funny faces at her. I can't help picture him with our own child. What, no, I can't think those thoughts. We are not even together, let alone having children together.

"I better take her back to see her mum and dad."

I grab the pram and the bag while Leo carries Molly back into the other room.

As we walk in together, I see that they are still sitting at the same table. Mum spots us, she turns to everyone and says something. As she does, they all turn and stare at us with worried looks on their faces.

Leo hands Molly over to Shelly.

"She's lovely, you guys. I'm going to speak to Alice." He touches my arm and leaves.

I sit down at the table they are still looking at me.

"What are you doing?" Xander asks me again.

I tell them all about what Leo told me about Sarah, Harriet and the contract. They look just as shocked as I was.

"You're not getting back together, are you?" Mum asks, she's worried.

"I don't know."

"I just don't want him to break your heart again."

"I don't think he would."

"Jacob, please don't rush into anything. You've just got yourself better."

"I won't."

I glace over to where Leo is talking to Alice and Oliver. Could I be with him again after everything that has happened? Did he hint he wanted to be with me after the contract has finished? I need to talk to him about it, but not today.

Leo makes his way back over to us. He is looking quite nervous and I don't blame him; there's Xander who he hasn't spoken to since the group split, Shelly who he has ignored at Harriet's office and then there's my mum and dad.

"Hey, Leo, why don't you join us," Xander says.

"Is that okay?"

"Yes, of course, it is," Xander replies.

He smiles at Xander with gratitude, he then smiles at Shelly who smiles back. He then looks over at my mum and dad.

"Hello, Mr and Mrs Adams."

I give Mum and Dad a look to say be nice please.

"Hello, Leo, and it's okay to still call us Lisa and Ron."

He nods, grateful not to be shouted at for breaking their son's heart.

The rest of the evening is wonderful. It feels so natural to be in Leo's company again, especially when he is so happy. Xander and Leo are back to how they used to be with each other, laughing and joking. We have been doting on Molly whilst Xander and Shelly have been up dancing. Leo even asked Mum up for a dance which she accepted gracefully.

I keep catching them all looking at me and Leo together at different times, but I don't care what they are thinking; I love being in his company again. If we do decide to get back together, they are going to have to accept my choice.

The evening is coming to an end.

"I've got to go. I haven't got a room booked," Leo says as he stands up to leave. He says his goodbyes to everyone.

"I will walk you out."

I see everyone staring at us again. This is why I want to say goodbye away from prying eyes.

We get to the hotel entrance.

"It's been lovely to see you, Jacob."

"Yes, you too. I'm glad we talked."

We just stand there looking at each other, not knowing what to say next. I don't think I can let him go again.

"Jacob, can I call you?" he says first.

"Yes, I would like that."

He gives me the biggest smile that make his eyes sparkle. This goes straight to my heart. I lean in put my hands on his face and kiss him. I feel his hand reach around to my back as he opens his mouth slightly and runs his tongue along my lips making me open my mouth and his tongue enters my mouth softly brushing my tongue. Fuck he is so hot but I have to stop. I pull away from him and I can see the desire in his eyes.

"Not now, Leo."

"I have waited so many years to be able to do that again."

"So have I, but we can't be seen. You are still under that contract and I'm sure it won't be good if you are caught with me. Let's not ruin it before we can get started again."

"You want to be with me again?" he asks, not believing what I've just said.

"Yes. I think so, but we need to talk about it."

"Oh, Jacob, that is the best news." And he kisses me again.

"Leo, we can't. Call me tomorrow. Goodnight."

"Goodnight, Jacob, sleep well."

He smiles at me and I make my way back through the hotel.

I reach the table. Molly is sleeping in her pram and everyone else is finishing their drinks and talking. When I sit down, they stop.

"Did Leo get off okay?" Dad asks.

"Yes, he did."

"What are you going to do, Jacob? You both looked so happy tonight especially with baby Molly. We just don't want you to get hurt again," Mum asks.

"We don't know yet. He is still stuck in that contract. He is going to phone me tomorrow and we need to talk about a lot of things."

"Just make sure you're happy before you jump back into anything," Xander adds.

"I will."

They don't look very convinced. I know I don't have a sensible head when it comes to Leo but I know seeing him today and sharing our problems has made me the happiest I have felt since we were first together.

I say goodnight to Alice and Oliver who look like they've had an amazing day. I will catch up with her on everything that has happened when they get back from their honeymoon. I kiss Mum and Shelly goodnight, I give Dad and Xander a big bear hug and make my way up to my room. I feel so happy.

I throw my suit off and jump into bed but before I turn over to sleep, I grab my phone and I want to send Leo a quick text.

Goodnight, sweet dreams x.

Almost instantly, he texts me back.

They will be after today xx

Chapter Twenty

That was the best night's sleep I've had in a very long time. I lay in bed going through the events from yesterday and I can't help smile to myself whenever I think of Leo. Would it be too much if I text him again? I pick up my phone and notice that he has already text me. Why didn't I hear that come through? I open it,

Good morning x

A huge smile appears on my face as I type a message back,

Good morning to you too. Did you sleep well? I had the best night's sleep I've had in a long time. Xx

I wait for his reply, I don't have to wait long.

I had a great night's sleep thanks to you. When can I speak to you?

I want to speak to him now but I need be downstairs soon for breakfast with everyone.

I'm driving home this afternoon. Can you call me tonight? xxx

Definitely, I will be thinking of you all day. Speak to you

later. xxxx

I will be thinking of you too. xxxx

Today is going to go so slow. I get out of bed, get myself ready and head downstairs.

As predicted today has dragged. I went for breakfast with everyone who stayed from the wedding. Alice and Oliver seemed to have had an amazing time. Mum, dad and Xander kept throwing me looks but I didn't take any notice of them. I just sat in my Leo bubble. Breakfast seemed to go on forever but eventually Alice and Oliver said their goodbyes to everyone which meant we were all able to leave. I said my goodbyes, grabbed my bags and hurry back down to my car as quick as I could. The drive home was the worst, there was so much traffic. It took me nearly two hours longer than it should have to get there. By the time I made it home it was the evening. Once I'm in, I sort out my bag, make myself a cup of tea in my 'L' mug and finally sit down.

I can't wait to talk to Leo. It's all I could think of all day.

I will text him to let him know I'm free to talk whenever he can.

Hi. I'm home xxxx

Hey, I can't talk right now Sarah is here but she is going out soon. I will phone you when she has gone. xxxx

I hate that she is there but I suppose he's still in that awful contract and can't just phone me when she is there. I need to do something to distract myself. I'm going into the studio. I need to write down how I'm feeling into a song.

An hour later and he still hasn't phoned. I have written a song, once I sat at my piano it all came flooding out of me. I have called it 'Back to Me' and it's about Leo finding his way back. I would love for him to hear it.

I'm making another cup of tea when my phone starts to ring, his name appears on the screen and my stomach fills with butterflies and shockingly a movement in my trousers too. It's only his name and I'm getting turned on what is the matter with me?

"Hello," I answer.

"Hi, sorry I took so long to phone. She didn't want to leave."

"It's okay. It's great to hear your voice now."

The bulge in my trousers has just got bigger. I need to calm down this will do me no good.

"How was you drive home?"

"It was a nightmare. Traffic was horrible."

"What have you been doing?"

"I've just been in the studio, writing. I was suddenly inspired to write a song."

"What inspired you?"

I can feel him smiling on the other end. He knows perfectly well what inspired me.

"You did."

"Well, I can't wait to hear it."

"I'm sure you will be able to soon."

"I would love to come to yours and listen to it in your studio."

"Would you?"

"Yes, Jacob, I can't wait to be able to spend some time with you but only if you want to."

"Yes, I would love to but what about the contract?"

"I have two months left on it and then I'm free."

He only has two months left on it that is great news but what about his contract with Harriet.

"But aren't you still under contract with Harriet for work?"

"Yes."

My heart sinks. If he is still with Harriet this is never going to happen, she will never let it. Why did I get so excited and think we could be together again?

"Surely, she won't let you be with me?"

He's quiet for a while then he says, "To be honest, I don't think she wants me any more. I haven't written anything or recorded any songs. I've even refused to record the songs that she has had written for me. I've just never felt good enough to do it."

"Of course, you're good enough, Leo. You wrote so many songs for the group."

"I had inspiration then. These last few years I've had none."

He sounds so down about it.

"How long is your contract with Harriet?"

"About six months."

Six months, I don't think I can wait that long to be with him.

"Jacob, are you okay? You've gone quiet."

"Sorry. I don't think I can wait six months for you to be totally free."

"So, what are you saying, that you don't want to be with me again?"

"No, that's not what I'm saying. Leo when I knew that I was seeing you yesterday I was so excited and then you explained what had happened to us, I knew that I wanted you back in my life. The fact that you want me too is just perfect. I know I have to wait until the contract with Sarah is up and I get that. But I don't want to wait any longer we've wasted so much time already."

"So, what do you want to do?"

"I know we didn't like it before but could we start dating again in secret just me and you, just to get to know each other again. Then once your contract is up with Harriet then we can announce that we are together. Unless you were planning on renewing your contract with her so you can carry on singing? Then I don't want you to not do that just for me. We would just have to be friends and I would rather that than not having you in my life any more."

"I definitely will not be renewing my contract with Harriet. She will be dropping me anyway. I have been a right pain since she signed me on my own. I think she will be glad to get rid of me."

This makes me grin. I bet he drove her mad with his moods.

"Jacob, I have missed you so much. I just want to be with you."

These are the words I have been wanting to hear for five years. I want to be with him but I feel he's being a bit reckless and I don't want it to blow up in his face and ruin it for us.

"You don't know what that means to me to hear you say that. But I think we need to be careful and take things slowly. I don't want you to get into any trouble with Harriet especially with the Sarah contract. I'm sure there are things in it about you contacting me and the consequences if you do can't be good?"

"No, they're not." He sounds angry by it.

"How about we stay in touch by phone until that contract ends. Then we will see how we feel about everything then. Although, I would love nothing more than to spend physical time with you."

Shit. There goes that twinge again.

"I would like to spend physical time with you too," he replies in a deep voice that goes straight to my pants.

"Leo, that's not what I meant!"

"I know but I do."

"Stop it that's not going to do us any favours."

"I don't know. I've not had that feeling in my pants for a very long time and it feels good."

I can feel my cheeks burning. Fuck even on the phone he is still hot. My trousers are now so tight I need to change the subject.

"Leo, you have to stop."

"You're such a spoil sport."

I laugh at him and I can picture him pouting and sticking out his bottom lip and that doesn't help either as all I want to do is lightly bite it.

We talk for another hour about everything and anything. It feels so right. This is my world right here. I wish we could be together now.

"Jacob, I've got to go. I can hear Sarah is back and I can't get caught talking to you she will let Harriet know. I will phone you again soon. Bye."

"Bye," is all I can quickly say before he hangs up.

That phone call was amazing but I didn't like the way it ended I was really enjoying talking to him. Just as I'm thinking about it my phone lights up again. It's Leo, he's sent me a message.

It was great talking. I've missed you so much and I will spend the rest of the night thinking of you physically!

That message again goes straight to my pants what is up with me. I am going to have to sort myself out. Before I do I text him back,

I missed you too. I need to go and sort myself out now with your comments.

I wish I could help xxxx

I wish you could too xxxx

Fuck I need some me time. I run up to my bedroom throw off my clothes and jump into the shower, with all the thoughts of Leo running through my head I'm not in there for long.

Two months have passed, very slowly. Leo is finally free from the Sarah contract. He leaked a story to the press saying that they had split up and she has moved out of his house. I can't say that I am sorry to see her go, I've finally got my man back.
 We have spent the last couple of months talking on the phone as often as Leo could and also texting each other daily. The texts have become more and more flirtatious and the sexual tension is diving me mad. I have never pleasured myself so much in my life but I've needed to release it or I would have exploded.
 Work wise I have been rehearsing for my tour which starts next month. It is only around the UK but I am doing as many cities as I can so I will be on the road for a few months. I'm hoping that Leo will agree to come on tour with me even if the first half of it will have to be done in secret as we don't want any issue with Harriet.
 I have been writing so much too with my new found muse.

The next album is going to be a much more upbeat one to reflect my new happiness I'm feeling.

Alice and Oliver are still blissfully married, when they returned from their honeymoon I filled them in on everything that has happened and they are just happy if I'm happy. Xander has finished his first film which is going to be released in the New Year. I can't wait to see it. Molly will be turning one very soon I can't believe where the time has gone. Xander and Shelly are throwing her a little party and I'm hoping to get to it as we made sure I had a break from touring around that time as I didn't want to miss my princess's birthday.

Everything seems to be fitting into place.

I'm in the studio at home putting some finishing touches to a new song when my phone rings. My stomach flips when I see his name flashes up on the screen.

"Hi."

"Hey, what are you doing?"

"I'm writing as usual, you?"

"Nothing, I'm bored."

"Well, why don't you pack a bag, jump in the car and come and see me?"

We've yet to see each other in person since the contract ended last week. I didn't want to push him to visit and he hadn't invited me to his but I just really need to see him.

"Really?"

"Yes, really."

"Okay, I will leave now and I will be there in a few hours. I can't wait to see you." And he hangs up without saying bye. I laugh as he is obviously very excited.

I finish up what I am doing as he won't be here for a while yet. I'm really happy with this new song maybe I will sing it to

Leo later to see what he thinks of it.

Right, I think to myself, *what needs to be done before he arrives.* I will cook him some dinner. Leo was always the better cook than me but I'm sure he will appreciate some food when he gets here. Looking in the fridge I find some salmon, I will do that with some potatoes and salad.

My bed sheets also need changing so I go and strip all the covers off the bed and put new sheets on but then I realise that I should sort a spare room out too. I can't just assume that Leo will want to sleep in here with me but I so hope that he does.

Sorting these rooms out waste a bit of time but not enough and I find myself pacing around the house. I need to do something else and burn some of this excess energy I've got so I change into some old joggers and a t-shirt and I spend an hour in the gym. I feel much better once I've done that.

I send Leo a quick text to see where he is and if he is hungry. He lets me know that he is an hour away and yes, he is starving. Surprise, surprise he is always hungry.

I have a shower and I'm back in my closet with the same question I always have what do I want to wear? I don't want to look too dressed up and look like I'm trying too hard but also I don't want to just throw on joggers and a hoodie. Although, I'm sure that's what Leo will be in, he doesn't seem to wear anything else lately from what I can tell from the photographs of him online. I opt for a pair of skinny jeans that hug my ass and a black t-shirt.

I take myself back down to the kitchen and start preparing the food. I'm busy sorting the salad when the doorbell goes. My stomach flips, he's here. I practically run to the door. I open it and there he is standing on my doorstep. I can't believe it I have to swallow back the tears that start forming.

"Come in."

I stand aside so he can pass as he does a familiar smell reaches me, he is wearing his old aftershave. I close the door behind him, he drops his bag and he embraces me in his arms. I wrap my arms around his back and rest my head in the crook of his neck breathing his scent. This is where we are both meant to be. I lift my head up and gently place my hands on the side of his face to bring those amazing eyes to mine. They are shining with tears as he looks back at me, one rolls down his face. I brush it gently away with my thumb as he leans in and places a gentle kiss on my lips. I smile at him, he smiles back and we let go of each other.

"Thanks for inviting me here. I have wanted to see you all week but I didn't want to invite you down to mine as I hate that house I'm in it's just full of bad memories and I didn't want to just invite myself up here."

He's rambling, he's nervous. I reach out to hold his hand to calm him down.

"I'm glad you're here. Come on in, we can't stand in the hallway all evening."

I pull him into the kitchen.

"Dinner is almost ready. Can I get you a drink?"

"Yes, please, a vodka if I could?" As soon as he says it, he realises what he's said.

"Oh, fuck, sorry."

"It's okay. I don't have any alcohol in the house, sorry."

"Jacob, I'm sorry I totally forgot."

"It's okay, honestly. Don't worry. Now do you want a cold drink or a cup of tea?"

"I will have tea please."

I put the kettle on and grab the 'L' and 'J' mugs from the

cupboard, I wonder if he will remember.

I make the tea and I hand him the 'L' mug wondering if he will notice he has the wrong one.

"Thanks."

He looks at the mug in his hand, realisation flashes across his face. He looks at the mug in my hand.

"Hey, you've got my mug." I give him a smile as I love that he still remembers and I hand him the mug and take mine off him.

"I can't believe you still have these!"

"I couldn't let them be thrown away so I brought them back with me when I cleared out the old apartment."

"What else did you keep of ours from there?"

"There wasn't much," I say as I continue cooking the dinner.

"There were the Christmas decorations from our Christmas at home together. I also found two photographs of us together."

"I didn't think there were any photos of the two of us together in private, not printed any way. Can I see them?"

"Yes, sure, one is in the studio." I walk out the kitchen and along to the studio. Leo follows me. The photograph of the two of us sat on the sofa in the apartment is on top of the piano. I grab it and hand it to him. He looks at it, then at me.

"You've got it framed?"

"Like I told you these things now bring me comfort."

"I don't even remember this being taken."

"No, I'm sure you don't, you got very drunk that night." I laugh at him.

"Where's the other one?"

"It's upstairs in my bedroom."

"You have a photograph of us in your bedroom?"

I nod, feeling a little embarrassed.

"Did you always have it there or just when we started talking again?"

"No, once I moved back here after my breakdown. I did it then as I saw them as a good thing not a bad thing."

"Can I see that one?"

I hold out to grab his hand and take him back through the house and upstairs. Leo grabs his bag on the way.

"I have sorted one of the spare rooms for you if you want to drop your bag in there?"

His face drops. "Okay," he says disappointingly.

"Or you can stay in my room if you want to, I just didn't want to presume you would want to."

His face lights back up, obviously he wants to sleep with me. That's fine with me.

We walk into my bedroom and I show him the photograph that's sitting on my bedside table. It's the one where we are naked in bed together.

"Wow, look at us. We look so happy."

"We were so happy, at the beginning."

"I want to be that happy again."

"Me too."

His lips are on me again. This time, it's full of desperation to taste me. His tongue runs along my lips urging me to open my mouth which I do with pleasure. Our tongues start to explore each other's and I start to feel a twinge in my pants as Leo runs his hands under my t-shirt and up my back. I put my hands on the back of his neck as we continue to kiss each other harder and harder. I can feel that he is getting excited too as he pulls me closer to him. I then remember the dinner is cooking, we can't carry on we will end up burning the house down.

"Leo, we have to stop."

"Why?" he says into my mouth.

"Because the food is cooking and if we don't, we will burn the house down."

He pulls away and sticks out his bottom lip. I lean forward and lightly bite it. I've wanted to do that for so long.

"Later," I say to him.

I adjust my trousers as I'm uncomfortable in them now as they are tight. I notice Leo watching me and laughing.

"That's what happens when you wear tight jeans, but that ass looks pretty fine in them though."

"It's all right for you, you seem to live in joggers now."

"Been keeping up with my fashion, have you?" he teases.

I go to walk pass him to go back downstairs and as I do he slaps my ass playfully.

"That's mine later."

I feel my cheeks burn red as I leave the room.

Luckily, dinner was saved just in time, we sit and eat, talking all the way through it. Just as if time has never passed. Once we have finished, we clean up the kitchen and predictably Leo is trying his hardest to wind me up as he always did with his little touches as we move around one another. He hasn't changed one bit and I love that.

We spend another hour snuggled up on the sofa, talking, laughing and reminiscing about the time in the group. It has been a wonderful evening.

"Shall we go to bed," I suggest, I have nervous butterflies in my belly.

"I thought you would never ask," he replies.

I hold his hand and pull him up from the sofa and take him upstairs.

Once in the bedroom, we can't stop ourselves. We are

kissing so passionately, tongues intertwined, hands running through our hair. I pull off his hoodie to reveal his toned body, I've missed that. I plant kisses down his neck and lightly bite and suck in his creases as he lets out a small moan which goes straight to my trousers. I continue as he closes his eyes and moves his neck to the side more so I can reach it better. His hands move under my t-shirt and around my waist. He moves his head back to kiss me again and he pulls my t-shirt up, our lips breaking for a second as he lifts it over my head and throws it on the floor. I pull him over to the bed where I lay down and he sits over the top of me running kisses down my chest and stomach. I can feel we are both very excited as he pushed himself into me. He slides further down and unzips my jeans and his kisses move down my body, I close my eyes, throw my head back and let out a loud moan as he goes further down.

Chapter Twenty-One

I wake up early and as I open my eyes there's Leo still snuggled up to me sleeping. Just where he should be. I can't believe last night. It was utterly amazing. I can't believe that after so long we can still read each other's bodies so well when we have sex. I can't move as I don't want to disturb Leo so I lay there staring at him, still in disbelief that he is here. I wonder how long he will stay. I need to be in London next week I hope he will stay until then.

I let him sleep another hour but I am starting to get stiff laying in one position so I gently run my hands through his hair. I feel him stirring. He lifts his head and those brown eyes are on me. He gives me a huge smile.

"Good morning," he says sleepily.

"Good morning." I lean down and kiss him. "Did you sleep well?"

"Yes, I certainly did. Did you?"

I nod back at him and he rolls over on to his back and finally I can move.

"What would you like to do today?" I ask him.

"I don't mind. What did you have planned to do before you invited me up?"

"I was probably just going to go into the studio and write."

"Okay."

"Do you want to do some writing?"

"No, I can't. But I don't mind if you want to. I would love

to hear some of your new stuff."

It makes me sad that he feels that he can't write any more.

"But before we do that, I want a shower with you." He leaps out of bed.

I watch him walk naked across my bedroom and into the bathroom. I hear the shower being turned on.

"Are you coming? I need some help scrubbing my back," he shouts out.

How can I refuse that offer? I go into the bathroom and he's in the shower foamed up with soap, he turns and smiles at me.

"Get in so I can foam you up too!"

I don't wait for another invitation I jump in with him.

We are both out of the shower with towels wrapped around our waist. I'm in the closet getting some clothes. I'm going to wear his clothes today. I pull out a pair of joggers and a hoodie from the drawer I keep Leo's clothes in and put them on with no underwear. It might be a nice surprise for him if he decides to explore down there later. I walk out and he is rummaging around in his bag pulling out clothes and I might add making a mess, another thing that hasn't changed. He catches me watching him, he looks me up and down.

"Hey! I recognise that hoodie, that's mine. I wondered where that had gone."

"These are yours too." As I look down at the trousers.

"Well, if you are wearing my clothes, I think I will wear yours."

He walks past me into my closet and starts rummaging around my clothes. I know most of it will be too small for him as he is taller and has a bigger build than me. It's a good thing for me as his clothes are always baggy on me. He chooses a white t-shirt and a pair of grey joggers then takes them into the bedroom.

I'm watching him the whole time and he knows it as when he reaches his bag he drops his towel on the floor giving me a full view of his amazing body. He sprays on his deodorant and to my disappointment, he pulls on a pair of boxers. He puts on my clothes and as predicted they are a little small for him but he still looks hot in them as they are a little tight in all the right places around his ass and chest. He sprays on some aftershave, looks in the mirror and ruffles his hair into place. I haven't taken my eyes off him and he is playing to that fact. I can feel movement again in my joggers. I can't be like this all day.

Once he has finished getting ready, he walks over to me and he can tell he has turned me on as I have flushed cheeks.

"Are you all right there, Jacob?" he says with a cheeky smile. He kisses me on the lips and shockingly shoves his hand down my trousers.

"Fucking hell, Leo. What are you doing to me?"

"Woah! Nice. No pants. Easy access."

He leaves his hand in there as he kisses me again. But then he pulls his hand out as quickly as he put it down there.

"Come on, I'm hungry. Not much of a host not feeding his guest." He laughs and walks away.

He's such as tease. I'm not going to cope today if he's like this all day.

I follow him downstairs to the kitchen, where I find him going through the fridge.

"I'm starving. What do you want?"

I laugh at him, he always got hungry after an energetic night or morning and we have had both.

"I don't mind. You pick. I will have whatever you are having."

He grabs bacon, eggs and bread and starts cooking. I take a

seat at the breakfast bar and watch him dance around the kitchen. Not knowing where anything is, he opens every cupboard to find what he is looking for. I don't want to tell him where things are, it's more fun just watching him. My heart feels with joy watching him in my kitchen.

He makes two cups of tea, in our mugs and hands me mine with a quick peck on my lips.

He is humming to himself as he is cooking, the tune sounds familiar but I don't know what it is.

"What are you humming?"

He looks at me with one of his cheeky smiles. What is he up too?

"Don't you recognise it?"

"No, not really, it sounds familiar but I don't know why."

He plates up the breakfast but doesn't tell me anything about the song. He puts the plate in front of me and joins me at the breakfast bar. This is the first time I've ever eaten anything up here, I always sit at the table. I like sitting here as I can feel Leo's leg touching mine.

After breakfast, we head into the studio. Just as I'm going in, Leo turns back around.

"I've just got to get something from upstairs."

He runs up the stairs and I go into the studio, get my note book out and I sit at the piano waiting for Leo to return. I don't wait long and he walks in with a book in his hand. He passes it to me.

"What's this?"

"Have a look."

I open the first page, recognising it immediately. I flash my eyes up to Leo who is now stood next to me.

"You kept it. I didn't know where it had gone."

"I wasn't throwing these away. I thought you would like them or at least some of them for your next album."

As I flick through the pages of the songs we started writing on our first holiday together at the Lakes, so many memories come flooding back and I can't help tears filling my eyes. I feel Leo's hand on my shoulder, he gives it a squeeze.

"I thought you would like them?"

Then it dawns on me that was what he was humming in the kitchen. It was the first one we wrote 'Far Away'.

"You were singing 'Far Away' in the kitchen?"

No nods. "It's my favourite."

"Are you sure you want me to have these, you wrote them too?"

"Yes, I'm sure. They make me happy and you singing them would make me even happier." He wraps his arms around me and kisses the top of my head.

We spend the rest of the day in the studio, Leo just choosing to sit, watch and listen. I try and involve him in writing but he refuses to. He pops out now and then to get drinks or food but he will not write anything. This makes me feel sad for him he was such a talented writer.

I have decided that I want to add 'Far Away' to the tour list. I will talk to the band to get some music sorted for it when I'm in London next week for our rehearsal.

We don't do much in the evening, just eat dinner and snuggle up on the sofa and watch a film. It all feels so natural and normal like this is what we do every evening.

We go up to bed and Leo is laying on my chest.

"I better head back tomorrow."

"Really? I don't want you to."

"You don't?"

"No. Why don't you stay a bit longer? I've got to be in London next week, why don't you stay until then?"

"Are you sure? I don't want to be in your way."

"You will never be in my way. I love having you here."

"You do?"

"Yes. I don't ever want you to leave again really."

His eyes are glistening.

"I don't ever want to leave you again either."

"Would you come on tour with me next month? I don't think I want to do it without you there?"

"Do you think I should? We are meant to be keeping us a secret."

"It was just a thought. It's just that I would miss you so much. Now you're back in my life I don't want you to be too far away from me." He can tell I'm getting chocked up.

"I would love to come on tour with you. But we are going to have to be so careful that I'm not seen with you."

"You will come?"

"Yes. You are my everything now and I have nothing keeping me in London."

"We will only have to be careful for the first part of tour after the new year you are free."

"I can't wait. I want to tell the world that you are mine."

The next few days have been some of the best of my life. With Leo here everything is so much better. Our days have just been very normal and domesticated and I love it but tomorrow I'm going to London and Leo is going back to his house.

I'm so happy Leo has decided to come on tour with me though, it will make living out of hotels much more fun. I have spoken to George and told him about the new song I want to add and that Leo is coming on tour. He was a little taken back by this turn of events especially as I told him that it has to be kept a secret for the time being. He totally understood once I explained about how we didn't want Harriet to find out.

I invited Mum and Dad around for dinner the other night to spend some time with the two of us before we go on tour. It was a bit tense at first but as the evening progressed, they could see how happy we make each other and it seems they too have now put the past behind them.

It's our last night before going to London and I won't be coming back here much over the next few months. Me and Leo are snuggling on the sofa discussing what we are going to be doing over the next week before we go away. There is something playing on my mind, something I want to ask Leo but I'm so nervous about it. He looks at me and he can tell.

"What's the matter? You look a little worried about something."

"I want to ask you something but if you don't want to or if you think it's too soon then don't worry about saying no."

"Jacob, what is it?"

"After, the first leg of the tour, during the break would you move in with me?"

He looks shocked at first, it's too soon. He's going to say no. But then his face lights up.

"Yes! Yes, I would love to but are you sure?"

"Yes, I'm so sure. We can live anywhere, I don't mind. I could sell the house and move to London, we can live at your house in London if you don't want to leave there. We could buy somewhere new I don't mind I just want to be with you always. I love you."

His smile gets even bigger at the last three words, that's the first time I've said those three words in a very long time.

"I love you too. I never stopped but I was worried it was too soon to tell you. I don't want to live in London especially my house. I definitely don't want you to sell this lovely house. I remember you telling me that you bought this house for us and I have enjoyed being here so much these last few days it feels like home. So, if you don't mind, I would like to move in here?"

I pull him into a hug. I can't believe he wants to move in here. It is just how I dreamed it would be.

"So, is that a yes to me moving in here with you?"

"Yes."

Tour is about to start. The first concert is in London. We are doing two nights here before we move on. Everything is set up for Leo to come along with me. Only a few people know about it, George, the band, some others on my personal team, my security and Jim.

I have arrived at the venue to do a final rehearsal. Leo has stayed at his house for now and will come along later once we have started and be secretly moved into one of the VIP boxes. I will know he's there but hopefully no one else will spot him.

I am so excited to kick off the tour, most of the shows have sold out and I know the fans are going to be amazing. I can't wait to see what their reaction will be to the new song and with the power of social media I'm sure it won't be long before they are all singing along to it.

I'm in my dressing room waiting to get the call to say we are ready to start, when a message flashes up on my phone.

Good luck tonight, you are going to be amazing. I'm leaving now so I should be there soon. Look out for me. Love you xxxx

That was just what I needed to settle my growing apprehension of doing this for the first time by myself. I will feel even better when he gets here.

See you soon. Love you too xxxx

Just as I finish sending my text back to Leo, George appears at the door.

"Are you ready?"

I nod, feeling slightly nauseous. I follow him to the side of the stage where the band are waiting. We wish each other luck and they make their way on to the stage with a big cheer. Shit! I'm so scared. What if it all goes wrong? I wish Leo was here now, he would be able to calm me down. He always did when we went on stage with the group.

The music starts playing and I take a few deep breaths and run on to stage. The cheer from the fans is deafening. How amazing this is as I look out over the crowd. I look up to the VIP box where Leo will be, I know he's not there yet. Hurry up Leo I need you here.

I've sung two songs and the nerves are slowly disappearing. I'm just about to sing 'Lost Love' when I glance quickly up to the VIP box and I notice movement up there. He's here at last, hopefully there were no problems getting him in. I glance up again and give him a big smile. I can't see him really as they have kept the lights off but I'm sure he is smiling back. This gives me the confidence to carry on, all nerves totally vanished.

Through some of the songs I can't help taking a look up at Leo and hoping he is enjoying the show.

I've now come to singing the new song. I start talking to the crowd.

"So, are you enjoying it so far?"

They all scream back. I look up to Leo, smiling to myself imagining him screaming yes back at me.

"I'm going to sing a new song that isn't on the album. It was written a long time ago with someone special whilst on holiday." The crowd go wild at this information and maybe I shouldn't have said what I did.

"It's called 'Far Away'. I hope you like it?"

The crowd go wild again. As I sing it I can't help but look up at Leo as if singing it to him. The crowd is quiet through it listening to every word I sing but once I finish the screams are once again deafening.

I come to the last song of the show and I am buzzing. That was absolutely amazing. I take one final look up at the VIP box but I know he's not there any more, the plan was to get him out before the end of the show so none of the fans would see him. He will be waiting for me in the car.

I thank everyone for coming and I leave the stage. Everyone is buzzing from that. I couldn't ask for it to have gone any better. But all I want to do now is see Leo and find out what he thought. I go to my dressing room, change out of my stage clothes, say my goodbyes and head to the back entrance. I have my security with me just in case any fans have worked out where I'm leaving from. They know Leo is waiting in the car so they want to get me out as quick as possible. But as we are leaving some fans have figured it out and are waiting. I say hi to them and let them take a few photographs, then the security team move me towards the car. Once I'm close enough Jim opens the door just enough for me to squeeze in without Leo being spotted. Once I'm in he quickly closes the door behind me and everything is quiet. Leo is sat there looking at me.

"What did you think?"

He pulls me into his arms.

"Jacob, you were amazing."

"Thanks," I blush.

"But you are going to have to stop looking at me in the box. You are going to give us away."

"Was I doing it that much?"

"Yes, you were."

"I wanted to sing to you."

"I know I like you singing to me but I'm supposed to be a secret."

He laughs and kisses me on the lips.

"It will be okay tomorrow night. I can look at you as much as I want because everyone else will be there with you."

Xander, Shelly, Alice and Oliver are coming to the concert tomorrow so it shouldn't seem strange if Leo is there too. He will be able to be there the whole time, before and after I can't wait.

It's day two of tour and I am so excited for this one because everyone is coming to see me which means Leo can be out in the open and not hidden away.

I am already at the venue, Leo is going to be picked up from the hotel we are staying in by Xander and Shelly on their way here. They are picking him up at the back entrance to avoid any fans or press that might be around.

It's half an hour before going on and they have all arrived. They are shown into my dressing room before they go to the VIP box.

Leo is looking happy.

"What are you smiling about?" I ask him.

"All this sneaking around it's like I'm an undercover spy. I'm finding it rather funny."

"You should have seen him coming out of the hotel. He was peering around the doors. He was covered head to toe in black, a black coat, sunglasses and a black cap. He looked hilarious," Xander adds.

As we are laughing at him, Leo walks over and kisses me.

"What was that for?"

"I just missed you these last few hours."

I give him a smile and slightly blush.

There's a knock on the door, it's George.

"George, come in and say hello to everyone."

He comes in and says his hello's and asks how they are all doing.

He then asks Leo, "Did you get out of the hotel okay?"

"Yes, I think so. I don't think anyone was around and they managed to park the car quite close to the door."

"That's good. Right are you all ready? I will show you where you are watching from."

Alice and Shelly come over and kiss my cheek and wish me luck. Xander and Oliver hug me then they all leave so I can see Leo alone. He pulls me into his arms and wraps them around my waist. I put mine around his neck. Then he kisses me, his tongue searching for mine. I let him for a little bit but I can't get wound up before going on stage so I pull away.

"You look so good," Leo says.

"Thanks, I will see you after the show. I hope you enjoy it again."

"I'm sure I will. See you after."

He kisses me again and joins the others outside.

The concert goes even better than yesterday. The crowd

went absolutely wild when I pointed out Leo, Xander and Alice in the VIP box. The crowd started singing 'I want to go dancing with you' to them so I joined in and so did Leo, Xander and Alice. It was a lovely moment. I wonder if we could fit it in on the other concerts, that would be fun.

It was lovely to see Leo properly throughout the show when I glanced up at him I could see him singing along. When I sang 'Far Away', I could see him singing that too. I hope no one spotted him singing it as no one is supposed to know the words to this song yet but it does make my heart soar.

We are heading back to the hotel to have a meal together. When we arrive at the restaurant and we are shown to our table I know we shouldn't have done it but I want Leo to sit next to me. I need to feel his touch.

We spend the next few hours just talking and eating, it feels just how it did when we were first put together. Throughout the meal I can feel Leo's leg and foot touching mine but I wish I could hold his hand but we don't dare as there are hotel staff and other guests around.

After the meal, I say my goodbyes to everyone and leave to go up to our room whilst Leo stays and has another drink with the others. This is so that we are not seen going to a room together and arousing suspicion.

I grab a quick shower and get into bed naked waiting for Leo, I need him so much. I wait for an hour and I know he will be on his way up as this was the plan. I fake sleep as I know this will disappoint Leo when he arrives back to the room.

Five minutes later, I hear the door open, I quickly close my eyes. I hear him come into the bedroom and let out a big sigh, he thinks I'm sleeping. I hear him strip off his clothes and gently climb into bed next to me. He drapes his arm over my waist and he feels cold. He moves closer and as he does I move my ass into him, I hear him catch his breath. I rub my ass against him more. He now knows I'm not really sleeping.

"You tease. I thought you were sleeping. I was very disappointed," he says, as he flips me over on to my back so he can see my face.

I lean up and kiss his lips. He holds my face and kisses me deeper. He runs his hands down the side of my body and turns me on to my side facing him and pulls me closer.

"I love you," he says, as he works kisses down my neck and my chest as I let out a moan of pleasure.

Chapter Twenty-Two

I can't believe little Molly is one already. We are gathered at Xander and Shelly's house for a party to celebrate.

I have a two-week break from touring so me and Leo have been enjoying a rest at home.

We travelled down to London yesterday and we are staying at Leo's house. He really didn't want to stay there but it seemed silly trying to sneak about in a hotel when he had a perfectly good house for us to stay in so after much persuading he agreed. Although, since we have been there, he hasn't been himself. He has been really quiet, he barely touches me and there has been no chance for sex, last night or this morning. He has stayed to one side of the bed not snuggling up to me like he usually does. I wonder if this is how he slept when she was in his bed with him. I haven't pushed him to open up to me about it as I can see him struggling.

I was looking forward to coming to London as I wanted to catch up with some people whilst I was here but I think it might be best if we make our way home tomorrow.

We have been at Xander's for a while enjoying watching Molly opening her presents and catching up with people. We are gathered around Molly's cake ready to sing happy birthday to her when Leo's phone goes, I see him look at it and put it back in his pocket and his face has dropped. He had been quite happy up until then. I wonder who the call was from. I focus back on Molly and laugh as Xander and Shelly are trying to get Molly to blow out her candles. They cut the cake and hand it around. Eating my cake, I glance over to Leo who is stood by the door and I can see worry etched across his face. He takes out his phone and walks out of the room. I follow him and I see him head towards the garden. I watch him from the kitchen window. He is on the phone and looks like he is having a heated conversation and he doesn't look happy. When he hangs up I go out to him. He spots me heading towards him and I give him a small smile which he doesn't return.

"Is everything okay?" I ask him.

"No."

"What's the matter?" I move towards him and reach for his hand but he pulls away from me.

"Leo, what's happened?"

I reach for his hand again and this time he lets me take it.

"Who was that on the phone?"

"It was Harriet. She wants to see me this week."

"What does she want to see you about?"

He just shrugs his shoulders looking worried.

"Maybe she wants to talk to you about the end of your contract. Don't worry until you know what it's about."

"She didn't sound very happy."

"Did she say when she wanted to see you?"

"No, she said she will let me know. So, it means we have to stay in London until I know. I wanted to go back to yours tomorrow. I hate that we are staying in that house. I hate it there."

"I didn't realise you hated it that much until we arrived. You have not been yourself since we got here."

I pull him close and wrap my arms around him.

"I know, I'm sorry."

"Shall I book a hotel room for us until you have your

meeting?"

"No, you were right, it is pointless as we would have to sneak around if we stayed in a hotel. Hopefully, the meeting will be in a day or two. And now you can meet up with who you wanted to. I know you were looking forward to coming down."

"If you are sure?"

"I am. I'm sorry I've been miserable."

"It's okay." I lean in and kiss his lips and this brings a smile to his face and he relaxes into my arms. "Come on, let's go back in and enjoy the party."

Two days later, Leo has been summoned to Harriet's office. He has left me at his house on my own and I don't know what to do with myself. Leo was so worried when he left and this has made me so anxious that all I've done is pace around the house since then.

I'm upstairs when I hear the front door open, I rush down the stairs but as I reach the bottom, I come face to face not with Leo but of all people Sarah.

"What the fuck are you doing here?" I snap at her as she glances around at me.

She gives me a smirk. "So, it's true. You two are back together?"

"What's it got to do with you?"

I can't believe she is here. What does she think she is doing?

"I'm here to see if I can find out anything that tells me you two are back together, but I didn't think I would find you here. Harriet will be over the moon with this information."

"How dare you come into Leo's house?"

"He wouldn't even know if you weren't here."

"Do you come here a lot when he is not here?"

"Yes. Harriet still pays me to see if Leo is up to anything."

"What the fuck? How dare you do that to Leo? The contract between you and him is over. You know that and so does Harriet."

"Yes, but he is still under contract with Harriet for his job. The job he seems to not want to do and he is breaking his contract because he is not keeping up with his regular meetings with her. She wanted to know where he was, so she asked me to keep an eye on the house to see if he is still in London, but he hasn't been here for months."

I can't believe what she is saying. Leo said nothing about having to keep up with meetings with her. If I had known, I would have made him go to them.

"Then there has been loads of rumours about Leo being with you at your concerts. You two still don't know how to hide your relationship. What with you singing up to darkened VIP boxes, shadows in your car and you being seen in clothes, Leo has been photographed in. Do you never look online to see what your fans are saying about the two of you?"

I look at her in shock. I don't do social media much any more but I know Leo always looks, so I have been asking him if anything has been said about us but he hasn't said that there was. I also wonder why no else has said anything to me either. I can see her watching me and she laughs out loud.

"You don't know anything about this, do you, Jacob?"

I won't give her the satisfaction of showing her that I know nothing about it so I don't say anything.

"Harriet will be pleased when I let her know that I found the biggest proof that you are together."

Just then the door opens again. We both spin our heads towards it and in walks Leo. He stops dead when he sees us both stood there.

"What the fuck are you doing here?"

"Good meeting with Harriet?" she replies to him.

"What! How do you know where I've been?"

"I know everything, Leo, and Harriet is going to be very pleased when I let her know that you two are together again. She had her suspicions but now we have proof."

"Get out of my house, you bitch," Leo shouts at her.

"Gladly. I don't need to be here any longer."

She heads for the door but before she opens it, Leo stops her.

"Give me your key," he says to her through gritted teeth.

She removes one key from the bunch she has in her hand and gives it to Leo.

"Now get the fuck out." He pulls open the door, pushes her out then slams the door on her.

He leans his forehead on the back of the door and I can see him taking deep breaths. I walk up behind him and rub his back to calm him down. I need him calm before I talk to him about any of this. As I rub his back, I can see his breathing return to normal, eventually, he pulls his head away from the door. He slowly turns around to face me, our eyes meeting. I can see that he is hurting. What happened at the meeting?

"Leo, why didn't you tell me you should have been having meetings with Harriet?"

His head drops, I place my hand under his chin and lift his head so he is looking at me.

"I didn't think it would matter if I didn't go as my contract was nearly up."

"And why didn't you tell me about all the stuff that has been online about us either?"

"I thought you would stop me from coming on tour with you

or that it would become too much again and you wouldn't want to be with me."

"Leo, I wouldn't do that. I would have made you go to the meetings, yes. But I need you with me I wouldn't stop you coming on tour I would have made sure we were a bit more careful."

"I'm sorry I didn't tell you."

"It's okay, but what I don't understand is why no one else on the team told me?"

Leo drops his head again, what is he not telling me now?

"Leo, what is it?"

"I asked George if I could look out for your social media stuff. I wanted to help with something, he agreed. He didn't say anything to you as I said I would tell you, they all must have assumed you knew what was being written. I didn't tell you as I didn't want all the rumours to ruin us again."

"Leo, you can't keep secrets from me. That's not how our relationship works. We need to be honest with each other."

"I'm sorry."

I pull him into a hug. I wrap my arms tight around him. I am annoyed with him for doing what he has done but he looks devastated as it is without me adding to it.

"What happened at the meeting?" I ask attentively.

"She wasn't happy. She wanted to know why I wasn't going to our meetings. She also said that she suspects that we are back together again because of the online stuff."

"But she didn't know for sure?"

"No, she didn't, but now Sarah has seen you here it's a bit obvious."

"What did she say she would do if it was true?"

"She will take me to court for breach of contract."

"What! What breach? Surely your private life has nothing to do with your work contract or is it and you didn't tell me that either?"

He doesn't say anything but I know the answer by the look on his face.

"For fuck sake, Leo, there is something in the contract about your private life. What is it?"

He still doesn't say anything. I need to walk away from him as I can't believe he didn't tell me this. As I start to walk away, he calls my name.

I turn back to him. "Leo, I just need a minute to myself. I can't believe you've done this."

I walk into the living room and sit on the sofa. What are we going to do? I need to talk to George about this. I take out my phone and pull up George's number.

"Hello."

"Hi, George. We have a problem."

I tell George everything that has just happened.

"Did Leo say what the breach to the contract was?"

"No, I couldn't talk to him any more."

"Are you still with him?"

"Yes, I'm just in a different room."

"Tell him I'm going to arrange a meeting with our lawyers as soon as possible and see if we can get this sorted. I will speak to them now and I will phone you as soon as I know what our plan will be. Don't worry, Jacob, we will get this sorted."

"Thanks, George. I have had enough of Harriet to last me a lifetime. The sooner Leo is away from her the better."

"I will call you soon."

"Okay, thanks again, George."

As soon as he hangs up, I go to find Leo. I open the door of the living room and he is sitting on the stairs with his head in his hands. As he hears me walk out, he looks up, he's been crying.

"Come here," I say to him gently.

He walks down the stairs and over to me and I embrace him in a hug. He buries his head into my shoulder and I can feel the tears falling on to my skin. I hold him for a while until I feel him calm. I then move him away from me.

"Listen to me we are going to get this sorted. George is talking to my lawyers to see what we can do and we are going to get you out of this contract and hopefully avoid going to court."

"I'm so sorry, Jacob. You really don't need this. You have enough to deal with. You've got to be back on tour next week."

"I know but you are my main priority. We will get this sorted, I promise."

I'm back on tour but I've had to come on my own. George advised Leo to stay at his house until everything has been sorted. Both of us were not happy about this arrangement but George said it was for the best.

Leo had a meeting with my lawyers last week and they are positive they can get Leo out of the contract early and not go to court. Leo told me that in his contract he was not allowed to have any relationship without management consent even though he was in the contract with Sarah. I can't believe they still felt the need to put that in his working contract and I'm still in shock that Leo signed them with all these agreements in, he must have been in a really low place when he did it. I was a little angry at Leo for doing it but I am absolutely fuming with Harriet for making him sign these ridiculous contracts, he basically had no freedom what so ever with them.

The lawyers have said that they are going to get him out of

it by using the fact that Sarah was caught going into Leo's house without permission and admitting that she had done it quite a few times and that she was being paid by Harriet to do it. They seem to believe that Harriet would not like the bad press about that so we think she will settle out of court.

I just can't wait to get this over with as it is putting unnecessary stress on us. Leo is feeling so down about it all and it feels like when he walked away from it all the last time. I make sure I call him every day even after I have done a show just to make sure he is okay but I can hear that he is struggling. I don't want to lose him again.

I can't sleep, Leo has his big meeting in the morning, with George, the lawyers and Harriet. I have been tossing and turning all night. I wish I could be there but I have a concert tomorrow night and I have to be here for rehearsal. I wonder if Leo is awake too I really want to talk to him. I will send him a text and if he is sleeping I won't wake him.

Are you awake?

I stare at my phone willing a text to be sent back but it rings making me jump and I almost drop my phone.

"Hey, you're awake too?" I say as I answer it.

"Yes, I can't sleep."

"How are you doing?"

"I'm not good. I'm so worried about the meeting."

"I know you are. But the lawyers are confident it will go our way."

"I know but you know what Harriet is like, she is such a bitch that she could pull anything."

"I know but we have to stay positive."

"I can't."

"I wish I was there with you."

"Me too. I'm missing you so much. I sleep much better when you're in bed with me."

"Just think after today you can hopefully move in with me."

"I hope so."

"I'm sure it will be all good. You need to try and get some sleep so that you have a fresh head. Ring me later before you leave. Don't worry what time it is I will keep my phone on me even during rehearsal."

"Okay. I will speak to you later."

"I love you."

"I love you too."

I hang up the phone, that call has done nothing to calm my fears about him not taking this very well. I hope he gets some sleep. He really isn't good when he is tired. I lay back down and try and get a few hours of sleep myself before I need to get up and make my way over to the stadium.

Three hours later and my alarm is sounding. I reach over still with my eyes shut and switch it off. I did not get much sleep after talking to Leo. I have to move I have a show to prepare for. I know my head is not going to be in the right place for the rehearsal. Hopefully, everything will be sorted before I go on stage tonight. I decide to have breakfast in my hotel suite today as I don't feel like facing the restaurant. I phone down to room service and order a small breakfast, I really don't want to eat as I'm just too nervous about later but I know I'm going to need some energy to get me through rehearsal.

I'm on my way to the stadium and I haven't heard from Leo, I thought he would have phoned me this morning but he hasn't. So, I decide to text him.

Good morning. I hope you are okay and got some sleep last night? Xxxx

He doesn't reply. I'm starting to get worried. I look at the time and he has his meeting soon but perhaps he was in the shower when I texted him.

When I arrive I check my phone again but still nothing so I text him again.

Leo are you okay?

Still I don't hear anything I'm now really worried but I am being made to get going on the rehearsal so that they can do the light and sound check and for me to run through the song list to make sure everyone is happy with the show.

A few hours later, during a short break, I check my phone again, he still hasn't texted me and he should be on his way to the meeting now. Why didn't he phone me he said he would? My mind is not on the job now and they are calling me back. I wish they would just leave me alone. I want to drink not jump around on stage.

I phone him but it goes straight to answer phone. I leave a message.

Why haven't you phoned me or answered my text. I'm so worried. I'm that worried I want to drink it away. Please phone me as soon as you get this.

I hear the team call me. Just fuck off. I don't want to do this. I storm over to see what they want me to do now.

I am at the rehearsal for another three hours as there have been so many problems, including me. The technical issues are finally sorted but my issues have not. The team keep giving me worried looks but I can't deal with any of it at the moment. I'm finally allowed to go back to the hotel and there is still no word from Leo.

As soon as I'm up in my room. I phone him again and once again it goes straight to answer phone. Surely the meeting is over, does it mean its bad news and that's why he's not talking to me. I have to phone George. It rings and rings but he doesn't answer either. I hang up and throw my phone across the room I am fuming why won't anyone tell me what is going on. I pick up the room phone and phone room service.

"Hello, room service how can I help?"

"This is room 375. I would like a bottle of vodka brought to my room."

"Of course, sir, right away. Would you like anything else?"

I stop and think for a second and I realise what I'm about to do.

"Actually, no, cancel that. I don't want it. Thank you."

And I hang up the phone.

I can't believe I was going to do that to myself again this is what happens when no one will talk to me. I am so angry with everyone. To distract myself I go to the gym. I need to burn off some of this anger.

An hour in the gym and a long hot shower has helped with the urge to drink but I'm still angry with everyone. I have no more time to think about it though as the show starts soon and I need to get ready to leave. As I'm throwing on some clothes to travel in there's a knock on the door. I told my team I would meet them downstairs, so who is knocking. I open it and standing there in front of me is Leo. I'm in shock and just stand there staring at him.

"Are you going to let me in?"

I come to my senses and nod and move away from the door.

"Jacob, are you okay?"

"No, I'm not fucking okay. Where the hell has everyone been? Why haven't you answered my texts or phone calls? I left you messages to phone me. Even George didn't answer his phone. I have been so stressed here not knowing what has been happening. Rehearsal was awful and I almost ordered a bottle of vodka to my room."

Leo looks absolutely devastated by my last statement.

"No, Jacob. I'm so sorry. I didn't phone you this morning because after we spoke, your voice calmed me down and I fell into a deep sleep and I over slept. I was late to the meeting. Then after that I wanted to be here to surprise you. I didn't see all your messages. I'm so sorry I caused you to want to drink. You had been so positive about everything I thought you would be okay."

"Well, I wasn't. I was just doing it for you as you had been so down about it all. If you knew I was struggling too, then that would have made it worse."

He pulls me into his arms and holds me tight. I wrap my arms around his waist and his scent calms me slightly. Then I wonder why is he here, I pull away from him.

"Why are you here?"

"Jacob, I'm free."

"What?"

"Harriet caved in. She couldn't do anything once she found out that Sarah had told you that she had been to the house to spy on me. She knew that if she took it to court then we would bring it up and that wouldn't look good for her."

"That's amazing news. So, the contract has ended?"

"Yes, but for that to happen, I had to pay back a year's wages as I obviously didn't make her any money whilst working for her."

"Fuck, Leo, that's a lot of money to pay back. Couldn't the lawyers do anything about that?"

"I didn't want them to. If it was going to make me free, I was paying anything."

I pull him back into a hug. I can't believe we are free at last after all these years.

"Why didn't you phone me to let me know?"

"I'm sorry I wanted to tell you in person, to be able to see your reaction. Also, I was sorting some stuff out on the drive up here. I've put the house up for sale. I want that gone as soon as possible. I want a fresh start, a new life with you."

He kisses my lips and I feel all the tension of the last few weeks fall away from me with that one taste of him. Just as I'm wanting to drag him into the bedroom my phone starts to ring. As I pick it up from the other side of the room where I had thrown it earlier, I notice the time. Shit I'm going to be late.

"I've got to go. I'm going to be late for the show. Are you coming with me?"

"No, I won't. I really need a shower as I haven't had time for one today, what with everything. You best go I will be here waiting for you when you get back."

I'm disappointed he's not coming with me but I have no time to argue. My phone rings again this time I answer it.

"I'm on my way." I give Leo a quick kiss and run out of the door.

"Where the hell have you been?" Jack shouts, one of my band members. "And what's with that stupid grin?"

"Leo's just arrived. He's got out of the contract."

"That's great news but we've got to go."

We all hurry to the waiting cars and make our way to the stadium.

The concert goes off without a hitch and I've really enjoyed this one everything feels so different now.

Once I run off stage, I say bye to the team and exit the stadium at the back into the waiting car. As I climb into the back there is a bunch of red roses with a note attached to it. I glance at Jim and I see him smile at me. I pick them up and take out the card.

To the love of my life
Hurry back
Leo xxxx

I smile to myself, when did he do this?

"Ready to go?" Jim asks.

"Yes, definitely," I say with a big grin on my face.

It feels like the drive back to the hotel is taking forever but eventually we pull up. Jim opens the door for me, I get out not forgetting my flowers and thank him.

"Have a good night," and he winks at me. What is going on with him?

I make my way up to my room and I can't wait to see Leo.

I open the door and as I do the room is dark apart from a flickering glow coming from inside. I walk in and the sight stops me in my tracks. There are candles lit around the room, the table is set up with a white table cloth, more candles and flowers. Leo is stood by the table dressed in a pair of black skinny trousers and a black shirt. Wow, he looks hot and I feel a familiar twinge in my trousers.

"Hi, I'm glad you're back."

"What's going on?"

He makes his way over to me and my heart is beating so fast. He kisses me and I want him here and now but he just takes the flowers from my hand.

"Thanks for those by the way they are lovely."

"You are welcome. Now go and have a shower. I've put some clothes out for you to wear after."

"I don't want a shower."

"You need a shower, you've just come off stage and me and you are going to have a romantic night. I have dinner waiting for you and I'm sure you don't want to eat in your sweaty stage clothes."

"Okay, I won't be long."

He smacks my ass as I walk past him. I go into the bedroom and notice the clothes he has laid out for me. It's the shirt and jacket from our first photoshoot. I always bring this outfit with me wherever I go I like to have it with me if I want to remember good times. It makes me smile and excited as I know what he wants to do to me later.

I jump in and have a quick shower, I dry, put the clothes on without my boxers again. I have a feeling I will need a bit a freedom down there tonight. I check myself in the mirror and I'm looking good.

I walk out and Leo is putting two plates of food on the table. He pulls out a chair for me to take, I sit down and he joins me.

"You still look amazing in that outfit."

I feel myself blush.

"How did you do all this?"

"I had some help from Jim."

"It's lovely thank you."

"I wanted to do something special for us. One to say sorry for making you so worried and two, to celebrate. Now eat up before it goes cold."

We sit and eat our food and we talk about how the show went and everything that happened at the meeting. It is so good to have him back and for us to be finally free.

Chapter Twenty-Three

A new year and a new start for me and Leo. We have been living together for three weeks and it has been amazing. I love having him here with me all the time. I love waking up with him in the morning, I love going to bed with him at the end of the day and everything else in between.

We announced that we are together on our social media sites just before Christmas. We posted a picture of us together in front of our Christmas tree with the caption, 'together forever.' The response we got from it was phenomenal, especially from the fans, stating that they knew all along and that they were right from the start.

We had a huge Christmas. Everyone came to us, our families and friends, the house was full of love and laughter and that is why I bought this house for such happy times.

Whilst everyone was here, over Christmas, we asked Xander if he would mind if our first public appearance was at his film premiere. He had invited us both and we didn't want to have to go separately but we also didn't want to take the limelight away from Xander. He was absolutely thrilled for us to do that. So we are very excited to go out together for the first time ever.

"Leo, are you ready? The car will be here soon."

"I'm coming," I hear him shout from inside the bathroom.

We are staying in a hotel for Xander's film premiere and we are running late.

"Leo, come on," I shout again as he still hasn't appeared out of the bathroom.

"Okay, stop shouting."

He opens the door and walks into the lounge area and my breath is taken away. He is looking stunning in a tight fitted black suit and black shirt. His eyes meet mine and he laughs at the look on my face.

"Like what you see, Jacob?"

"You look stunning."

"See I scrub up okay. I'm not all joggers and hoodies."

I walk over to him, place my hands on his waist and pull him into me. I kiss his lips and I feel the familiar feeling inside me and I want him. Leo can feel what I'm feeling and he pulls me away.

"You were just shouting at me that we are running late. There's no time for that," he laughs at me.

"But you look so hot. I want you."

"You look hot too but you will have to wait. We've got to go."

"I'm sure Xander would understand if we don't turn up. Maybe we could stay here and I could make love to you all night?"

"No, we cannot. Now come on, we really are late."

Leo holds my hand and I follow him out of the room and down to the waiting car.

"How are you feeling?" I ask Leo.

"I'm good. A little nervous but good. You?"

"Yes, me too."

"I hope we get a good reaction?"

"I'm sure it will be fine. It's not as if it's going to be a surprise us being together."

I reach over and hold his hand. I can see that he is worried, it shows so much on his face. I lift his hand and kiss the back of it. He gives me a small smile in return.

The car slows down and the butterflies have suddenly become worse. I take a moment before I exit the car. After a deep breath and a kiss for Leo, I open the door. I am greeted with hundreds of cameras flashing and screams from the crowd that have gathered. I reach back into the car for Leo to hold my hand as I help him out of the car. When everyone see that we have arrived together they scream louder. The journalist are shouting so many questions but I can't hear them over the noise of the crowd. I squeeze Leo's hand and we make our way along the red carpet. We pause to have some photographs taken. I put my arm around Leo's waist and we smile for the cameras. We then make our way into the cinema. Before we go in we wave out to the fans that have been shouting our names, we want to acknowledge that we heard them and are grateful for their support.

Inside we meet up with Xander, he introduces us to some of the team he worked with on the movie. We then spend some time talking to Shelly, Alice and Oliver as Xander greets other people who are arriving. It is then time to go in to watch the movie.

Three hours later and the movie has finished and I am full of pride for Xander. The film was great and Xander was outstanding. He is definitely made for acting. We congratulate Xander, he seems very relieved that we like the film.

We are all going to a club to celebrate, so we head back down the red carpet into the waiting cars and head to the club.

We have been in the club for a few hours and everyone is having a great time. Leo has had quite a few drinks and has a glow on his cheeks and has started hugging everyone. He's definitely drunk. As I'm sat at our table watching Xander and

Leo laughing and joking about something, I notice a familiar figure standing at the bar. Shit, is that Ryan?

He turns around and spots me. He smirks and I can see he is coming over.

"Jacob," he says in his slimy voice. What did I ever see in him?

I don't reply. I just want him to go away before Leo spots him. He doesn't move, he just looks at me.

"What are you doing here?" he finally asks.

"Fuck off, Ryan. I don't want to speak to you."

"Well, that's not very nice. I only asked you a question."

"It's none of your business what I'm doing here."

He looks around and spots Leo and Xander.

"What's this, a group reunion?"

"Actually, we are celebrating Xander's film release. Now just fuck off."

Just as I say this, I see Leo making his way back over to me. He reaches my side and he puts his hand on my shoulder. Not looking at Ryan.

"Are you okay?"

I nod. He then looks at Ryan.

"What are you doing here?"

"It's a free country. I can be here having a drink."

"This is a private party so you can just fuck off and leave Jacob alone."

Ryan looks down at me.

"What you need your boyfriend to talk for you now, do you, Jacob? You were always such a push over."

Leo looks like he is about to attack Ryan at any minute. I put my hand on his that he still has on my shoulder to try and calm him down.

"Congratulations are in order. I saw online you two were back together. I was right all along. You didn't have to pay me all that money after all to protect him. You are such an idiot, Jacob, but thanks for it all. My life has been made so much easier living off your money."

It all happens so quickly. Leo dives at Ryan and punches him in the face and as Ryan falls to the floor, Leo tries to hit him again. I've jumped from my seat trying to grab Leo. Xander and Oliver rush over to help me get Leo off Ryan. Some other people come over and try and pull Ryan off the floor. They must know him as they are shouting his name. Leo is just uncontrollable, in the process of the three of us trying to pull him off Ryan we almost get hit by his flying punches.

Eventually, Xander and Oliver manage to get hold of Leo. Ryan's mates manage to pull him off the floor and drag him away, his face is bleeding.

"You fucking prick," he shouts at Leo. This causes Leo to try and pull away from Xander and Oliver again.

"Leo, calm down," I shout at him.

"He can't talk to you like that, Jacob."

"It's fine. He's not worth it."

I see Ryan's friends drag him out of the club.

"He's gone. Now calm down."

Xander and Oliver let him go.

"What happened?" Xander asks.

"Ryan just being a dick," I reply.

"What did you ever see in him?" Leo asks.

"Leo, I was lonely and he was someone who showed me some attention. I didn't know what was going to happen."

"Well, he's a fucking prick."

"Leo, calm down. I think I better take you back to the hotel."

"I don't want to go back. I was having a good time."

"I think you've had enough to drink. Come on, let's go."

"No, I'm not going back. Just because you can't have a drink and enjoy yourself doesn't mean you have to stop me."

What the fuck! Where did that come from?

"Hey! What's your problem?"

"Nothing, I'm getting another drink."

He storms off towards the bar.

"I'm going to go. Sorry, Xander. Congrats on the film again. I'm so proud of you." I hug him.

"Are you okay?"

"Yes. He's not going to come back with me. He's got himself wound up about Ryan. He will make his way back later. Can you keep an eye on him for me?"

"Of course. We will see you soon."

I say my byes to everyone else and before I leave, I go to Leo who is still at the bar.

"I'm going back to the hotel. I will see you later."

"Fine," he snaps at me.

A few hours later and I hear him sneak back into the room. I'm in bed and I pretend to be sleeping. I don't want to talk to him. I hear him get undresses and slip into bed beside me. I have my back towards him and I feel him move closer to me and put his arm around my waist.

"Jacob, are you awake?" he whispers.

I just ignore him. He has upset me tonight with his comment.

"I'm so sorry."

I wake up early. It's still dark outside. Leo is sleeping so I quietly get out of bed. I don't want to wake him yet. I make my way out into the lounge area and close the bedroom door behind me. I put the kettle on to make a cup of tea and I want to see what has been said about us last on social media.

I take my tea and make myself comfortable on the sofa. I open my phone and there is lots of love for us from the film premier from our fans. There are also some articles from the press and they are all mainly positive. There is also a lot of love for Xander's film which makes me happy. Just as I'm about to close everything down a new headline pops up. 'Jacob Adams lover's fight for him.' Shit it's about Leo in the club. Someone got a photograph of Leo fighting with Ryan. I can't believe it. It says that Leo attacked Ryan when the three of us were talking. It then says that I left the club alone and they insinuated that I had gone to the aid of Ryan and left Leo in the club by himself. Leo will be fuming but that's what happens when you lose you temper.

As I'm sat there looking to see if anything else has been written online about it, I hear the bedroom door open. I'm sat with me back to the door and I don't look around at him but I hear him walking over to me. He stands behind the sofa puts his arms around me and kisses the top of my head.

"Good morning," he says quietly.

"Morning," I reply without looking at him.

He leans over my shoulder to see what I'm looking at. I purposely pull up the article about the fight.

"Shit. It's online?"

He continues to read it, leaning over to move the article up so he can read more of it. He gets to the part where they said I went to see Ryan after leaving Leo in the club. I wait for his reaction but he doesn't say anything.

He finishes it and stands up from leaning over me and walks around the sofa and sits next to me.

"I'm so sorry, Jacob. I didn't mean what I said to you. Ryan just got me so wound up."

I don't say anything, his comment really hurt me.

"Jacob, look at me."

I turn my head to look at him.

"You have to believe how sorry I am."

"There was no need to talk to me like that."

"I know. I really ruined the night."

He pauses for a while.

"Please tell me that the article isn't true. You didn't go and see Ryan after you left the club, did you?"

"Are you fucking seriously asking me that?" I raise my voice. I can't believe him sometimes.

"Sorry. I know you didn't."

"No, I didn't." I'm so pissed off with him.

"I'm sorry."

We sit in silence for a bit. I can feel him glancing over at me.

"I'm going to have a shower."

I stand up and make my way back into the bedroom. I throw off my joggers and t-shirt and get into the shower letting the warm water run over me. I stand there with my eyes closed when I feel Leo's hands run down my back, it makes me jump. He wraps his arms around my waist and I feel his forehead rest on the back of my shoulder.

"I'm so sorry," he whispers.

I hold on to his hands which are resting on my stomach. He starts placing kisses across my shoulder blades. As he does I don't want to fight any more I just want to forgive him. I turn around in his arms.

"I'm so sorry, Jacob. I didn't mean any of what I said. I'm sorry I hit Ryan too but he did deserve it. I hate what he did to you."

"I know but I didn't like what you said to me and you really need to control your temper."

"You're right but he made me so mad but I shouldn't have taken it out on you."

I lean in and kiss him running my tongue along his lips. He opens his mouth and my tongue searches for his as I kiss him deep and hard. Leo runs his hands up and down my back as my hands finger his wet hair.

"I love you," he says into my mouth and I let out a moan at his words and his touch.

We have been back on tour for a while and we only have a few shows left to do. Leo is travelling with me and it is so different this time as there is no more hiding or sneaking around which is great but I have noticed Leo's moods seem to be like a roller coaster. He tries to hide it when he is feeling down but I can see it. When he smiles or laughs it doesn't reach his eyes. I wonder if touring with me and not doing anything for himself is getting too much. I wish he would do something for himself.

We are back home. It is only for a couple of days but it's always nice to be here. Even Leo's mood has lifted since we have been back. He seems much happier when we are home just the two of us. When we are here we are just a normal domesticated couple and not famous pop stars. I think Leo really enjoys this side of us. I need to talk to him about how he is feeling about touring with me and what he would like to do for himself in the future. Especially now, as there have been a few articles written about how sad he's been looking at the concerts and the media have been giving him some stick about how he just follows me around and doesn't do anything for himself.

We are sat eating dinner and Leo seems to be in a fairly good mood so I decide this is the perfect opportunity to bring it up.

"Leo, I've been wondering something?"

He stops eating and looks over to me.

"What is it?"

"Are you happy touring with me?"

"Yes. Why do you ask that?"

"You haven't really seemed happy lately. I know you have been hiding it but I can see you are unhappy at times."

"No, I'm fine."

"I'm worried that just following me around is not fulfilling you. You seem happy when we are home together but when we are touring your moods are up and down."

"Well, I'm sorry I'm not happy all the time like you are." He is starting to get annoyed and that's not what I wanted.

"That's not what I'm saying. I don't want you to feel you have to come with me all the time. There must be something you want to do. Why don't you start writing again?"

"I don't want to start fucking writing again."

"Okay, well maybe you want to do something else?" I try and keep my voice calm.

"Jacob, just fucking leave it. I'm fine."

He pushes his plate away.

"Are you not finishing that?"

"No, I've lost my appetite."

"Leo, I'm sorry. I just don't think you are happy."

"Fucking hell, Jacob. Would you just leave it?"

He stands up and storms out of the kitchen.

That didn't go as I had planned. I clean up the kitchen, thinking Leo just needs some time alone to calm down. After I'm done I go and look for him. He is nowhere downstairs so I go to see if he is up in our bedroom but he's not there either. I look in one of the spare bedrooms where I find him sat on the bed scrolling through his phone.

"Why are you in here?"

"I just need some space."

"I didn't mean to upset you. I just want you to be happy."

"I am happy."

"I don't think you are."

"I am," he shouts.

"Okay."

"I know what the media have been saying about me, Jacob. I've seen the articles saying that I just follow you around with nothing else to do. I just didn't think you felt like that too. Just leave me alone."

"Leo, come on, don't be like this. Come to bed with me."

"No, Jacob just go away."

"Look we leave for Liverpool early tomorrow let's not be like this on our last night home for a while."

"You brought it up. It's your fault. Just go away."

"Please, Leo."

"No, I'm pissed off with you."

"Fine."

"Good."

I walk out of the room slamming the door behind me.

I haven't slept at all. I could hear Leo walking around the house until late. I didn't go to see if he was okay and he didn't come into me either. I hope when I see him this morning he is in a better mood. As I really don't need this, I have a busy day of rehearsal before the show tomorrow night.

I have a shower and throw on some comfortable clothes for travelling and make my way down to the kitchen to grab a quick bite to eat before setting off. Leo is not down here. I eat my breakfast quick and go to find him as the car will be here soon. I find him still in bed not even ready to leave.

"Why aren't you ready? I want to leave soon."

"I'm not coming."

"Why?"

"You obviously don't want me there so I'm not coming. We seem to be back to how it was before, you telling me what we should and shouldn't be doing."

"What! No I'm not."

"Yes, you are. You want me to move in, you want me to tour with you. Now you want me to find something to do."

"But you wanted to move in and come on tour and I just wanted you to know if you wanted to do something then you could."

"Well, I am. I'm not coming on tour with you," he snaps.

"Leo, please I do want you there."

"Well to bad. I'm not going. You better hurry up you will be late."

"Leo, please."

"No, just go."

I can feel the tears welling up in my eyes. I don't want to leave when he's like this.

"Leo, please come to Liverpool, if not now come tomorrow to see the show."

"Jacob, I won't be coming to any more shows. Now you've got to go as you will be late."

"What! You're not coming to any of my last shows."

"No."

My phone is ringing. It's Jim to let me know he is here.

"I've got to go. I will phone you later. Please think about coming tomorrow."

I go over to kiss him goodbye but as I do he moves away.

"Leo." I'm heartbroken and the tears I've been holding back flow down my face. He looks at me with those glorious eyes and they are full of sadness.

My phone rings again.

"You've got to go," he says and looks away.

I know the conversation is over he won't say anything else now I can tell. So I leave the room, I grab my bag from our bedroom and head out of the door. Jim is waiting to take my bags.

"Where's Leo?" he asks.

"He's not coming," I reply sadly. Jim gives me a look but doesn't say anything.

On the drive, I text Leo but he doesn't reply. I can feel the fog coming over me.

We arrive at the hotel and I check in. Jim informs me that he will be here in two hours to take me to the stadium for the rehearsal.

I spend the next two hours in my room texting and phoning Leo but he still won't talk to me. The fog is getting heavier.

My phone rings and I grab it quickly hoping its Leo but it's Jim to tell me he is waiting for me.

The rehearsal is the worst I have ever done. No one says anything but I know in myself that it was. I basically walked through it in a daze.

When I'm back in the hotel room I phone room service for them to bring a bottle of vodka and some bottles of lager up to my room.

When it arrives, I pour a glass and the first taste burns my throat as I swallow it. The second and third feel the same but the more I drink the better it feels. I pour another glass and I feel the fog lifting through the alcohol. I then have a bottle of lager and another glass of vodka. I'm now feeling brave so I dial Leo's number. As expected it goes to answer phone.

"Leo," I slur down the phone, "you don't have to come to my concerts if you don't want to. Just stay at home and be boring. I will look after you and support you. You obviously like being a kept man. I don't know when I will see you next as I'm not coming home for ages. By the way the vodka is going down a treat." I hang up the phone.

I return to drinking what is left.

What's that banging? Is it in my head? That feels like its banging. No, it's not my head.

Thank god it's stopped. Back to sleep.

"Jacob, Jacob. What the fuck have you done?"

Now what. Who is shouting?

"Jacob, wake up. For fuck sake, why?"

Someone is shaking me. Shit, I feel like I'm going to be sick stop shaking me. No, I am going to be sick. I lean over the edge of the sofa I'm lying on and throw up.

"Fucking hell, Jacob, that was nearly all over me."

I open my eyes. There he is, my Leo. He's come back to me.

"Leo," I say very quietly and I'm going to be sick again. I lean over and throw up on the floor again.

"Well, it's better out than in I suppose," I hear him say. I feel his hand running through my hair moving it out of my face. Where am I, what has happened?

"Jacob, are you okay?" I hear Leo's voice, he sounds worried.

I shake my head but wish I didn't I feel awful.

I feel Leo move off the sofa. Now where are you going, don't leave me.

"Don't leave me," I say out aloud.

"I'm not leaving you. Here drink this." He hands me a glass of water.

"Leo, don't ever leave me."

He pulls me into him and wraps his arms around me and hugs me tight.

"I'm never going to leave you again."

"But you did and you don't want to be with me now," I cry into his chest.

"Jacob, I do want to be with you I was just mad with you and myself. And I promise I will never leave you again. You have to believe me."

I continue to cry into his chest. After a while I look up into to amazing eyes they are now filled with concern.

"Why are you here now?"

"The last message you left me got me so worried. You were slurring your words so I knew you had a lot to drink and you said that it was going down a treat so I knew you were going to carry on drinking, I was so worried what you would do to yourself so I jumped straight into the car and drove here. But I was too late to stop you drinking again. I should have been here and you would have never had a drink."

He lays me back onto the sofa and gets up.

"Where are you going?"

"I'm going to phone down to reception to see if we can have a different room and I will tell them about the mess you have made on the carpet. That's going to be a big cleaning bill for you, Mr Adams."

I see him on the phone but I can't really hear what he is saying. He hangs up and goes into the bedroom, throws all my stuff into a bag. He throws it over his shoulder.

"I will be back in a minute, you stay there and drink that water."

"Where are you going?"

"I'm going to get the key for the new room. I won't be long."

I take a sip of the water and watch him go out of the door. I close my eyes and the realisation of what I have done comes over me. I did it again. I had done so well and then when Leo pulls away from me and I can't cope, look what happens. I can't help but cry, the tears stream down my face. Leo comes back into the room.

"Hey, what's the matter?"

He rushes over to me and sits on the sofa next to me. He wipes away my tears from my cheeks.

"I can't believe I did it again. I hate when you pull away from me and don't talk to me about things. Then you ignored all my calls and I thought you were leaving me again." I drop my head.

"Jacob, come on, let me take you to the new room, get you showered and changed and then we can have a talk. Come on, let's get you sorted."

He helps me up off the sofa and I stumble as I still have the effects of the drink still in me. He makes sure there is no one around, the fewer people who know about this the better. When he is sure no one is there he takes me to the new room which is just down the corridor. Inside he guides me to the bathroom. He leans me against the wall and turns the shower on, then he removes my t-shirt and joggers followed by his own clothes and gets us both in the shower. I am holding on to him so tight, as I feel wobbly on my feet. He lets the water run over us both then he proceeds to wash my hair and my body. I look into his eyes and I can see they are full of love and care. I give him a small smile. He smiles back at me and I realise how grateful I am for him.

He turns the shower off and wraps me tightly in a fluffy towel. He throws one around his waist. He gets me out of the shower and dries me off.

"You need to brush your teeth, your breath is not good," he laughs and I give him a small smile back feeling a little embarrassed.

I brush my teeth and he takes me into the bedroom, sits me on the bed as he grabs some clothes out of the bag and puts them on me. He finally gets me into bed. Once he knows I'm settled. He dries himself and puts his clothes back on.

"You need to eat something. It will make you feel better."

He leaves the bedroom and he is on the phone again.

"I've ordered you some food, it will be here soon."

He comes and lays on the bed next to me.

"Do you think you will be able to perform or shall I get them to cancel?"

"No, don't cancel it. I don't want to let the fans down."

"But are you going to be okay?"

"I will have to be."

We sit in silence for a bit then there's a knock on the door. It's room service. Leo brings in the plate of food. Its toast, egg and avocado. He then goes to make us both a cup of tea. He places mine on the bedside table.

"Jacob, you need to eat that, drink your tea and then sleep for a few hours if you want to perform later tonight."

I wonder what the time is but I don't have my phone to check. As if he reads my mind, he says, "Its three in the morning. You have plenty of time to rest."

I eat some of the food but my stomach is feeling too delicate to eat much, although, I do enjoy the tea.

When Leo is satisfied that I have ate and drank as much as I am able, he says, "You need to sleep."

"You said we could talk once I was sorted."

"Yes, but I need you to rest."

"I want to talk."

"Okay but then you need to sleep."

I nod but don't say anything. He looks at me and he knows I'm waiting for him to start.

"You were right," he finally says.

"About what? You leaving me."

"No, Jacob. I've told you time and time again I'm never leaving you ever again. You are my world but you were right about the fact that I haven't been totally happy. I love being on tour with you and I have immense pride when I see you on stage but maybe deep down I do miss being out there. I miss being in the group, I miss writing and recording. But with all I've gone through I don't have any confidence to do any of it on my own. I don't know if I could do it even if the group was to ever get back together again. And this got me down at times. I thought I hid it well but I didn't. You noticed, then the fans noticed and so did the press. My bad acting coming out again. I hated reading the press reports as they had it spot on to how I was feeling."

"Why didn't you talk to me about it?"

"I don't know. You are so happy when you are touring and I didn't want to spoil it for you."

"Leo, we are a team. We need to work through things together."

"Yes, we do and you do too. We can't have another incident like this. I can't lose you."

His eyes tear up. I hate myself for hurting the people I love when I do this to myself.

"I'm sorry but I tried to talk to you about it as I felt it coming over me but you didn't answer your phone and the fog just descended more and I couldn't stop it."

We are both now crying. We pull each other into a hug. Holding each other tight. When we release, we look into our eyes.

"We both have to promise from now on we talk to each other and I promise I will never not answer my phone."

"Why was you phone off any way?"

"Like I said, I was mad at you and at myself. I just needed to shut myself away and think about what I wanted to do. I went into the studio and I did start writing some songs. I don't think I ever want to sing them myself but I really enjoyed writing them. I couldn't wait to tell you what I had been doing. I was going to come here today. I wouldn't never want to come and see you perform. I came out of the studio and switched my phone on to let you know I was coming. I saw all your missed calls and listened to your messages and suddenly, with the last one, my world stopped turning."

I see worry etched on his face.

"I'm sorry," I say to him.

"I'm sorry too for not telling you how I felt."

"I'm so glad you want to write again. You are so good at it."

"I wrote a song for you, maybe for your next album."

"I can't wait to hear it."

"Now you need some sleep if you are going to be in any fit state to perform later."

Leo gets under the covers with me, I slide further into bed and turn on my side. Leo moves closer to me and wraps his arms around me and he is running his hand through my hair as I fall to sleep.

Chapter Twenty-Four

It's the last night of my solo tour. It has been one hell of an experience. We are doing my last show in Manchester so I am in front of my home crowd and I have invited everyone to be here with me. Xander, Shelly, Alice and Oliver have travelled up from London. Mia and George are here. As are my mum and dad. It is hopefully going to be an amazing show.

Everyone has gathered in the VIP boxes and I'm ready to go on stage with the band. We are all in great moods, although, I have noticed Leo seems to be a bit off tonight. Before I said bye to him, he seemed a bit nervous about something. I hope he's okay. I will make sure we talk it over after the show but first I have a job to do.

Again, the band goes onto the stage first and I hear the crowd go wild. I wait a little while, then the music starts and it is time to go on. There are no nerves any more, there is only pure enjoyment.

The crowd scream as I start singing the first song. Looking up to the VIP boxes I can see all my family and friends singing along too. I am about to sing 'Far Away' when I do a quick glance up to Leo but I can't see him anywhere. Where is he? This is his favourite song. I'm starting to get a little concerned by his behaviour today. I have no time to dwell on it as the band starts up and I need to keep going.

As I knew would happen, the fans now know all the words to this song and they join in as I start singing but when I'm half way through the song the crowd start screaming really loud. This hasn't happened before, then I notice that they are screaming Leo's name. I look up to the box he was in but he's not there. I then hear his voice singing along with mine. I stop dead and look around the stage, I can no longer sing as I see him walking towards me. He is singing as he moves closer to me. He looks amazing he has changed into a suit. I am so confused with what is going on. We never discussed him coming on stage to sing with me and I'm surprised by it as he's said he never had the confidence to sing on stage again.

He finally stands next to me smiling his biggest smile. He puts his hand on the small of my back and encourages me to carry on singing with him. I look up at everyone else and they all have big grins on their faces too. What is going on? I manage to get to the end of the song.

I look at Leo; he is still smiling. I just don't know what to say or do. Leo then starts talking to the crowd, who haven't stop screaming since Leo came on the stage.

"Hello, everyone. I'm Leo. If you didn't know." He laughs as the crowd scream at him.

"Sorry for disrupting your show, but I have something important to ask Jacob. So, I hope you don't mind if I borrow him for a minute. You will have him back singing to you in just a bit."

Leo looks at me and I stare back at him in total bemusement. He laughs at me.

"Now Jacob has no idea what is going on as you can see by the look on his face."

The crowd laughs.

"If I could have some silence, I want to ask Jacob something."

The stadium falls silent.

His eyes are back on me. I really don't know what is happening until he gets down on one knee in front of me pulling something out of his inside suit pocket.

Oh my god is he going to propose right here, right now. I am now a total nervous wreck. I start to panic, I know we have discussed that one day we would get married but not to the extent that we would do it so soon. Is it too soon?

Leo starts speaking and it snaps me out of it.

"Jacob. We have been through so much. So many downs but also lots of ups. I have loved you since we first met at our audition right here in your home town."

The crowd screams again and quietens down straight away.

"I want to be with you forever. We always said that when we could, we would tell the whole world that we are together. Well, today I am doing that. I want the whole world to know that you are mine and I am yours."

My heart is pounding so hard I'm sure the whole place can hear it. But I am lost in Leo's eyes, it is as if it's just me and him and all those worries that I was just feeling melt away with every word he says.

"Jacob, will you marry me?"

He opens the ring box and inside is a ring with two coloured metal bands, one inside the other and two small diamonds set in the inner band. It's simple but beautiful. I look at the ring then into Leo's sparkling brown eyes that are pleading me to say yes.

I hold out my hand to help him up off his knees. I pull him into me.

"Yes, I would love to marry you."

He kisses me deep and lovingly and the crowd erupts in the biggest cheer I have ever heard. Leo hugs me so tight and whispers in my ear, "Thank you."

He pulls away, takes the ring out of the box and he places it on my finger, he then places a kiss on top of it.

I'm just speechless, I just don't know what to do, am I just supposed to carry on with the show after that. I need to take a minute. I need to leave the stage to compose myself.

I still haven't said anything or moved so Leo starts talking to the crowd again.

"Thank you for letting me have my moment. Thank you, Jacob, for thankfully saying yes. Now I will let you all get back to enjoying my wonderful fiancé."

He turns to me looking a little concern as I haven't said anything. "Are you okay?"

I nod but I need to take five minutes before I start again. I finally find my voice and I turn to the crowd.

"You are all going to have to give me five minutes to pull myself together. I'm a bit emotional and in shock. I will be back out in just a bit."

I hold Leo's hand and I leave the stage. Leo is still looking concerned.

Once off the stage I take a few deep breaths.

"Jacob, are you sure you are okay?"

I pull him into me and kiss him so passionately. He wraps his arms around me and I can feel the tension release from him. I think I worried him for a second.

"I love you so much. That was the most romantic and special moment of my life. Thank you."

I can see he has tears in his eyes.

"I was worried for a second, I thought that you wished I hadn't done it like that. But I just wanted everyone to know how much I love you."

"No, it was the best way you could have done it. I was just a little taken back. I didn't have a clue. I assume everyone else knew about it?"

He nods at me with a lopsided smile as if to say sorry we had been sneaking around hiding things from me.

"You better get back out there and finish the show or you are not going to have very happy fans."

"They will be fine for a minute more, they have just witness something amazing and unique tonight. I just want one more kiss from my perfect fiancé."

I grab hold of his suit lapels and pull him into me, lips locking together as they were meant to be.

The rest of the show goes by in a daze, it feels like I'm floating over the stage. It is a whole different atmosphere in here since Leo's proposal. The crowd are just super hyped, more so than normal and my performance has gone through the roof.

Leo has re-joined everyone in the box and they look like they are having the time of their lives too.

Once the show is over, I make my way back to my dressing room and I'm surprised to see Leo is waiting for me.

"You were amazing the best you've ever been."

"I had some extra adrenaline tonight."

"Get in the shower. I brought you a suit to change into then we are off to have a party to celebrate our engagement."

"Leo. When did you organise all this?"

"I had lots of help from everyone. But I had to do it when you were at rehearsal and lots of sneaky phone calls and conversations when you were occupied doing something else. It wasn't easy. Come on, get ready everyone is waiting."

We are in the car on our way to the party. I don't know where it is being held as Leo said that it's a surprise. I keep looking out of the window trying to guess where we might be going. Jim turns the car round a corner and I recognise the hotel we are pulling up to. It's the one where we first met at the audition.

I look over at Leo. "Is it here?"

He nods. He has thought of everything.

Jim stops the car outside the hotel entrance, he gets out and opens the door for us.

"Thanks, Jim. We will see you inside," Leo says. He nods his head and gets back into the car. "I have given him the rest of the night off, so Jim and his wife can join in the celebrations with us. We are staying here tonight. I've booked the honeymoon suite."

We walk towards the entrance and there are a few fans and photographers waiting outside. How do they know we would be here? I'm amazed how they know things before even I do.

Leo holds my hand as we say hi to the fans and let them have a few photographs then he takes me inside the hotel. As soon as I walk through the doors a million memories flood back to me. I can't believe I'm back in the place we first met.

Leo is watching my every move and I can see he is feeling emotional too.

"Come on, everyone is waiting for us."

He leads me to one of the ballrooms and as soon as he opens the door we are greeted with cheers and clapping. The room is amazing, decorated all in black and gold.

Mum and Dad are the first ones to come over to us. They both hug us.

"Congratulations you two. We are so happy you got your fairy-tale ending. We are so proud of you both," Mum says to us both.

Then Leo's mum, Mark and Tessa come over.

"Why didn't you come to the show?" I ask them after I have hugged them.

"Leo thought if too many of us were there, then you would have definitely guessed something was going on," Penny answered.

"Thank you for coming and thank you for this wonderful boy you brought into this world for me to find and fall in love with."

"You're very welcome, Jacob, and we are so pleased you are in his life too."

Penny hugs me tight, then she hugs her son and I can see there are tears in both of their eyes.

We then make our way over to where Xander, Shelly, Alice and Oliver are standing, they all hug and congratulate us.

"Welcome to the married peoples club," Xander laughs at us.

"Who would have thought that eight years since we first met here that we would be stood in the same place all of us married or nearly married," Alice says with tears glistening in her eyes.

"I am just so happy that we are finally all happy together. We had to put up with some awful things," I say to everyone as Leo grabs my hand and squeezes it. I look around at him and add, "But we made it through and it has made our love and bond as friends, no not just friends, family stronger. I hope in a few years' time, when we've all settled down and finished having our families that we can reform UsFour again."

"Definitely," Xander says, "I would say let's give ourselves five years and we will meet back here and reform in the place where we were first made. What do you all say to that?"

"Yes, that sounds like a plan," I say.

All four of us put our hands in the middle, one on top of each other, just as we did when we were about to go on stage and we shout, "UsFour."

We say it a bit louder than we thought and everyone else turns around and stares at us.

The rest of the evening is spectacular. Leo has invited so many people that we love and who we haven't seen for so long. I've enjoyed talking to them all but now I am utterly exhausted, emotionally and physically. I just want to go up to our hotel room, make love to my beautiful fiancé and fall to sleep in his arms.

We say our goodbyes to everyone and make our way up to our room. Once inside I pull Leo into my arms.

"Thank you for tonight. It was amazing. And thank you for asking me to be your husband. I can't wait to marry you."

"You are welcome. I can't wait to marry you either. I have one more surprise for you before I'm taking you into that bedroom and making love to you."

"What else can there be, you've surprised me so much already?"

Leo reaches into his suit jacket pocket again and pulls out an envelope and hands it to me.

I open it, inside is a piece of paper with a holiday itinerary on it.

"I'm taking you away. You have been working so hard and you need a rest. We are going to Greece for a two week break just me and you."

"Oh, Leo you've already done so much but that will be amazing."

I can't wait any longer, I need to have him now. I grab his hand and pull him into the bedroom, Leo laughing the whole time. I throw him on the bed and I can't contain myself any more.

We are back from our two weeks away in Greece and it was so special. We had our own private villa and beach. We just spent the whole time relaxing, eating and being together. It was just what we needed after the manic few months of tour.

We talked lots about what we would like to do for our wedding whilst we were away and once we got back we started our search.

I knew Leo would love planning our wedding, he is so excited about everything we look at.

Xander, Shelly, Alice and Oliver are travelling up to us tonight to have a celebration meal. Leo has been cooking up a storm in the kitchen and the house is full of wonderful smells. I have been pottering around the house, getting the guest bedrooms organised for them to stay in. I have tidied the rest of the house and I have set the dining table ready for dinner later. Once I have finished, I join Leo in the kitchen. He is busy checking something in the oven and he is bending over and his trousers are tight around his ass, I feel a twinge in my trousers. He turns around and he has a rosy glow on his face from the heat and his hair is messy from being so busy. I stand in the doorway just watching the hot mess he is. He catches me staring.

"Like what you see, haven't you got anything to do?"

"Yes," I give him a cheeky smile, "I would like to do you."

"Jacob!"

I walk over to him, "Have you got time for me?"

I can see him blushing. I wrap my arms around his waist pulling him close to me. I kiss his lips and feel him relax in my arms.

"I might do," he replies.

That's all I need to hear. I kiss him deep and can't wait to taste his mouth. He lets me in and I search for his tongue. I push my hips towards him and I can feel we are both excited. I put my hand down his trousers and he takes a deep breath then he moans as I move my hand. He pulls at my hair as I continue to kiss him hard. I feel his legs becoming week so I lower us both onto the kitchen floor and this is where we end up making love.

We are sat leaning against the kitchen cabinets. Leo looks absolutely beat, what with cooking and our time together. He still has his eyes closed, I lean over and kiss his lips. He slowly opens his eyes and gives me a smile.

"I love you," he says quietly.

"I love you too. We best get ourselves sorted they will all be here soon and you better have a shower before you finish dinner."

"I can't you've taken the last of my energy from me."

I stand up and sort myself out a bit and I go to the wine fridge, which is normally empty but we did get some wine in for everyone else this evening. I open a bottle and pour Leo a glass.

"Here see if this helps to perk you up."

He takes a slow sip of the wine.

"That's good."

"I'm going up to have a shower and change. I will see you up there when you've recovered." I give him a wink and make my way upstairs.

Two hours later and they have arrived and we are all in the kitchen catching up with each other, whilst Leo is putting the finishing touches to the dinner. I notice that Shelly or Alice are not drinking I wonder if they have any news for us.

We sit down for dinner, which is delicious. Leo is such a great cook. The conversation is flowing when Xander says, "We have some news."

We all look at Xander and Shelly, was I right?

"What is it?" Alice asks excitedly.

"We are expecting another baby."

"Oh my god, so am I," Alice blurts out.

We are all shocked and so happy. We get up the food abandon and hug everyone.

"I can't believe we are pregnant at the same time," Alice announces as we all sit back down.

"How far along are you?" Shelly asks Alice.

"Four months, you?"

"Me too. They are going to be born at the same time."

I watch our friends celebrating their wonderful joint news and I'm overwhelmed with emotion. I feel Leo hold my hand. I look at him.

"I can't wait until we have a baby," he says.

"One thing at a time. Let's get married first."

"Seriously though could we look in to finding a surrogate as soon as we are married. I would love our child to grow up with Xander and Alice's children."

I see the emotion and longing in his eyes.

"Are you sure you want a child so soon after we get married. Don't you want to work on our music for a bit longer?"

"No, I want to be a Dad and I want you to be a Dad too. You would make an amazing one."

Leo would make an amazing dad too but is it too soon. What about work? I love my music and wouldn't having a child now stop me from doing that. I do want children but do I want them yet? I look over at Xander and Alice they are so happy. Xander and Shelly have continued working after they had Molly. Could I do it too?

I feel Leo squeeze my hand.

"Hey, you okay?" he asks gently.

"Yes. I was just thinking about how it would work if we were to have a baby."

"Jacob, I would never stop you from doing your music. I know it's your passion and it always has been and always will be. We would work this out together. I could just stick to writing which I can do from home or with you on the road and I would look after our child when you were working."

"Would you be happy doing that? Wouldn't you miss singing?"

"It was never my passion. I haven't told anyone this but when I went to the audition for the group, I went because Mark saw the article and said I had a good singing voice and that I should try it. So, I went for a laugh, a day out away from London. I didn't think any of this would happen to me. I never wanted it, unlike you, Alice and Xander, this is what you've always wanted to do."

I'm shocked by his confession. Singing isn't his passion but he's so good at it. It makes me feel a little sad that he has done this job for so long and it wasn't what he really wanted to do.

"Why didn't you ever tell me? Leo, what was your passion, what did you want to do?"

"I didn't know. I was young and didn't really have any idea of what I wanted to do with my life. I was grateful to get into the group it gave me a future that I didn't see. And, of course, I met you and every day I'm thankful that I did go to that audition joke or no joke."

I lean over and kiss him.

"What is your passion now, what do you see happening in the future for you?"

"I want to build our family and be the best husband and dad I could ever be. My dad wasn't around and I don't want that to happen to my child. I also love writing. I did in the group. I found a love for it that I didn't know I had and I would be happy to write for you or anyone else."

I look into his eyes and I can see our future reflecting back at me and I know that we could make this work.

"Leo, let's do it."

"What are you serious?"

"Yes, as soon as we are married, let's start trying for a baby."

"Jacob. That's amazing."

He pulls me into the biggest hug ever, I am so pleased I have made him this happy. I can see everyone else is now looking at us.

"What just happened?" Xander asks.

"We've just decided we are going to have a baby too," Leo says very excitedly.

"Not until after the wedding," I add touching Leo's hand to try and calm him down but I love that he is so excited.

"That's great," Xander says.

"We will have to have our own travelling nursery with us if we get the group back together with all these babies," Alice laughs.

"Anyway, enough baby talk. How are the wedding plans going? Have you set a date yet?" Shelly asks.

"Well, after today's announcements, I think we will pick the date after you two have given birth as we would like you both to be our bridesmaids. If you would like to?"

"Yes, I would love to," Alice screams. She jumps up and runs around the table to hug us both.

Once Alice has let us both go, I look over at Shelly.

"I would be honoured to be your bridesmaid, thank you."

I can see she is tearing up and Xander wraps his arm around her and kisses the side of her head.

"Now then for you two," I say, looking at Oliver and Xander.

"Oliver, we would love it if you would be one of our groomsman?"

"That would be great, thanks. But you didn't have to include me."

"Yes, we did. You helped me out when I was going through a very rough time. You put up with me stealing Alice all the time and I want you stood up there with the rest of us. You are part of this family too I'm afraid."

"Then yes, I would love too, thank you for asking."

I then look at Xander.

"Xander you have been by my side through everything. The good and all the crap and I would be honoured if you would be my best man?"

Xander looks a little taken aback but a huge smile suddenly appears across his face.

"Yes," is all he can say. I get up from the table and go around and hug him.

"Who is going to be your best man, Leo?" Alice asks.

"My brother Mark. I'm going to ask him next weekend when we visit my family."

"So is that all the wedding party?" Xander asks.

"No, Jacob wants Jack from the band to be a groomsman with Oliver and we would love little Molly to be our flower girl?"

"That's so lovely. Thank you," Shelly answers.

We spend the rest of the evening discussing different things about the wedding and this has made it feel so real and exciting.

Chapter Twenty-Five

Our wedding is here. Leo is driving us to the wedding venue and I'm sitting in the passenger seat thinking back over everything that has happened this past year.

Alice and Oliver had their baby first, a little boy they named Oscar. They have taken to being parents really well.

Three days later, Xander and Shelly had their baby, a little girl called Evelyn. They are both precious little things. Thankfully, Molly dotes on her new sister which we are all grateful for. Xander and Shelly love having the two girls but they do look exhausted every time I see them.

Me and Leo have looked into surrogacy for us to have a baby after the wedding. We have decided that Leo will be the biological father and we will use an egg donor with similar features to myself so hopefully the baby will look like the both of us. We are both really excited to start our journey.

Not only did we have all the great baby news, I also released a new album. Me and Leo wrote it together so this meant he could come and promote it with me. I could actually have him at the interviews with me because I'm not that keen on doing them on my own. The album did amazingly and the fans are still as supportive as always but more so because they know Leo wrote it with me.

The rest of the time we have been busy organising the wedding, which has been so much fun. Hopefully, everything will fall into place tomorrow.

I look over at Leo and I can't believe this day has finally arrived what with everything we have been through. At one point, I thought this would never happen. I keep staring at him.

"Stop staring at me," Leo says without looking around at me.

"I can't help it. This will be the last day I get to see you as a single man. Tomorrow you will be my husband. I'm taking it all in."

He smiles a huge smile but still doesn't take his eyes off the road, he just moves his hand and rubs my leg.

"I love you."

"I love you too," I reply.

He pulls up to the venue, this is it, the next time we are in the car we will be married. We both get out of the car, we hold hands, Leo gives mine a squeeze and we make our way into the venue.

We are greeted by our wedding planner Julie. She shakes Leo's hand and goes to shake mine but I reach in for a hug, we have got to know Julie really well.

"How's everything going?" Leo asks.

"Everything is nearly set up come and have a look."

We follow Julie into the magnificent stately home, we fell in love with this place the first time we saw it. It's big enough to accommodate all our guest but still has an intimate feel to it.

As we enter there is white flowers and green foliage on ever surface, it looks spectacular. We follow her into the area where we will be having the reception and it takes my breath away. The room is full of round tables covered in white table cloths, each table is surrounded with black chairs. On the centre of each table is a magnificent display of white flowers. Around the room there are so many flower displays and candles. It all looks stunning. It's just how I pictured it in my head. I turn and look at Leo.

"What do you think?"

He squeezes my hand.

"It's amazing. It's just how we wanted it."

"I'm so glad you both like it," Julie adds.

"It's perfect, Julie. Thank you. Can we see the room where we are getting married?" I ask.

"Yes, sure."

Again, we follow her through the house and arrive at another room, she opens the door and we step inside and again I am taken back. There are rows of black chairs with an aisle down the centre. White flowers and candles all around the room. And all of a sudden, I'm overcome with emotion and tears well up in my eyes. I feel Leo watching me, he notices that I'm getting emotional.

"What's the matter, Jacob?"

He pulls me into him and wraps his arms around my waist and his eyes are on mine.

"Nothing. These are happy tears. I'm just feeling a bit emotional. This is where you become mine forever."

Leo pulls me even closer and holds me tight. I rest my head on his shoulder as I wrap my arms around his waist. Leo runs his hand through my hair as I release the tears I was trying to hold back.

When I settle down, he brings my head up to his and places a loving kiss on my lips.

"I love you," he says.

"I love you too," and I kiss him again.

I am then aware that this moment was witnessed by Julie and I become a little embarrassed but as we break apart, I notice that Julie has moved herself outside. We leave the room and find her waiting by the stairs.

"I thought you two needed a moment. Do you like the room?"

"Yes, we love it, Julie. Thank you again," I say to her.

"Great. There are a few more bits to sort out but apart from that we are ready for tomorrow. We've set a room aside for your meal later today with your family but until then you are free. I will get someone to get your bags from the car and take them to your rooms. Now, Jacob, you are staying in the wedding suite, is that right?"

"Yes, Leo insisted that I stay in that one. I wanted us both to stay in it but our mums said we weren't allowed to see each other the morning of the wedding."

Leo looks at me and shrugs his shoulders, we both wanted to spend tonight together but our mums were not having it.

"Okay. I will show you up to your rooms."

We follow her up the stairs, she stops outside the first door we get to.

"This is the wedding suite."

She opens the door, she stands to the side and me and Leo walk in. The room is lovey. There's a big four poster bed and a free-standing bath on the other side of the room in front of large window with views over the acers of garden.

"I'm going to be so lost in that bed tonight," I say to Leo.

We then follow Julie a little way along the landing to the next room, which is also lovely but much smaller and it makes me sad that Leo will be sleeping in here on his own.

"I'm going to leave you for a while to sort some bits out and keep a look out for your family when they arrive. Feel free to explore."

When Julie leaves, I need to feel Leo's touch. I pull him into me and instantly his arms are around my waist.

"What is it, Jacob?" He can always tell when something is bothering me.

"I don't like the fact that we are spending the night before our wedding apart."

"I know but we've discussed this so many times and my mum and yours are very keen on us not being together tonight and in the morning for luck."

"But surely we've had all our bad luck?"

"I hope so." Leo kisses me softly. "Come on, let's go for a walk around the gardens."

It's much later in the day and we have spent it relaxing and greeting our family. Leo's mum was the first to arrive. She became very emotional as soon as she saw Leo. She held him in her arms for so long, tears streaming down her face. She then did the same to me.

"Thank you for making my son so happy," she whispers to me.

Then Mum and Dad arrive, they both look so happy. Then Mark and Tessa, followed by Alice, Oliver and baby Oscar, they came with Alice's sister Chloe and her girlfriend Meg. Then Jack and his boyfriend Sam and finally Xander, Shelly, Molly and Evelyn. Everyone is staying here with us tonight and tomorrow so we have arranged a meal for this evening.

The meal was delicious but it's now time to depart for bed. Everyone makes their way to their rooms and Leo takes me up to my room. As we reach the door, he stands in front of me and rubs my arms and I am instantly taken back to the first time we stood in front of a hotel door together, we have come so far since that day.

He brushes my hair out of my face and kisses me.

"I will see you at the ceremony. I can't wait to be your

husband."

"Me too," I reply.

We kiss each other one last time as two single men, the next time I kiss him, we will be husbands.

"Good night, Jacob, sleep well. I love you."

"I love you. Goodnight. I will miss you."

He then walks towards his room and I go into mine. Inside, it's very quiet and lonely in this big room by myself. I take off my clothes and put on a pair of shorts and a t-shirt then climb into bed.

I close my eyes and try to sleep but I spend the next few hours tossing and turning. Eventually, I've had enough. I sit up and reach for my phone, I pull up Leo's name and start typing.

Leo are you awake?

Its only seconds until my phone lights back up.

Yes, I can't sleep either.

Come in here with me then.

No we can't we said we wouldn't to our mums

I know but they won't know and I need you here to help me sleep. We want to be fresh for tomorrow.

Okay I'm coming.

I knew he would if I told him it would help me sleep. Not a minute later, the door to the room opens and he walks in. My stomach flips, will I ever get over the sight of him?

"Hi," I say as I pull back the covers for him to climb in next to me.

"Hi. I'm going to set an alarm so I can get back to my room before Mum comes to get me."

"Okay then we get what we wanted and they think they got what they wanted."

"Now snuggle in and let's get some sleep."

I move over closer to him and he wraps his arms around me and instantly his scent and warmth makes me relax.

Leo's alarm goes off at seven, he reaches over to turn it off without moving me off his chest. I slowly open my eyes and look up at him. His eyes are still closed so I stare at him for a while taking in all his wonderful features.

"Stop staring."

I let out a little giggle.

"How do you always know I'm staring? You have done since we first met."

"I can feel you."

I pull myself off his chest and kiss him. He slowly opens his eyes and there they are the deep brown eyes I never want to stop looking into.

"I better get back next door, Mum will go mad if she gets there and I'm not there."

"Five more minutes, please. We are not going to see each other until the ceremony and that's not for hours."

"Okay but only five minutes more."

I snuggle back down and Leo kisses the top of my head and starts to run his hand through my hair.

Leo has gone back to his room, I've had breakfast in bed and I'm about to start getting ready when the nerves come from nowhere. I'm taken aback by the feeling, why am I nervous it's only Leo I'm marrying. As I'm trying to get my head around these feelings there is a knock at the door. I open it and Mum and Dad are standing there.

"Mum, you look beautiful."

She is wearing a black and white fitted skirt suit with a black and white hat to match. She gives me the biggest smile and hugs me.

"Mum, you are going to mess up your outfit."

"I don't care I want to give my son a hug on his wedding day."

Mum pulls away and holds me at arm's length.

"Are you okay?" Why does she always know when something is wrong?

"I don't know. I've come over really nervous."

"It's only natural but you will be fine," Dad replies and I feel a little mean as I've ignored my dad only focusing on Mum. He looks very smart in his suit.

"Sorry, Dad, you look great too."

I step out of the doorway to where he stood and hug him too.

"Jacob, get back in this room, what if Leo walks out of his room," Mum shrieks.

"Mum, it's fine." I roll my eyes at Dad and she playfully smacks my arms.

"I saw that."

"Best get inside, Jacob. Don't make your mum mad."

This makes me laugh and I suddenly feel so much better.

I spend the next hour getting ready. When I have put my black suit, white shirt and black and white patterned tie on I look at myself in the mirror not believing in two hours I will be marrying Leo. This time the feeling I feel is excitement.

I walk out of the dressing room into the bedroom where Mum and Dad are waiting for me. As Mum sees me for the first time, tears well up in her eyes.

"Don't cry, Mum, you will ruin your make-up."

"We are so proud of you, Jacob," and she hugs me again. I look over her shoulder to Dad and see he has tears in his eyes too. He comes over and joins us in the hug.

"I love you both. Thanks for everything."

Mum kisses my cheek and finally she lets me go just as there is knock on the door. Dad wipes his eyes and goes to open it.

Xander, Shelly and Molly are waiting to come in. Xander is dressed in a black suit like mine with a slightly different tie design, Shelly has a black evening dress on and looks stunning in it. Molly is wearing a white flower girl dress. She is the cutest as she runs in swishing her dress.

"Uncle Jacob, look at my dress."

She runs over to me and I scoop her up into my arms.

"You look beautiful, just like a princess."

"Mummy, Daddy, Uncle Jacob says I'm a princess."

"That's because you are a princess, sweetheart," Xander replies to her.

I kiss her cheek and she wraps her little arms around my neck.

"Come on, Molly, get down, you are going wrinkle Uncle Jacob's suit. Uncle Leo won't be happy if he is not looking pretty today, will he?" Shelly says to Molly.

She looks at me not wanting me to put her down.

"Uncle Leo loves Uncle Jacob whatever he looks like."

We all laugh at her. I kiss her cheek again but this time I lower her back down.

"You are right, Molly, he does," I say to her as she runs off.

"Are you ready? Leo has already gone downstairs to have photographs taken then it will be our turn," Xander informs me.

"Yes, I'm ready. I've been ready for a very long time."

I hug everyone and we make our way downstairs. Leo, Mark or Penny are nowhere to be seen. They must be in the room waiting for the ceremony to start as he will walk down the aisle first.

Alice, Oliver and Jack are waiting for us in the hallway.

"Have you seen Leo, how is he?" I ask Alice.

"He's good, Jacob, he can't wait to see you though."

"I can't wait to see him too."

Julie appears from the side room where Leo is waiting.

"Jacob, how are you doing?"

"I'm good, thanks."

"Let's get some photographs taken and then get the two of you married?"

"Yes. I can't wait."

We have a few photographs taken with everyone and finally it's time.

Julie calls for Jack and Oliver to enter the room, once they have gone in, she closes the doors again. Then she gets Xander and Shelly in place, followed by Alice and Mark. They will walk down the aisle first and finally Molly will follow them. She is hopefully going to throw rose petals along the aisle but she wasn't very keen to do it yesterday when we had the rehearsal.

Me, Mum and Dad are waiting around the corner from the entrance as Mum will not let me see Leo until we walk down the aisle. I'm glad she didn't find out about me and Leo sleeping together last night.

Julie must have opened the doors, as I can hear chattering

coming from the room but it quietens down once the music starts. The music is very special to me and Leo as it is a song we wrote especially for our wedding day and we wanted to walk down the aisle to the music.

I hear Julie instruct Xander, Shelly, Alice and Mark to make their way down. I can then hear her talk to Molly and say that she can walk down to see Mummy and Daddy.

I then hear a door open and I know Leo is making his way out to walk down the aisle. I just want to run around the corner to him, before I can Julie appears.

"Ready?"

"Yes, definitely."

Mum holds my hand and Dad rubs my back as we make our way to stand in front of the doors. As I reach them and look inside for the first time, I see all our family and friends stood watching Leo walk down the aisle. I focus on him too and as he reaches the front he turns and looks back up the aisle our eyes meet. My stomach flips and I give him the biggest smile. He looks so handsome in his suit. He wouldn't let me see what he had chosen. He is wearing a tight fitted black suit that really hugs his waist. A black shirt and black tie. He looks hot.

Julie snaps me back to the moment by letting us know we can go.

I start walking down the aisle with Mum and Dad by my side but I don't look anywhere but at Leo.

I finally reach his side and he takes my hand and squeezes it.

"Hi," he whispers.

"Hi," I say back to him.

We turn to face the registrar but don't let go of our hands.

She smiles at us both and continues, "Good afternoon, ladies and gentlemen. I would like to extend a warm welcome to Brinsopcourt Manor House and an extra special welcome to the grooms, Jacob and Leo."

As she says this Leo squeezes my hand again.

"My name is Mary and I will be conducting the ceremony. This place which we are now met has been duly sanctioned according to law for the celebration of marriages.

You are here today to witness the joining of matrimony of Jacob Adams and Leo White.

If any person present knows any lawful impediment to this marriage, they should declare it now?"

At this precise moment, Molly decides to shout, "Uncle Leo, have you seen my pretty dress?"

Everyone laughs out loud, Xander and Shelly go bright red from embarrassment and tell Molly that she needs to be quiet.

"We will ignore that," Mary says to the both of us, with a smile on her face.

"Before you are joined in matrimony, I have to remind you both of the solemn and binding contract of the vows you are about to make. Marriage is a deep and lasting commitment that should not be entered into likely or without thought. Of course, you both know that anyway." She smiles at us and I turn to Leo and give him a smile too.

"Furthermore, marriage is a desire of two people to share themselves and their experiences with each other and a willingness to except each other for who they are. Marriage means making a commitment to the development of friendship and mutual respect, it calls for honesty, patient and of course a sense of humour. Marriage is where each cares for the other and supports them in all that they do. It demands courage, the courage to be open, the courage to grow and change and the courage to sort tasks of everyday life. A good partner, in such a marriage, will be loving, caring and above all a best friend.

Now if you could both turn towards each other and hold both hands."

We turn and our eyes meet, Leo reaches out for both my hands.

"Jacob and Leo have written their own vows. So, Jacob, if you would like to go first."

I clear my throat and look deeply into Leo's eyes.

"From the first time we met you stole my heart. I looked into those deep brown eyes of yours and I was lost forever. I am amazed by everything you did and do for me and I promise that I will try every day to do the same for you. I will always be by your side through whatever comes our way. I love you now and forever."

I see Leo tear up.

"Leo, now it's your turn. Just take your time," Mary says to him.

I see him take a couple of deep breaths, then he starts.

"Jacob, I love you and I have always loved you even when I didn't or couldn't always show it, you always had my heart. I promise to love you forever and I will spend my whole life making you as happy as you make me."

Once we have finished, we give each other a huge smile and squeeze each other's hands.

"Stay holding hands and you both need to reply with I do. Jacob, today you have come to promise to share your life with Leo. Do you promise to love and protect him, to be faithful to him and to be always supportive and understanding?"

"I do."

"Leo, today you have come here to promise to share your

life with Jacob. Do you promise to love and protect him, to be faithful to him and to be always supportive and understanding?"

"I do."

We both smile at each other.

"I call on the best men, Xander and Mark, to bring forward the rings."

Mary says looking at them. Xander and Mark reach into their pockets and pull out a ring box each, they take out the rings and place them both onto the table.

"Jacob, if you could take Leo's ring and place it on his finger."

I pick up Leo's ring from the velvet mat on the table, I hold his hand gently in mine as I place the ring on his finger.

Then looking at him I say, "All that I have I bring. All that I am I give. Leo, wear this ring forever as a sign of our unbroken love. May we love as long as we live and may we live as long as we love."

As I'm saying these words to the love of my life I feel tears run down my face. Once I've finished Leo reaches up and wipes the tears from my cheeks.

He then takes the other ring and places it on my finger and he says, "All that I have I bring. All that I am I give. Jacob, wear this ring forever as a sign of our unbroken love. May we love as long as we live and may we live as long as we love."

Mary then continues, "Jacob and Leo you have both made the declaration prescribed by law. You have made a solemn and binding contract with each other in the presents of friends, your lovely family, your witnesses and before me. So, I am delighted to pronounce that you are now husband and husband."

We did it, he's mine forever. The room fills with cheers as we lean into each other and kiss for the first time as husbands. My heart could not be more filled with love.

Epilogue

I am sat in the driver's seat of our car. I look in the mirror to see a sight that I never grow tired of. Leo is placing Ellie into her car seat, he is talking quietly to her and they both have big smiles on their faces. I still can't believe how lucky we are to have her in our life. She looks just like Leo and can also be as stroppy as him at times.

Two years ago, she came into our world and life has never been the same since. We both love her more than we ever thought we could.

Once Leo has got her strapped into her seat, he walks around to the passenger seat and jumps in.

"You ready for this?" he says as he puts his hand on my leg.

"Yes, definitely. Are you?" I reply.

"I don't know."

I know he has had his doubts about what we are going to do today. We have spent many hours discussing it as the time got closer to today. He didn't want to let anyone down, but he is still a little unsure if he wants to give this a go again.

"It will be okay. Let's go, I would like to be there first," I say as I start the car and pull out of the drive. It's only a short drive to the hotel. I park the car in underground car park and we make our way to the reception.

I go up to the desk as Leo waits with Ellie in his arms.

"Hello," I say to the receptionist.

"Good afternoon, sir, how can I help you?" She looks up and

I see that she recognises me but doesn't say anything.

"Hi, my name is Jacob Adams-White, I have a private room booked. I just wanted to let you know we have arrived and to make sure the room is set up with the drinks and snacks I requested."

"Of course, Mr Adams-White. Your room is ready for you. You are the first to arrive, would you like someone to show you where to go?"

"No, thank you. We know where it is."

I walk back over to Leo and Ellie.

"Everything is ready and we are the first here, shall we go?"

Leo nods, he looks worried again. If he really doesn't want to do this, I really don't want to pressure him into it.

"Come on," I say as I hold his free hand and lead him to the room that changed our lives forever.

We reach the familiar door. I open it and I see Leo take a deep breath before carrying Ellie into the room. It is such a weird feeling being back in this room where everything started all those years ago.

"Are you okay?" I turn to look at Leo. I'm not sure what he is thinking as obviously this place not only started good things but also a lot of bad things too.

"Yes, I'm good."

We take a seat at the table, Leo puts Ellie down. As she starts exploring the room, I watch her and I can't believe she is in the room that changed her daddies' lives.

The door then suddenly opens and a pram is being pushed through. Ellie stops what she is doing and turns towards the door.

"Molly, Evelyn," Ellie screams as she runs towards the two girls coming into the room.

Xander and Shelly walk into the room pushing the pram with

their newest addition to their family, Emmett, in, he is only eight months old.

I stand up to great them both.

"Hi, how are you all doing? How did you get on staying at the hotel with these three?" I ask.

"Not as bad as I thought it was going to be," Shelly replies.

"You should have stayed with us at the house, like I said."

"I know but it was just as easy to stay here it is only the night."

I look over to Ellie, who is now playing with Molly and Evelyn. I'm so glad they get on so well. Ellie loves it when they come to stay with us and she is always asking to go to London to see them.

Leo is suddenly by my side. I can see worry etched on his face.

"How are you doing, Leo?" Xander asks him.

I have confided in Xander about how Leo is having trouble deciding whether he wants to do this again.

"I'm still not sure."

"Well, once Alice and George arrive, we can all sit down and talk about everything and see how you feel then," Xander says to him.

Leo nods and goes over to Shelly who is with the girls and he picks up Emmett out the pram and starts playing with him. I notice that a little of the stress has gone once he has a baby in his arms. The smile never left his face when we first brought Ellie home with us.

As I'm watching Leo, who is now surrounded by all the little ones, the door opens again. We all turn to face it and see Alice walk in with Oscar as Oliver follows with William in his arms, who has just turned one. All three of the girls jump up and run towards them, they all love each other so much. They pull Oscar over to play with them.

We all take a seat around the table, talking about everyday things when there is knock at the door. Molly runs over to open it.

"It's Uncle George," she announces to the room.

George walks in and says his hello's. I look at Leo and worry is back on his face since George arrived. Shelly and Oliver offer to take the children out of the room so we can talk in peace but none of us will hear of it we are all in this together. So, they gather them all up and decide it's a good time to give them some food to keep them quiet for a little while.

Me, Leo, Xander and Alice sit back around the table and ask George to join us. I hold onto Leo's hand he looks like he needs a bit of comfort.

We sit in silence for a few minutes and I can't take it any more so I speak up.

"Well, we said five years ago at our engagement party that we would meet up here again and talk about reforming the group. I know we have talked about it but we have never actually sat down formally and discussed if it is something that actually could be possible. So now we are here what is everyone's thoughts?"

I look around at the other three. Leo has his head down; he's not going to say anything yet.

Xander speaks first. "Well, I think it would be a good time to reform. Me and Shelly have finished having our family. Shelly has quit her job at Harriet's firm so we are free to do what we want now."

Alice then speaks, "Oliver and I have discussed it and obviously Oliver has to stay in London as his job with the theatre is there, but he has said if I want to do it then he supports me."

"Do you think you want to do it?" I ask her.

She smiles and nods her head.

"What about you two?" Xander asks.

"I'm happy too. I've actually been working on a few songs that I think might be good for us," I say to them all.

We are then all looking at Leo.

"Leo, if you really don't want to do it, we would totally understand," I say to him squeezing his hand.

He lifts his head and gazes into my eyes and for the first time I can't read him, I really don't know what he wants to do.

"You know I have been struggling to decide whether I want to get back into the group or not. With everything that happened before my confidence is not where it used to be regarding this. It's not like it used to be when I was a confident, cocky kid who thought nothing could touch me. But so much shit happened that I'm worried about going through it again."

"But it will be totally different this time. We have George to help us through everything and we are one big family now who are always here to support each other," Alice says to him gently and she reaches over to hold his other hand.

George then speaks up, "I know you have worries, Leo, but Alice is right this will be totally different. We will take it slow and at your pace. No rushing to get albums out, no rushing to get you on tour. None of that. You all have families now and we need to take that in to consideration whenever we plan anything."

Leo nods at George.

"So, are we doing this?" I ask everyone.

"I'm in," Xander says.

"Me too," Alice replies.

"I am definitely," I say. We then look at Leo again. I can still see that it is bothering him. He doesn't speak straight away.

"Okay, let's do it," he says with a smile on his face.

I can't believe he said yes. I pull him into me and hug him tight.

"Okay, okay that's great," say George, "so UsFour has reunited. That is amazing news and your fans will be over the moon. Should we do something to mark this moment and post on your social media to announce it?"

"I think that would be a great idea, let's have a group photograph and post it," I say to the others.

"Yes, let's get everyone in, including the kids because they are part of the group now too," Alice responds.

We gather everyone together and try to get everyone to face one direction. I have Leo next to me, he has Ellie in one arm and the other around my waist. My arm is also around his waist and before we take the photograph, I kiss Leo.

"I love you and thank you for doing this."

"I love you too," and he pulls me closer to him.

"Everyone, look at me," George shouts over the madness.

We all turn to George.

"After three, everyone say UsFour. One, two, three."

"UsFour!" we all shout, as George takes the photograph. We then all end up in a group hug.

Once we separate, I open up our social media site, which hasn't had anything posted on it for a long time, and post the photograph with the words...

A new chapter.